SKIN ARTIST
By R.W. CLINGER

Herndon, VA

Published in the United States by STARbooks Press, PO Box 711612, Herndon, VA 20171. Printed in the United States

Many thanks to graphic artist John Nail for the cover design. Mr. Nail may be reached at: tojonail@bellsouth.net.

Herndon, VA

CONTENTS

CHAPTER ONE – MAN-BOND

Rocco Malonni sleeps inside the beach house at Flamingo Cove, Florida. His flight from Springbok, South Africa was the absolute worst: a lot of turbulence; mechanical issues with one of the Boing 777's engines; an overweight bitch sat her flabby ass next to him and took up most of his space. I never hear him cuss so much regarding a rough flight.

Frankly, he can complain all he wants because I'm just glad he's home again, safely returned from his dangerous escapade to Africa and retrieving four million dollars' worth of diamonds from a voodoo practicing bad man named Zulan Cane.

This is the man I'm going to marry, I think, studying a naked twenty-six-year-old Rocco at sleep on our king-size bed: motionless on his back with his muscled arms stretched out at his sides; onyx-black military cut; heavy scruff on his thin cheeks and chin; thick cords line his neck; swollen pecs and abs covered in thin, black fur; nipples at attention, ready to be kissed and licked by my straying tongue; V-patch of curly pubic hair above his six inches of decompressed shaft; fuzzy Ping-Pong-size balls drooping between his chiseled thighs.

I am so hungry and horny for his bare skin and want to jump him right now. When was the last time we devoured each other in a sexual manner? It's burned in my memory: November 24. The day after Thanksgiving, and the night before his flight to Africa. That was over two months ago, almost nine weeks that I have not felt his steeping erection pressed against my needy bottom. Nine weeks of pure hell, suffering from pneumonia; the reason why I couldn't travel with him to South Africa. None of these facts matters now that he's back in Florida and the Gulf from his foreign trip, here at my side. Now I can take advantage of his skin all I want, and devour him with sexual energy in ways that will only astonish him.

For now though, the man of my dreams must sleep, build up his energy, and rest from his travels. When he becomes fully recuperated

1

from his mad-capped, African adventures, I will surely find a means of sexually pleasuring the Mafia man from head to toe, in full.

# # # # #

Well after midnight, I undress inside the bedroom, ready to accompany Rocco in a good night's sleep. A mirror on the far wall exemplifies my twenty-three-year-old body: a toned and hairless chest; mediocre-pumped biceps; blond curly hair; azure-colored eyes; delicious-looking blond treasure trail between a divot of navel and the man-scaped and triangle-shaped patch of pubic hair above a five-inch limp tool that will surely grow into ten inches at some point in the man's future company; narrow hips and muscular legs that exemplify a jock's sexy body.

After turning out the yellow-dim light, I join him on the king-size bed and spoon him in my boyfriend arms. Here, I center my deflated cock at his rigid buttocks in hopes that he will wake during the night, roll over, face me, and have every intention of seducing my skin. How hungrily I want to finally expel my nine-week pent load over his internationally traveling and muscular core. Why not, right? Particularly since he is now back in my life. Who wouldn't want to spray him down with man-churn?

This greedy sexual longing doesn't transpire, though. Instead, he begins to snore, entrapped inside his dreams, comfortable at my side, safe in my arms, and at peaceful sleep.

# # # # #

January 31. Early this morning, Rocco stirs awake at my side and whispers my name in fear, "Derek? ... Derek Reed?"

I squeeze his body close to mine, seal his back to my chest, compress my skin to his, and let him know that he's safe in my arms. Calmly, I faintly reply, "I'm here, Rocco. You're okay now. You're with me."

"Zulan was after me again," he puffs, heaves for breaths, and perspires everywhere.

2

I graze a palm against one of his rigid pecs, kiss the nape of his furry neck, and say, "You're safe now. It was just a dream. You're with me. You're home."

He drifts back to sleep, lightly snores again, lost in a sublevel of dreams.

Awake now, I wonder what he encountered in Africa during his diamond excursion. Voodoo. Murder. Bloodshed. Apartheid. Revolution. My fully-awakened mind drifts to the most darkest places, which prevents sleep. How close was Rocco Malonni to death in Springbok, South Africa? What transpired with that evil man he calls Zulan Cane? How happy is he to be back in Florida, close to my side, entrapped in my arms, and out of harm's way again?

# # # # #

The diamonds currently are kept in the beach house, hidden in a secret safe under the conservatory's floor. Instead of Rocco delivering the four million-dollar package to his father – the godfather of bad guys, Antonio "Boss" Malonni, and hopefully my future father-in-law – in Miami, Rocco keeps the jewels in our care. Tomorrow he has every intention to deliver the prized gems to his daddy, fly from Tampa Bay to Miami with me, and visit the king mobster, staying for a family dinner. For now, though, the mobster's youngest son has some heavy-duty sex to catch up on with me, which I won't reject.

# # # # #

A heated, Gulf dawn offers two erections and fiery libidos. The godfather's son wakes me from sleep, kneels over my body, and kisses my neck with his sultry lips. His fingers toy with my chest and roll their fingertips over firm nipples. His eight inches of cock aligns with my ten-inch one and adorns our heated flesh with pre-bubbles of pent goo. Rocco's tongue strays against my corded neck, blond-stubbly chin, and slips into my mouth. Here, it finds my own tongue and meets after nine long weeks of restless sleep and unlimited loneliness.

Hungry for his explosion, he slides his rod against my rod and builds friction between the two. His palms move up and down my sides

3

and cause goosebumps of excitement to rise on my touched skin. Helplessly, he delves his tongue into my sliver of mouth, pulls out, and quickly enters again.

Our passion develops to the fullest degree as our naked male bodies connect. I caress his strong back and meet my rough palms against his manly bottom, pulling its bulbous cheeks apart. I graze two fingertips against his pink-tight opening, drive the goon mad, and force a hearty moan out of him. Besieged by his pole-touching, my own pole releases more droplets of pre-ooze out of its capped head, which is expected since our recent away-time from each other.

Overtop me, twinkling dark-purple eyes and a five-o'clock-shadowed smile is shared. He pulls his mouth away from my mouth and wittingly begs, "Fuck me with your big dick, Derek. I want you inside me. Stop teasing me."

Although I try to please the bad boy to the fullest, wanting to spend the rest of my life with him, I reply, "I can't, or at least not yet. I haven't seen you in so long and I'll shoot my load in a second. Neither of us want that, I'm sure."

He laughs above me, deciding to kiss me again. One of his palms brushes through my blond curls as his other palm caresses a left hip. Breaking for air from the potent kiss, he promises, "I understand. I feel the same way. You can fuck me later if you want to."

Again, I graze the two digits against his bottom, which prompts him to murmur in pleasure. He sits up, sports his eight inches of hard tool between his chiseled legs, arches his neck and back with unstoppable passion, and leaks droplets of man-sap out of his stick and onto my own stick. As our balls connect, he takes his right palm and wraps it around our throbbing extensions of meat. Vibrantly he begins to shift the cocks up and down, working their elastic skins together.

"Rocco, if you continue that … I'm going to blow." I melt beneath him on the bed, zealous for our man-bond. Unstoppable vibrations skirt through my center, which cause my temperature to rise and the Earth to fall off its axis. Burning pleasure races up and down my shaft and spine with his every stroke. The clouds separate over Flamingo Cove and the Gulf's post-oil spill water begins to boil because of our connected spell or concoction of unstoppable heat.

"Shoot," he whispers. "Go for it, guy. I can always get you hard again."

And so this is done. I heed the Italian's instruction and will my creamy load to surface. Burning desire churns within my stem and I'm almost ready to erupt and spray man-fluid everywhere.

Above me, he shivers and manhandles our meaty devices with the rhythm of lust. His movement is fierce, wild, and massages our skins to the nth degree, which causes me to helplessly give into his own orgasm. One quick groan escapes his red-lipped mouth, which is followed by a husky growl. Chaos brews as he bucks his fist, acquires bliss, and wills himself to eventually burst his sticky cargo.

The hold on our flesh-covered masts is still strong and unyielding. We gasp for air together and naked poetry in motion occurs, our lust discovered again, the sexual connection we have temporarily put on hold because of his trip to Africa and my bout of pneumonia. This is what we have lost, but embraced again, passionate sex between male lovers, a sweaty and sticky reunion of sculpted bodies after nine long weeks.

Goo flies out of our solid bars at the exact same time. The white liquid rises between our bodies, melds together, and rains to his thrusting hand, our tangled cocks, and my perspiration-covered chest. The vat of ooze sticks us together, seals our bliss in a tangled mix, pivots our sexual connection, and pushes us into a shared stage of utter delight.

Our moment is not over just yet. He is still hungry for me and slowly releases his palm from our kissing cocks. He moves his hand up to his morning mouth and begins to lick his fingers and palm clean, removing all of the sap away that he can with tender tongue-strokes.

After his protein-induced breakfast, he climbs between my legs, faces my still-hard tool, and desires nothing less than to suck me off. The mobster opens his mouth, slides the tip of my semen-slick rod between his red-plump lips, and cordially invites the rest of its sticky length down the back of his throat. Stringent sucks are applied; a dozen or more, which cause me to feel as if I will burst a second load of dawn's gluey churn.

Just when I believe his craving is fulfilled, he releases my hose from his throat, takes oxygen into his lungs, and begins a fruitful tongue-licking adventure on my plated and hairless stomach. Here, he dips the tip of his slippery appendage into the torso-pools of our thick spurts and laps up every drop of spunk, completing our sexual union by satisfying his hunger.

# # # # #

Spent and nestled in his muscular arms on the king-size bed, I heavily pant like an animal in the wild. He kisses my forehead, the tip of my sloped nose, and now my pursed lips. When he finishes, he slowly pulls away and laughs, "You're still sticky."

"I'll just have to take a shower with you."

"And let me pound your rump under the spray?"

"I've been dying for you to thump me for the last nine weeks," I admit.

"That was a long nine weeks without you. I missed you, Derek Reed ... Everything about you. All I could do was think about you while I was on my diamond-business in South Africa."

"And jerked off to a vision of me, I hope?"

"Almost every day," he replies.

"Same here," I giggle, exploring his chest with one of my open palms and a few fingertips.

We entangle our bodies yet again with arms and legs. More kisses are shared and eventually we shower together. As promised, he finds himself behind me, takes advantage of my tight bottom with his eight inches, and proceeds to fulfill his sexual intentions with relentless bumping.

# # # # #

Mantabaun Choaa, a chocolate-skinned, Incan descendent is our eighteen-year-old houseboy. The boy-thing is fresh out of high school,

6

tidies up the house, prepares waffles and fresh strawberries for our breakfast, and asks my returned lover, "Did you see the present left on the beach, Mr. Malonni?"

My lover runs around the beach house bare-chested again. He wears nothing more than his navy pair of Rufskins, sports nipples that are fully erect on his furry chest, and looks lip-smacking yummy and sexier than hell. I've told him numerous times that Mantabaun adores his Italian skin, and to cover up his delectable goods while in the help's presence. The last thing we need is a houseboy popping wood next to the kitchen counter while adorning wheat waffles with fresh slices of market strawberries and whipped cream. Rocco doesn't listen to me, though.

I have yet to tell my boyfriend that while he was away in Africa, during my almost-fatal episode of stage two pneumonia, which prevented me from joining him on his diamond adventure, that Mantabaun thieved an 8x10 glossy picture of Rocco from our bedroom. The picture was of my Mafia boyfriend in a Nautica trunk along the Gulf two summers before: bare chest sporting hard nipples; canary yellow trunk snug against his middle, molded to his skin; glistening thighs of steel; smiling from ear to ear in the beaming sunshine of a sizzling August afternoon. Unbeknownst to Mantabaun, I have watched him jerk off to the photograph numerous times, tugging on his nine inches of uncut stick between his boyish legs, spraying Incan semen over his bronze and thin chest. Nor has this detailed information been shared with Rocco.

To prevent our houseboy from gaining a stiff wanker in the kitchen during breakfast, sporting a sausage in his white capris and Oakley sandals, I pull Rocco off to the side and whisper into his left ear, "Mantabaun has a secret crush on you. Go into the bedroom and slip something over your sexy chest before he bursts a load over our breakfast."

My partner listens, escaping the sixties-style kitchen. He returns in less than a minute wearing a chest-tight tee the color of the Florida sky. His granite-hard nipples poke through its cotton and turn me on to the fullest. So much for him trying not to be sexy, right? Talk about an impossible mission.

Mantabaun serves glasses of freshly squeezed orange juice at our two-person table and repeats, "You didn't see the present left on the beach?"

Rocco is a little grumpy this morning, having been told to put some clothes on for our shared meal. He forks waffle into his mouth and gruffly mumbles, "What present?"

"The man," Mantabaun says, and points over his right shoulder to the beach.

I look across the table at my lover, over his right shoulder, through the window, and down at the beach.

My lover asks our help, "What man?" He turns around in his chair and also scopes out the low tide and beach.

Truth is we see the body at the same time. Approximately one hundred feet away from the back patio – a place where Rocco likes to share blowjobs with me after dark – the body lies face up, naked with bloody knife wounds on its chest.

"Holy shit," my lover exclaims and drops his fork to the plate in front of him. He quickly bolts out of the kitchen and onto the cobblestone patio.

I'm right behind him and gallop to keep up with his speedy pace. Together we are blinded and warmed by the morning sun, traipse through the sand in bare feet, and close in on the male body.

# # # # #

At approximately ten-thirty, positioned over the cadaver like a chiseled member of a CSI unit, Rocco says, "He was stabbed to death four times."

"How can you tell with all the blood?" I inquire.

The naked corpse has a five-ten frame, weighs about 285 pounds, body piercings in his ears, nose, mouth, forehead, and nipples. The victim is covered from head to toe in a variety of tattoos: dragons, crucifixes, skulls, headless horsemen, fiery torches, a fire-breathing wizard, hieroglyphics, and other symbols.

Mantabaun takes residence at my side and surveys the body. He informs, "The skin artist."

I look over at him and ask, "Who?"

The houseboy replies, "Tang Meadow ... He owns of The Skin Artist. A tattoo parlor on Castle Street."

My soon-to-be husband says, "I know him," and crosses himself while bowing his head, beginning a short prayer.

I impolitely interrupt and ask Rocco, "How do you know him?"

My sexy-hot beau finalizes his prayer and lifts his head. He now whispers, "He was one of my childhood friends. We grew up together in Miami. My father has always hated him."

CHAPTER TWO – BEACH BODY

Having survived the Baskin Fish Company drug smuggling case together last September, Rocco and I decide not to panic regarding the body on the beach. Mantabaun, on the other hand, drops to his knees next to the body, flings his arms up to the heavens, and begins wailing an Incan prayer that he probably learned from his great grandmother.

My lover and I stand back and watch the Incan and disbelieve what we see. Eventually, sexy Rocco leans into me and inquires, "What the fuck is he doing?"

"Praying. Cleansing the body before it gets to heaven. One of those white magic spells, I think."

"How do you know that?"

"While you were on your diamond gig he taught me a few things about his people."

"And Incan prayers just happen to be one of those things?"

I whisper, "Yes, and spells. Tell me why you sound perturbed."

"It's not that I'm perturbed, he just looks ridiculous doing it."

Without sounding cold or uncaring, Rocco is right. Approximately ten feet away from the cadaver, Mantabaun rises and falls on the sand, flails his arms up to the sky, prompts them to fall, and swings them upward again. Spanish verbiage is heard; a mix of baritone and alto howls become lost in the Gulf's steady wind.

Rocco walks away from the body and begins to head back to the beach house. I leave our houseboy with Tang Meadow, and rush up to my lover's side. "Where are you going?"

He trudges quickly through the sand and explains, "I have to call my father. Maybe he knows something about this."

"What about the police?"

"I've learned never to get the police involved in these situations. My father will know how to handle it."

My pace quickens, attempting to keep up with him. "Isn't that breaking some kind of law, though?"

He freezes on the sand, turns to me, places his palms on my shoulders, provides both with a gentle squeeze, and says, "You're going to marry into the mob someday. It's a very high-powered family with connections. There's nothing to worry about. Tang will be in good hands once I get my father involved."

I have a dozen or more questions for him; none of which will be answered anytime soon: Why was Tang murdered? Why does Boss Malonni not like Tang? What kind of friendship did Rocco have with Tang when they were boys who played together?

Before rushing to the beach house for his cellular, he adds, "Go back to the body and make sure our Incan boy doesn't touch it, okay?"

I nod my head, agreeing to carry out his command.

He dots a kiss to my forehead and provides a sure sign with me that his pissy instruction isn't personal. Following the peck, he turns and heads back to the beach house. In doing so, he rips the sky-blue tee off his chiseled body and drops it to the beach, reluctant to wear it any longer.

# # # # #

Mantabaun Choaa undresses next to the murdered body. He strips out of his white capris, skin-tight briefs, and sandals. The Incan piles his clothes and shoes at the bottom of Tang's feet and begins to dance around the skin artist, clapping his palms together and singing another Spanish prayer.

I admit, Mantabaun is rather cute for his age: twinkish with narrow shoulders, brown skin, dark nipples, and a flat stomach; hairless beneath his navel and above his extra-long snake that droops between his boyish legs. The houseboy continues to dance in circles about the corpse, jumps up and down, throws his arms to the light wind, and howls his Spanish prayer with glee, wishing the victim on the beach a final farewell and safe travels to a beyond place in the unknown afterworld. I watch carefully, learn his custom, listen to his Spanish, and obtain some sense of his practiced ritual.

Again, my eyes travel to the bloody cadaver and study its serrated appearance. The four stab wounds in the bald man's chest – gashes that are approximately three inches long and just as many apart, creating a circle of sorts over Tang's heart – cause me to determine there was very little struggle by the overweight man, if any. Was Tang already dead before ending up on our private beach? Did someone carry the corpse through the sand or transport the deceased into shore by boat? Obviously Tang is a very large man, consequently far too heavy to carry. Nor are there footprints in the sand, besides the Incan's, Rocco's, and my own, which tells me that the corpse was dumped on the beach by boat, approximately two feet from the water's edge. Also, I'm quite certain that the murder is fresh because rigor mortis has yet to set in; an executed killing that has taken place within the past two hours, perhaps occurring while Mantabaun was practicing yoga and Rocco and I were showering after another session of heated sex.

Rocco interrupts my mental investigative procedure and returns to my side. Shirtless with just a hint of perspiration dotting the center of his chiseled chest, he holds his cellular in his right hand and proclaims, "I called my father about the body. Fortunately a few of his men are in the area and will be here in a matter of minutes to take care of the situation."

"What will your men do with Tang?"

He shrugs a shoulder. "I don't know. My father doesn't ever share things like that with me."

"Any guesses why Tang was killed?" I inquire, wanting to know.

He shakes his head, but doesn't say anything.

"And why was he on our beach? Do you think Tang was purposely left here so we could find him?"

Again, Rocco shakes his head. A heavy sigh escapes him and he replies, "No. I think I was supposed to find him, not you."

"Why's that?" I interrogate my lover, which he doesn't seem too pleased about.

He rolls his eyes at me, heavily sighs, and prattles, "Tang worked for my father years ago. Some bad business went down. Trust issues became a concern. Tang liked to say too much regarding my father's cash flow at Milo's Laundry in Miami. My father gave him the option of dying or moving to Flamingo Cove. Tang opted for the latter."

"And now Tang shows up dead, which your father could be connected to in some way, right?"

"I believe so." The look on Rocco's face explains frustration and deep concern. Mafia matters always disturb him, particularly when they involve his father so closely.

"I'm sure it's not that," I say, talking out my ass. "My gut tells me this isn't about your father, or the Malonni family." Frankly, I really don't know anything about his father's connection with Tang, or all of Rocco's family's past business ventures. Not that I ever will either. My comments are merely support that pertains to this morning's chaotic drama. To not care will certainly label me a bad boyfriend or criminal, someone no different than the killer at large.

"I'm glad to know you have my back, Derek," he says, winking at me.

"And your front. Don't forget that," I correct him.

He jostles the beef between his legs for my personal pleasure and admits, "You really like my front, don't you?"

I lick my lips, wink back, and reply, "Yum."

# # # # #

I send Mantabaun to the local market for a long list of groceries; a time-consuming chore to keep him occupied until the body on the beach is removed by Boss's men. The houseboy insists he can do the shopping later today, which perturbs me.

I hand him an extra thirty bucks and tell him, "Have lunch on me."

He snatches up the money, finally agrees with me, finds the keys to Rocco's ink-black Hummer, and vanishes into town before I know it.

# # # # #

Dragon and Brit arrive at the beach house looking like FBI agents. Both are dressed in black suits, ebony-colored shoes, and Ray-Ban sunglasses. Dragon, a Chinese-American cutie with the most beautiful hazel eyes, carries a body bag. Brit is from Liverpool and has a thick English accent, is uppity, and a delicious Jude Law look-alike; he follows his partner. Both take notes in black leather books before toting Tang's cadaver away. Neither speaks to anyone, having gained this instruction from Rocco's father.

Rocco and I sit on the back patio drinking glasses of orange juice with splashes of vodka. Our shoulders gently rub together in a romantic manner. I inquire, "Who do you think killed Tang?"

"I'm not sure."

"You think a boat floated up to shore and someone dropped Tang's body on the beach while we were showering this morning?"

"Something like that."

"I don't see any footprints in the sand besides ours."

"I noticed that."

"Who dumped him on our beach?"

Rocco turns to me and musses my hair with a palm. "Damn, you're definitely in Agatha Christie mode."

"It's not every day I wake up to a dead body on our beach."

I want to ask him about his childhood with Tang, but drop the subject. He obviously seems locked in a state of deep thought, possibly contemplating my questions and choosing to be silent, absorbing the moment. Instead of further questioning him, I watch Boss's men bag up the body and carry it away. The duo eventually place the dead guy into the trunk of their 2013 Caddy, climb inside the sleek vehicle, and drive away, leaving me with a silent Rocco.

# # # # #

Ten minutes later Rocco jaunts into the beach house, snatches up a pad and pen, and returns to my side. He makes a list of my questions, including a few of his own: Why does my father despise Tang Meadow? What did Tang do to become murdered? What does his childhood have to do with Tang's murder? Why was Tang naked?

"Nicely done, Rocco. A true investigator," I coach. "Who is Agatha Christie now?"

He kisses me on my cheek, points down to his notes, and confesses, "I have a very bad feeling about this."

My full attention is directed on him. "Why? What do you know that you're not telling me?"

My boyfriend shakes his head and replies, "I don't know yet. I just have a vibe."

"Are you using your Scooby senses again?" I joke, and cause myself to laugh.

"A little of that and a little intuition."

"I love intuition. Tell me more."

Again, he shakes his head. "I don't know if I can."

"Spill it, guy. What happened between Tang and you? How old were you?"

He looks out at the Gulf with squinting eyes, inhales, exhales, and finally admits, "Sixteen."

"What happened?"

"Tang tried to seduce me. My father found out. He hit the roof. Tang was badly beaten a week later, which I'm sure my father was behind."

I reach over and squeeze one of his hands, applying support to him regarding the ugly situation. "I'm sorry. Some things come back to haunt us."

"We were at Milo's in Miami. Tang found me in the bathroom. He grazed fingers along one of my cheeks. Nothing else happened, but it was enough. My father walked in and just about shit a brick."

"Tang's lucky he wasn't offed."

"I'm sure my father thought about it numerous times."

"And that's really the reason why Tang was booted from the Mafia business, right?"

"Spot on," he said. "Tang was thrown out of Miami. My father did it himself."

"To protect you, of course, right?"

"Yes. It's always about protection."

I caress his fingers with my own. "Thanks for spilling it to me."

He pulls his attention away from the Gulf, leans in my direction, dots my nose with a fingertip, kisses my forehead again, and shares, "You're my partner in crime, Derek. Who else would I tell?"

# # # # #

Rocco calls his father again in Miami. Their conversation is about twenty minutes long, which I'm not privy to. Maybe the two men are talking about a bathroom incident that transpired when Rocco was sixteen. Maybe not. Truth is Rocco and I have agreed to allow each other privacy in our relationship. I feel that if the conversation is at all important, he'll share the details with me following the call. Otherwise, it's none of my business. Situation dropped.

The bad boy doesn't let me down, of course. He hangs up with the Mafia kingpin, finds me in the glass conservatory among potted orchids, cacti, and a bench to read on. Here, I review his handwritten notes regarding Tang Meadow's murder. He kindly interrupts me and shares, "My father says the murder has nothing to do with Tang's bathroom gig with me. Boss thinks Dane Duncock is involved with Tang's murder."

"Who is Dane Duncock?"

"Tang Meadow's number one enemy."

"Why did the skin artist have an enemy?"

"Why does anyone have an enemy? If you ever figure that out, let me know."

"There has to be a reason why Dane Duncock hated Tang. How is Dane involved?"

He tells me that Dane and Tang used to be business partners, opening up a tattoo shop called The Ink Den in downtown Flamingo Cove. Things soured between the two men. Dane insisted Tang was ripping him off, embezzling more than his share of the profits. The relationship ended badly. Dane attacked Tang and put the man in the hospital for over three weeks. Rocco adds, "He broke Tang's legs and one arm. Tang almost lost an eye out of the deal."

"And Dane hasn't forgiven Tang?"

"Tang wasn't the one stealing money. Dane was skimming funds off the top."

"Sounds like a pretty deceptive guy."

"Dane has a history of doing meth and men. He likes his drugs and fast guys. They can be expensive, of course, and he always has to find a way of paying for both."

"Where is he now?" I inquire, fully interested in Rocco's details.

"Both men ended up opening their own tattoo shops. Tang stayed in Flamingo Cove and started The Skin Artist. Dane moved to Tampa Bay and started a business called The Ink House. Both are very successful."

"Is Dane still using meth?"

He shrugs his shoulders and responds, "I don't know. But why wouldn't he?"

I lift my eyebrows and ask, "Should we find out?"

"What's into you, Nancy Drew?"

"I prefer being one of the Hardy Boys, if you want to know the truth," I confess.

He laughs. "Of course you do. Shame on me for thinking otherwise."

Our conversation ends because the doorbell at the front of the beach house chimes. I escape Rocco's notes and his side. In a matter of seconds I'm at the front door, pull it open, and welcome an old friend inside.

# # # # #

Walter Landing, Flamingo Cove's famous gay mystery writer, presents a hardback copy of his latest bestseller, *Bottom Tales*, to me. Walter is round, bald, and quite the sleuth. The sixty-nine-year-old is a joy to be around: funny, charismatic, and sinfully horny at all times. Yet today, he seems most irritated and grouchy, frowning at my doorstep.

Excited to see him, I welcome him inside the beach house, provide a lemon iced tea for his thirst, and sit across from him in the black and aluminum-colored living room.

Rocco excuses himself and vanishes somewhere in the house to review his notes regarding the dead body on the beach.

The mystery writer takes off his sunglasses, straw gardening hat, and asks, "How long has it been since we saw each other last?"

"Two days after Thanksgiving," I reply. "Rocco was in South Africa. I was sick with pneumonia. Fisk and you brought a vat of homemade chicken soup and warm rye bread to me, which I treasured. Do you recall?"

"I do," Walter concedes, nodding his head. "You look much better these days with Valentine's Day lurking around the corner."

"Speaking of the day for lovers … How is Fisk Deveraux these days?"

"Missing again. I cannot keep that man under lock and key. He wanders the world's countryside again. The last I heard he was in Lima, Peru working on a science project."

"Doing what?" I inquire.

"Visiting a friend … Or so he tells me." Walter sounds a bit irritated; perhaps he finds the topic of his boyfriend's whereabouts grating. Honestly, Fisk is hard to keep a leash on according to the mystery writer's stories. The Italian man with his model-perfect looks has the naughty reputation of enjoying drugs, and will travel around the globe to fetch them for his use.

"Is he dealing drugs again?" I inquire, taking a sip of my own iced tea.

"Not that I'm aware of. Those days are over. I believe he's interested in a Peruvian field worker at the moment, which I can't blame him for, since I'm almost three times his age." Walter sounds sad, almost brokenhearted by Fisk's doings. "Obviously we'll never marry. Not if he can't keep his cock in his pants."

Long story short: I know Fisk Deveraux through my once-friend, Felicia Horodowski, who died of stomach cancer last year. When I was living in one of Flamingo Cove's most attractive apartment buildings and running errands for its tenants to pay for my monthly rent and meals, Felicia, upon her deathbed, needed marijuana for her pain. Fisk was the local drug dealer. Whatever I wanted in the pharmaceutical area, he supplied. When Felicia needed pot, Fisk was the guy to go to and my friendship with the dealer grew throughout the years at the apartment building. As Walter's assistant, I introduced Fisk to him, and the two have been faithful lovers ever since, until now, by Walter's confession.

"Such a shame," I admit. "I thought you and Fisk were a match made in heaven."

"We are. But only if Fisk stays faithful, which I think is impossible for him to accomplish since he's just so damn sexy."

I find some strength to be positive and suggest, "Maybe Fisk is buying you something extravagant. A coat made from llama. A rare Incan bracelet. What do you think?"

"I'm sure he's fucking the field worker, or scientist ... or whoever the man is," Walter admits with a frown. "The boy knows nothing about fidelity."

I decide to change the topic for fear of adding fuel to the mystery writer's anger. Money and hefty bank accounts are somehow brought up and Walter becomes nosy, "Have you spent all of your twenty million dollars, kitten?"

Another long story made short: When Felicia Horodowski, a retired actress, passed last year, she willed me twenty million dollars. My life is a rags to riches tale. Truth is I would give all the money back if I could spend one more day with the woman, adoring her as an aunt-like figure in my life, someone whom I will always love and miss, dearly.

Although my financial situation is none of the novelist's business, I supply, "I have used just a small portion of the money."

He looks at me in a smug manner and inquires, "And Rocco isn't taking any of it from you?"

"Rocco has his own money. His father is very wealthy and takes care of him."

The writer is snippy today, which is out of his character. I imagine it's because Fisk is in Peru, maybe bedding a Latino man and laboring over a foreign cock. "His father is a notorious man who runs the mob."

"Be kind, Walter. Stop pointing fingers." I sound rather curt and to the point, but say exactly what's on my mind, unable to hold back.

Fisk's daddy lover is perturbed with me. He places his lemon iced tea on a nearby table, stands, and informs, "I just wanted to drop my new novel off. I've taken the liberty of autographing it for you on the title page."

I want to tell him thank you for stopping by, and for the novel, but Walter seems impatient and trots from the living room into the foyer. Before I can hug and share a light kiss of goodbye with him, he vanishes from the beach house, bolting outside, into Florida's warm January.

CHAPTER THREE – INTERRIGATION

"Derek!" Rocco screams at top of his lungs inside the conservatory. "Derek, we have a huge problem!"

After I watch Walter Landing pull out of the gravel and seashell-covered drive in his Mercedes, I immediately bolt through the house and end up in the conservatory.

My lover is on his knees and reaches into a square-foot hole hidden in the floor. An unused Everready flashlight lies beside the secret compartment in the floor. He turns his view to me, resembles a ghost, and informs, "The diamonds are gone."

"You're kidding me? This is a joke. They can't be gone."

"The safe is empty. There's nothing in here."

"Are you sure you put them in the floor last night?"

He sounds irritated and flummoxed by my question. The man raises his eyebrows with more alarm and says, "Of course I'm sure. You watched me put them down here."

I did. Last night when his flight came in from South Africa. He removed a dozen or more glittery diamonds worth four million dollars from inside his winter jacket. I wanted to hold them, just to say I did, but he wouldn't let me. Immediately, he hid the diamonds away in the underground safe, sealed and locked the device tightly closed, and went to bed with me. Now, I wonder what happened to them. Where are they? Who thieved the precious stones, and why?

I move up to the safe and fall on my knees at his side. I grasp the Everready flashlight in my right palm, feel its cold and sleek barrel, flick it on, and shine the beam of golden-white light into the square-shaped abyss under the floor. "Nothing," escapes me. "It's empty. They're gone, just like you said."

Rocco's face drains of color. He looks scared to death, like a pantomime, and obviously knows he's going to be held accountable by his father for the loss, who was expecting the diamonds in his care today. Almost crying, he whispers, "My father is going to kill me."

I try to soothe him to the best of my ability. The flashlight is useless and I turn it off, setting it on the floor next to the safe. I squirm my way over to his side, become a little closer, and wrap an arm around his shoulder. "You went halfway around the world for the diamonds, Rocco. If we have to travel a second time to get the glitteries back, we will."

His eyes light up with the first hint of faith, and now he asks, "You'd do that for me?"

"And for your father," I reply, squeezing him close to me.

In the back of my mind, I think the stolen diamonds have everything to do with the body found on the beach this morning. As Rocco obtains some of his composure, pulling himself together, I try to piece together a connection. To no avail, I triumphantly fail. Instead, I whisper, "Mantabaun. We have to ask him about this. Maybe he knows something we don't."

My partner calculatingly shakes his head and explains, "We can't get him involved in this. He's a houseboy who can't be trusted."

"That's exactly why we have to get him involved. Only the three of us knew about the diamonds in the safe. Mantabaun included. I don't know if he knew the code to get in the safe, though. If the young man can't be trusted, then we have to involve him."

The mobster's son thinks this over for a second or two. Eventually he agrees with me. "Call the houseboy's cell phone and tell him to come home. Explain to him that there's been another emergency and we need to speak with him."

"Of course," I respond, stand, and fetch my cellular out of my front pocket. Quickly, I dial our help's number, listen to his cellular ring a few times, and hear the Incan pick up. "Maunty."

"Mantabaun," I gruffly say his name, "where are you?"

"The Tinder Box. I'm picking up cigarettes."

It's a habit I have always abhorred. Thank God he only smokes outside, although I can still smell the nicotine on the young man when he walks about the beach house afterward. "There's an emergency here at the house. Can you come quickly?"

"I can, sir. Let me pay for my cigarettes and I'll be home in minutes."

"Thank you, Mantabaun." I press the END button on the cellular, pull Rocco up and off the cherry-colored floor, and share, "He'll be here in a few minutes."

"Can we grill him?" Rocco questions. This is truly an unexpected side to the Mafia son that I have only seen on Paragon Island when I was a prisoner in a bamboo cage for over a week last September. Rocco became a hero then and saved my life, was super-testosterone boosted, hungry with power and aggression, sort of like now.

"Perhaps. Let's get a good read of him first. Then we can decide."

"Did he sound guilty?"

I shake my head. "He sounded like Mantabaun shopping."

The mobster rolls his eyes at me, gaining all of his confidence back. He admits, "We have to find the diamonds before my father learns that they are missing."

"And Tang's murderer," I supply.

He nods his head and closes the safe's door with his right foot. "Let's take one thing at a time, Joe Hardy. What do you say?"

"I'm game. Like always … with you."

# # # # #

Mantabaun is delightful in all aspects. Think Ricky Martin in Menudo back in the eighties. Think David Archileta on American Idol. His dark eyes appear mysteriously sweet under bushy eyebrows. His white teeth gleam with a Colgate semi-smile as he sits in one of the living room's palm-shaped reading chairs. Innocently, he asks, "What's going on? What did I miss?" and raises his open palms up like a show monkey with naïve puzzlement.

"The diamonds were stolen," Rocco says from across the room, pacing with his hands on his hips.

"Stolen?" Mantabaun asks. "How could they be stolen when they were in the safe?"

My bed partner turns his attention to the young man and spits at him, "That's the question we have for you. Who took them? How did someone get in the safe and steal them?"

The houseboy's smile deflates. His face quickly turns somber. "I don't know."

"The three of us were the only ones who knew where the fucking diamonds were stashed!" Rocco barks, evidently agitated. He walks up to our help and raises his right hand into a fist, willed and capable of blasting the boy with some of his rage. "Do you know the code to the safe?"

"Rocco, don't do it!" I warn, attempting to calm him down. Speedily, I move up behind him and push his arm down to his side with my hand. I nuzzle my lips against his right ear and whisper, "Keep your temper out of this. If Mantabaun says he doesn't know where the diamonds are, or how someone got into the safe ... then we have to believe him."

My lover has a pretty bad temper when tested. Of course he has access to a Colt 45 or a Derringer or .9mm, but doesn't plan to use such weapons on the houseboy's skull, chest, or whatnot, shooting the young man. Fortunately, all of his weapons are stashed away in our bedroom, most of which are hidden under our shared bed and safely stored in plastic cases. Frankly, he calms down before fetching a handy sidearm, turns around, and smiles at me.

I admit, it's a little bit sinister, sexy, and loving – exactly how I believe the mobster is most of the time. Now, I step in front of him and politely say, "Let me handle this."

The Mafia man shifts to his left, out of my way, and responds, "Give it your best shot."

"Thank you."

"My pleasure." He finds a seat on the living room sofa, a black and leather Swedish piece that cost him a gazillion dollars.

I step up to the houseboy and ask, "Do you know the code to the safe?"

"No. I'm not privy to that information."

"Did you hear anyone enter the house last night or this morning?"

Mantabuan shakes his head. "I didn't. The house was quiet and relaxed. "

"Was the security system set?"

He thinks about my question for a few seconds, rubs his chin, and finally replies, "To my knowledge it was. I'm not really sure."

"Didn't you turn it off this morning with your own personal code?"

The houseboy nods his head in agreement. "I did, which means it was set. I disarmed it around eight o'clock. The monitoring company can tell you that."

"Did you notice that any of the doors or windows were tampered with?"

Vehemently he shakes his head. "I didn't. I got up and accomplished my normal routine. Coffee. Retrieve the paper from the front deck. Prepare freshly squeezed orange juice for you and Mr. Malonni."

"Did you happen to go into the conservatory?"

"I did not. There was no reason to. I usually water the plants in the evening, never in the morning."

I get nothing out of Mantabaun regarding the safe and missing diamonds, even though I want to. Half of me wishes he will say something to pin him to the crime, but he doesn't. The houseboy claims his innocence, a coincidental suspect in the ordeal and nothing more.

Behind me, Rocco blurts, "Ask him about the body on the beach … Do it, Derek … I want to hear what he has to know and say."

I turn to my right and look over my shoulder. A scowl is shared with my lover that screams: Let me handle this! Keep quiet! I have everything under control! Calmly, I turn back around and stare at the boy in the reading chair. Is he nervous? No. Is he bright-eyed and excited? No. Does he act like a smartass? No. Mantabaun is quiet and reserved, still, rather calm, and acts like himself: a houseboy who likes to do a lot of shopping. Perhaps the young man is innocent and has nothing to do with the cadaver on the beach and missing diamonds. Maybe not, though.

Again, Rocco blurts, "The body on the beach … What does he know about it? … Ask him."

I raise my voice at the mobster again, turn around, share daggers with him, and supply in a condescending manner, "Calm down and let me finish."

Rocco raises his arms, surrendering. He backs away from me, stopping approximately three more feet behind me. Cordially he says, "Go for it. He's all yours. I won't say another word."

Again, my attention is drawn to our help as I attempt to ignore my lover. I clear my throat and ask, "The body on the beach, Tang Meadow, when did you find him?"

Mantabaun thinks about this for a second or two, calculating time in the folds of his mind. He nods his head, surfaces an answer, and replies, "Around ten o'clock. You and Mr. Malonni were just getting in the shower."

"Did you see anything at all regarding Tang?"

The houseboy shakes his head.

"Was Tang inside the beach house?"

Again, the young man shakes his head. This time he responds with: "I told you that I was doing my morning routine. I gazed out the kitchen window, which looks over the beach, and … I saw something on the shore. Curiosity got the best of me and I went to investigate. I only walked halfway down the beach, though, knowing what was there. I then returned to the house. By this time, you and Mr. Malonni were out of the shower. I then told you both about the body during breakfast."

"You're sure about all of this?" Rocco chimes in from behind me. His voice is brusque and not at all pleasant.

Our houseboy nods his head and replies, "I'm very certain."

I thank the employee for his time and give him the rest of the day off. Mantabaun relishes days off, spending them at the local shopping mall where he buys things he really doesn't need. He scurries out of the living room, into his bedroom, gathers a few of his personal items to accompany him on his day off, and eventually leaves the beach house.

# # # # #

"He's lying," Rocco says, after Mantabaun leaves. We're in the kitchen, standing side by side and overlooking the beach, munching on fresh strawberries. The day is crisp and beautiful. A blue heaven opens over Flamingo Cove without a single cloud in the sky. A light wind teases the brass chimes on the back patio, creating a rather tranquil melody.

I shake my head and respond, "He isn't. All of his times match up. There were no footprints around the body. We can call the monitoring company and find out if the security system was set, which I believe it was."

"You're defending him," Rocco shares.

"I'm not. I'm merely absorbing all the information he has kindly fed us. Rationally, I'm attempting to analyze all the details. Besides, you still have a few negative feelings for him that you're holding in, which is manipulating your opinion regarding this situation."

My lover knows exactly what I'm talking about. Before leaving for Springbok, Rocco placed two hundred dollars on the top of his dresser in our bedroom. Mantabaun took the money, claiming he needed it for groceries. Rocco believed the man spent the cash on a frivolous shopping spree at the mall, since he didn't come home with any provisions. The houseboy, of course, was interrogated, humiliated, and badgered by the mobster. I had to step in the middle of their tawdry argument and end the battle. Rocco requested the money back from Mantabaun. He also wanted the houseboy to resign from his position, which I opposed, protecting him. The houseboy agreed to return the two hundred dollars to Rocco, calling the incident a misunderstanding that he felt terrible about. He stayed on as our houseboy, and money has not been an issue since. Rocco still holds contempt for the young man, believing him to be a thief, untrustworthy, and sinister.

"If the shoe fits ..."

"Rocco, be nice. Mantabaun helps us in many ways. He's faithful and devoted to our care. You need to get over your hard feelings for him and move forward."

I believe he's ready to explode on me, rehashing the tale of how he still believes Mantabaun thieved money from atop his dresser, pocketing it and frivolously spending the sum. Such an outburst does not occur, though, since his cellular rings on the kitchen counter and we hear the familiar ring tone of his father calling.

As he takes Boss Malonni's call from Miami, I gently pat his bottom, exit the kitchen with a cup of Madagascar coffee, and find the Dell computer in the sitting room, having every intention of catching up on my e-mails.

# # # # #

Seven e-mails desire my attention. I study the communication with much enthusiasm:

Hurricane Brass, a sexy bodyguard hired by Rocco's father last summer, writes: The Undergear gig is working out great. Can't wait to see the final pics. Glad I got out of bodyguarding. I'll keep you posted.

Fisk Deveraux, Walter Landing's pup of a lover, provides his whereabouts and involvements: Lost in Peru. Found the Internet. Studying a new drug for malaria. Be home soon. Take care of my beloved, who I'm sure is extremely worried about me.

Mr. Chaz, my so-called architect boyfriend prior to my involvement with Rocco, shares: Pounding Steven Daigle's bottom tomorrow afternoon in a new skin flick. Can't wait to get next to that sexy flesh. Love him. You can watch the XXX movie when it comes out in the fall.

Mother preaches: Your Aunt Sophie is dying to see Rocco and you in Jacksonville. Call her and make arrangements to visit. Don't abandon your family now that you're rich, honey. I taught you better manners.

Walter Landing explains: I know Fisk is having sex with guinea pigs. The man is sick. How can I keep loving him?

Rocco sends a reminder: Valentine's Day coming up. Don't make plans. I want to treat you like the knight in shining armor that you are.

The last e-mail completely catches me off guard. The sender is Tang Meadow. Sent at four o'clock this morning. I open the e-mail and read: being watched. croon. the stash is no secret. taking. africa shadows.

Behind me, Rocco enters the sitting room and blurts, "It looks like we're not going to Miami. My father decided to cancel dinner today because of the body on the beach. He said the death of Tang Meadow is opening up a can of nasty shit and we should be careful. He's sending Dragon and Brit to watch over us."

I half hear what he says, rereading the e-mail from Tang, having no clue what it means. Quickly, I turn my head to the left and say, "Rocco, read this. I received an e-mail from Tang this morning."

He reads the e-mail over my shoulder. He sounds quizzical when he says, "What the fuck does this mean?"

"I have no idea."

"What is croon?"

"Or, who is Croon?"

He points to the flat-screen and says, "Send that to my father. I'll text him and let him know it's coming."

"Does he know about the missing diamonds?" I don't know why I ask, but I do. Perhaps intuition tells me that it was a topic of discussion between the father and son only minutes before.

"He does. Banco told him about it an hour ago."

Balls Banco works for the badass Chain Chan, a sweet looking Asian musclehead who happens to be Boss's ally in Miami. I ask Rocco, "How did Balls find out about the missing diamonds?"

"I'm sure Mantabaun leaked it. The man has very loose lips, even in just a few hours."

When you marry into the mob, you know everything about organized crime. Murder. Drug smuggling. Payoffs. Sex scandals. Ponzi schemes. Gambling. The works. Obviously my love for Rocco Malonni has placed me into this lifestyle, and now there's no getting out. Not that I mind, though, since it keeps my days occupied and interesting. Truth is I wouldn't have it any other way.

Rocco says he has a couple of calls to make about Tang Meadow and exit's the sitting room. I'm left with the dead man's e-mail on my screen, which I read again. Attempting to keep all of my knowledge straight, I pull out a piece of paper and pen from the mahogany desk and create a list:

Tang Meadow

Murder on the beach

Dane Duncock, enemy

Mantabaun Choaa, thief

Missing diamonds

E-mail from Tang

Croon/croon

Africa shadows

I read the list a number of times, scratch my jaw in confusion and curiosity, and whisper to myself, "Rocco, we've got a lot of things stirring up. It looks like we have some work ahead of us."

CHAPTER FOUR –
OFFICER HAUTE

Approximately fifty minutes later, Barbara Reed, my mother, phones and tells me, "Did you know Melvin's going to be arrested?"

Melvin Caspi owns Carpet Ride, a rug store on Tarpon Street in downtown Flamingo Cove. He's been dating my mother for the last two years. I predict the two will marry soon, if he stays out of jail, but the man has a record of not paying his parking tickets.

Officer Garrett Haute of the Flamingo Cove Police Department has had it out for the man for the last eighteen months. Garrett and I go way back, and I know mother is calling me to somehow involve the cop and get her boyfriend out of trouble.

As a junior at Mirmanda High School, Garrett was my first tug-buddy. The black-haired and blue-eyed cutie had an unstoppable libido at sixteen. Rape could have easily been declared in those days, since he was all over me, tugging on my meat and eating creamy things that boys of sixteen usually don't eat among friends. Garrett was so horny for my blond ass that he numerously sneaked into my bedroom window at night, pulled the sheet away from my body, removed my boxers, and had his dick-hard way with my skin.

Not that I ever objected, of course. Perhaps I had craved his skin as much as he had craved mine. Because I too was a boy with certain pre-manly needs, testosterone-filled, and willed to fuck anything that resembled the same gender, I never pushed him away. For eight months our relationship continued. It ended rather bluntly the following spring, breaking my soul a touch, of course. Garrett found Whitney Hockingstock and her vagina, leaving my ten-inch cock and rigid ass behind. Other things were on his mind. Girlie things. Whitney things. Garrett had found what we believed was his soul mate. A certain someone that he had fallen in love with and would surely spend the rest of his life entertaining. I wasn't that person. Whitney won the prize. Oh well.

To this day, Garrett and Whitney are still together. They live on Dolpher Street in the Cove, have three very young and lovely daughters, and spend two weeks of summer in North Carolina along the coast. Whitney teaches English at Flamingo Cove High School. Garrett took up criminology after high school and is a blue for the city.

Long story short, I use Garrett whenever I need to. He erases speeding tickets from my driving record and will do the same with Melvin's parking tickets. Truth is he is still smitten for my school-pal skin, longs for its tanned beauty, desires its bulbous bottom, and craves the cut knob between my legs. Although our flesh has not united since those naked junior days of high school, I'm sure he would love to reenact such a hand-wrapped-around-cock event that transpired in his bedroom, inside the woods behind the house he grew up in, or in my parents' basement. Oftentimes he tells me he is supremely in love with Whitney Hockingstock, but desires my skin with an untamable lust. Honestly, it's no surprise to me. Garrett's confused and sex-driven, but I still consider him one of my best friends.

"You have to call Garrett," mother demands. "I can't have him spend another week in jail like last time, all over parking tickets."

Yes, Melvin has a history of parking anywhere he wants in the city and not paying his fines. The silly bastard is lucky to have me around, and I'll have to remind him of this soon.

I picture mother as I have always seen her: round with red flaming hair, forest green eyes, two chins, beaver bucked teeth, dangling faux earrings, low-cut blouse showing her wrinkly jugs, no bra, and too much lipstick. Barbara is a beloved train wreck all the way and hasn't changed in looks since the day I was born; not that I expect her to, of course. Everyone has a cross to bear, and Barbara's looks just happens to be mine.

"Did you pay the tickets?" I'm far too curt with her; shame on me. I should love and respect the woman more, but sometimes it's just too hard. It's not that I don't love Barbara, because I really do. Honestly, she can just be a little overwhelming at times, difficult, and overbearing. She likes to have things her way at all costs. If I don't live up to her requests, our relationship then becomes stringent and I avoid her. A smart son knows not to fuck with her, because she will fuck back doubly. No shit. Honest to God. Trust me, I know.

"The check is in the mail, darling." This is her subtle way of telling me that the tickets have not been paid, and that she has no intention of paying them from her funds in the near future, if ever.

I roll my eyes. "Mother, you're lying to me."

"I never lie, Derek. That was all your father's doings."

My father, Gregory Hillton Reed, is dead. The poor man died of a heart attack when I was eight-years-old. Mother, I believe to the fullest, caused his demise; I have yet to prove this today. But maybe someday I will. Gregory was a pharmacist. My hero when I was a young boy. My inspiration to become a man someday. The god I wanted to grow up and become. How sad that I wasn't given the opportunity to enjoy him longer; sometimes God just sinks his claws into our most loved, rips them off the earth, and pulls them into heaven.

"Call Garrett," mother demands, sounding viperous.

"I will. As soon as we end this call."

"Thank you, darling." Now she is going to be nice to me, obviously getting what she wants. Leave it to Barbara to be bitchy and catty until she obtains her desired outcome. "And by the way ... I hear Rocco is back from his trip." Mother has been told that my boyfriend was visiting relatives in Italy. The woman doesn't know I will someday marry a mobster's son who occasionally accomplishes not-so-legal matters for his father like murder, stealing money, and transporting drugs around the globe. Some secrets need to be kept untold; this just happens to be one of them.

"Yes. Rocco is back from Italy. We were planning on having you and Melvin to the beach house for dinner some evening." It's a white lie, but whatever. Frankly, she doesn't need to know that Rocco finds her boyfriend a touch grating. In fact, Rocco says he's going to off Melvin, just for the fun it.

"Melvin would love that."

Melvin Caspi needs to stop parking his Toyota where it doesn't belong. Or mother needs to find a man to sleep with who knows how to abide by the city's laws.

Before our call ends, she snippily adds, "Don't forget to contact Garrett."

"I'll visit him in person. I haven't seen him since Thanksgiving. It will be good catch-up time for the two of us."

She's pleased with my admission, seems soothed at the moment, and I'm sure she smiles from ear-to-ear on her end of the call, but who really knows for sure, right? "You're such a good little Derek. Momma loves you."

I roll my eyes, end the call, and feel like puking.

# # # # #

The Flamingo Cove Police Department is rather small is size but big with attitude. Seven officers work out of the two-floor red brick building on Tequila Street. Ages range from Garrett at twenty-three to Officer Tiger Manning at forty-eight. All of the officers are steamy hot with chests of steel; no wonder the community wants to produce an annual charity calendar of the beefy boys and men, but the idea never comes into fruition.

Tiger greets me at the front desk, manning the phones. The guy is ruggedly cute with salt and pepper-colored hair, sharp blue eyes, thick jaws, and a tiny line-scar over his upper lip. The shade of his skin screams Hawaiian, which is utterly beautiful. He lights up with a blistering smile and says, "Derek, you came by for a cavity check, right?"

I laugh out loud. "Yeah, right. Haven't had enough those lately. Bring it on, man."

He offers me a cup of coffee and a glazed donut, which I decline. He asks in his rugged-alluring voice, "You here to see Haute?"

I nod my head, replying to his question.

He cocks his balled, right hand and extended thumb over his shoulder and says, "He's in his office working on a case. Go in and see him. He won't rip off your fucking head for not knocking, since he finds you adorable."

I pass the office area and head left, through a glass door marked PRIVATE, enter a second hallway, and read the pale wooden door: Officer Garrett R. Haute. I twist the door's knob, open it, slip inside, and ...

Garrett is the only one in the office. He has his black boots cocked up on the edge of his desk. His cowboy-bulky legs are spread wide open. White boxer-briefs and his tan uniform slacks are comfy around his ankles. His khaki-colored cotton shirt is open and he sports erect nipples in a patch of curly dark chest hair. The strands of hair fall into a thin strip on the middle of his chiseled chest and lead to his puckered, comma-shaped navel. Beneath the navel lies a V-area of coal-black tangles of pubic hair and nine whopping inches of stiff and uncut cock. He holds the cock with both palms and jerks the slab of beef up and down. On the desk in front of him are three naked mechanics on a nineteen-inch Sony flat-screen, all of which are accomplishing some naughty garage overtime against the hood of a red MX-4 Miata.

My high school friend makes eye contact with me, broadly grins, and inquires, "Want a lick for old time's sake, Derek?" He continues to stroke his pole a few times, provides a hearty groan, arches his neck back, and shoots a spray of white ooze up and over the plates that design his stomach.

Honestly, if I didn't want to marry Rocco and spend the rest of my life with the mobster and become a future member of his family, I'd be on my knees, in front of the crime scene investigator, and take full pleasure in licking up his bittersweet ooze-treat. Rocco means the world to me, though. I'm in love with the man to the nth degree, and his family. The last thing I want to do is ruin my relationship with the guy, and fuck up my future.

"Thanks for the offer, Garrett, but I'm kindly going to have to pass."

As the mechanics carry out their three-way on the flat-screen, my high school jack-buddy draws two fingertips through the puddle of gunk next to his puckered navel and slips them into his mouth. He smiles a semen-covered grin with me, winks in my direction, and says, "You don't know what you're missing."

Right now, I miss Rocco. Our sex gig from this morning was just not enough to tide my needs over until I see him again. Truth is I desperately want to eat up my mobster's sticky goo from his Italian hairy chest, fulfilling my needs. Rocco is across town, though, on business. His current adventure entails a search to find Dane Duncock and question the bad boy about Tang's murder on our beach.

Garrett continues to feed himself the goo, using his fingertips as a spoon. Between sucks, he says, "You know I should have never fallen in love with Whitney. I'm gay and need to tell her that. All I want is a cock like yours to be jammed into my ass for three days in a row."

"I'm sorry, but you can't get that from me. I'm in the mob, as you already know."

He finds some tissues and swabs up the sticky residue from his perfectly designed chest, and at the corners of his mouth. The sexy cop tosses the tissues in his waste basket and sighs with contentment. He now leans forward, exits the naughty website he jacked off to, and stands up. His shaft is still hard: throbbing, veined, and quite a mouthful for a guy with a narrow throat, in my opinion. A bubble of pearl-colored semen dots the end of it. He politely offers me a last lick before putting the stem away, which I also cordially decline. Now, he eventually pulls up his cotton boxer-briefs and slacks, belting them around his waist. Following this act, he begins to button his shirt and says, "I'm going to have to divorce Whitney. I've been going to Pallyo every other night."

"What do you do there?"

"I pick up the hottest guys. This happens about three or four times a week. I take them to local hotels and let them fuck me. They jam their cocks into my mouth and ass. Sometimes they don't even wear condoms, although they should, but I don't make them. Whitney doesn't know about any of this. The guilt regarding the issue is starting to kill me inside. I'm sure I have an ulcer because of it."

"You have to be honest to the both of you," I say, pull out my imaginary therapy card and decide to use it at freewill, even if I don't have a degree in psychology, although I have always wanted one. Then again, I was raised by Barbara, which entitles me the degree without even spending a single class at a university or college. The woman can gift anyone a degree in psychology after living twenty-plus years with her.

"Whitney deserves someone better than me. One of those men that doesn't think about cocks all day long."

"You mean a straight guy, right?" It sounds like a joke, but it's not. Shame on me.

"I should have never married her, if you want to know the truth. I should have known that on our wedding day when I found her older brother unbelievably sexy. Can you believe I wanted to fuck him in the men's room at the church before my wedding gig with Whitney? All I wanted to do to the guy was suck his cock and nail him against one of the bathroom walls. That should have been a clear sign that I was not meant for Whitney."

I want to laugh, but hold it in. "People get divorced all the time." Honestly, I don't know what else to say. It sounds like good advice, right? Who knows? I'm an ex-errand boy, not a psychiatrist. Maybe a degree in shrink-work is a bad idea after all.

He has his shirt buttoned, sits back in his chair, and says, "I'm worried about my three girls. I'm going to have to break our family apart. This is just the beginning to one fucked-up mess."

"You'll be helping them out in the long run. Stay honest to yourself. Someday you will be completely happy. This is just a rocky patch you're going through. Keep your chin high and move forward. Life is too short to be miserable."

He sits up, clears his throat, reviews notes on the blotter in front of him, and says, "Enough of my bullshit, Derek. Wasn't there a murder on your beach this morning?"

I nod my head. "How do you know about that?"

"We're the police department. Of course we know things like that." He reads from his blotter, "Tang Meadow. Owner of The Skin Artist. Son to Tai and Shae Meadow. Comes from a wealthy family of Koreans. Stabbed four times. Naked. No footprints around the body."

"That's him."

"Is that why you're here?" He looks up from his blotter, rubs the side of his nose in a boyish manner, and winks at me again.

I shake my head this time. "Mother needs a favor from you."

He vigorously laughs. "It's about Melvin isn't it?"

"I'm afraid so."

"She wants me to make his parking tickets vanish, doesn't she?" A sneer crosses my handsome friend's face. He's still adorable following our childhood: sharply sexy and terribly masculine. The guy should have went into modeling instead of criminology.

One wrong look at the guy can suggest that I'm interested in him and want to secretly have a sexual tryst, which will then spark Boss Malonni's interest and have the mobster man on my queer and cheating ass in less than two seconds. So I keep my look clean and very businesslike, exactly what's expected out of me as a future don's son-in-law. "You got it."

He shakes his head. "I'm not removing the tickets, Derek. The man parks wherever he wants. Near fire hydrants. In school zones. Blocking driveways. He's lucky I haven't had his car towed and impounded. Last week he was parked in two handicapped places in front of the First Episcopalian Church on Dora Street."

"I get it. Can you do one favor for me, though?"

He stands from his desk, closes the gap between us in his office, and practically dots the tip of his nose to my nose. "Anything for you, Derek … You know that I have always adored you. Something about your skin and good looks make me hard. Shame on me for dumping you for Whitney so many years ago. What the fuck was I thinking?"

"Can you keep Melvin out of jail? No lock up time. What do you say?"

"What about his fines? I just can't overlook them, Derek."

I feel the cop's right hand on my hip, which casually strays to my middle and presses against my tight stomach where it plays with my rigid abs.

"We can maybe go get a hotel room and ... I can forget about the fines. What do you say?"

Rocco will kill me if he learns about this somewhat intimate moment with Officer Garrett Haute. It's better not to tell him, breaking a rule of honesty in our relationship, of course. My future husband can easily call his men in Miami and have Garrett buried in cement, which is out of the question. The police officer's body can be missing for decades in the future if this little pony show continues anymore.

I back away from him and say, "I can't do that and you know it. How about I just pay his fines? You know I've got the money to do it."

Garrett knows about my twenty million dollars in the bank, and my relationship with Rocco Malonni, a kingpin son. "You're Mafia boyfriend wouldn't approve of you having a sex-round with me, would he?"

"I'm afraid not, Garrett. We're getting married someday and ... I don't think he's into threesomes."

My former tug-buddy gushes with embarrassment. He pulls away from me and whispers, "My apologies. I should have known."

"It's alright. I know you have a thing for me. Mr. Right is out there somewhere for you. Never give up and find him."

When Garrett becomes nervous or on edge, he always changes the subject. This is what happens right now. He finds his comfortable chair again, sits down, reviews the scrawled notes on the blotter, and says, "Dune Duncock hated Tang Meadow. I think he can be a number one suspect."

"And others," I add, glad that the somewhat intimate and uncomfortable moment between us is over.

My high school fling looks up from the blotter and shares, "Tang has a lot of enemies. He wasn't a very nice man."

I have a seat in the block-like chair to the right of his desk and ask, "How do you know that?"

"Tang was a dick. A heartbreaker. Mean. Uncivilized. Some of us believe he's better off dead."

This catches me off guard. Garrett now sounds like a suspect. I tilt my head with question and ask, "You know Tang personally?"

"Maybe."

He's not telling me truth. I know him well enough to sniff this fact out. Plus, he won't look at me; his eyes shift back down to the blotter and stay there.

"What kind of secret do you have?" I ask, now intentionally playing the cop role.

The guy leans back in his chair, toys with a pencil, rolling the tool between his fingers. "You really want to know?"

"I do," I respond, having both ears open and on a mission to discover a murderer with Rocco.

An arrogant smile surfaces on my jack-buddy's face and he happily responds, "We fucked like dogs a few weeks ago. I met him at Pallyo, picked him up, went back to his tattoo parlor … and he nailed me over a sofa there. The guy didn't have the biggest cock, but he sure did know how to use it."

I'm not surprised. The cop is going through a stage of finding himself, searching out some honesty and reality regarding his sexuality. I'm sure that lately he's been bouncing from one bed to the next, fucking anything that can slide into his ass. Some guys are like this. Others are like me, I guess. We're all the same, though, which means we're just in need of some closeness in our lives, some happiness, and a gay gig.

Garrett confesses, "He fucked me a few times and ended it. He said he wasn't the type of guy to be committed to one man. He admitted that he liked to play the field. One cock wasn't enough for him. Nor was two or three at the same time. No surprise there."

I don't know why I play *Spencer for Hire*, but do: "You kill him?"

The dude looks at me and shakes his head. "Why the fuck would I do that?"

"Cause he wouldn't stay with you?"

"Maybe I didn't want to stay with him."

"Maybe you killed him."

He admits, "It sounds like a good theory, but I didn't do it. I was with Whitney all morning."

"Wives will do anything to cover up a murder for their loving husbands, won't they?"

Again, the cop becomes uncomfortable, shifting in his seat. He changes the subject and says, "The money for the fines. Write a check out to me."

"You going to personally pocket it?"

"Fuck yeah," the officer of the law answers. "Your badass boyfriend would."

I don't know what to say to this, pull out my checkbook from my back pocket, write out a check for one thousand dollars, and pass it to the guy who used to give me the best handjobs in high school. "Don't spend it all on hustlers," I tell him.

He looks at the check to see if it's filled out right, pockets the piece of paper, and says, "Thanks for stopping by, Derek. It was nice to see your cock again."

When I leave his office, I shake my head. Half of me doesn't know who Garrett Haute is anymore. He lies to Whitney Hockenstock every day about his sexuality. He jerks off on company time. And he just pocketed a bribe of one thousand dollars over parking fines. Does a man like Garrett have the potential to murder one of his former lovers? Does he have more secrets that he's obviously not sharing with me? Is he a bad cop or just playing one for me? I really don't know. But then again, I'm not Spencer.

CHAPTER FIVE – BLOW ME AWAY

Upon returning to the beach house, I fetch the mail. A few bills arrive, the newest issue of Instinct, and a naughty DVD from Mr. Chaz. The XXX flick is titled *Man-Break*; his newest porno produced by Worthington Lewis, his husband, and the owner of Gladiator Media Limited. I'm about to watch the DVD in our bedroom when I receive a call from Rocco on my cellular.

My favorite guy in the world sounds rushed and on edge, "I need you over here right now."

"Where are you?"

"At The Skin Artist. How soon can you get here?"

I tuck the XXX DVD back into its plastic case and snap it closed. "A few minutes. What are you doing there?"

"Looking at a second dead body."

"Jesus," I whisper. "Who is it this time?"

"Just get over here, Derek. I need all the help you can give me." He ends our call, hanging up on me; someday I'll get even for his abruptness.

# # # # #

Approximately seven minutes later I make the drive in Rocco's cherry red 182i convertible BMW to 7291 Castle Street. This area of the city is a dive with litter on the streets, broken windows, vulgar graffiti everywhere, cheap hustlers, and betraying drug dealers. The smell that lingers throughout the street is rank: a mixture of burning diapers, blood, smoke, and alcohol. There are more rats and cockroaches than citizens that accommodate the dilapidated apartment buildings and illegal businesses.

Rocco waits for me on the sidewalk. He waves for me to park.

I've never been the greatest driver in the world and accidentally back into his Hummer. Frustrated with me, he investigates the damage to his front bumper and the BMW's rear bumper. Both are scratched. The BMW suffers a fist-size dent.

My boyfriend pulls me out of the BMW in a pissed off manner and presses my back against the driver's door frame. I think he's about to slam a fist into my face and break my nose due to the accident, but the guy will never hurt me, head over heels in love with me. Instead, he leans into me, provides me with a kiss that about knocks me off my feet for eternity, and asks, "Where were you for the last two hours? I was trying to reach you, guy. Did you have your cellular off?"

I choose not to share this information since he knows about my past buddy-tugging festivities with Garrett Haute in high school. Rocco will surely become jealous if he finds out I was with the cop. Frankly, he doesn't really like Garrett. A fight would certainly break out between the two of them if they were in the same room for more than ten minutes, I'm sure.

Instead, I mention his affable affection, and eventually ask, "Where is the second body?"

"Inside. I don't think you want to see it, though."

Of course I do. Why not? I viewed Tang Meadow on our beach just a few hours ago and didn't vomit. I'm sure I can handle a second body. To get this point across to him, I say, "Walk me inside."

"My father's men are inside."

"Dragon and Brit?"

"Yes. They're going to take care of the body."

"Does your father know about this murder, too?"

"He does. Whatever I know, my father knows more about it. It's the way our family operates and why he's the don." Rocco walks at my side. We close in on a graffiti-painted wall with a steel door. He opens the door in front of us and steps inside. What appears is a small room with floor-to-ceiling tattoo paintings; examples for paying clients to choose from to be their permanent body art. Each tattoo is numbered and priced with an orange yard sale sticker. Beyond the room is another small room with a desk, cash register, radio, and television set. Sitting at the desk is Dragon, rifling through papers. His hazel eyes meet my blue ones and he genially nods his head, approving my presence.

Brit is with the second body in one of the small studio ink rooms. Rocco leads me to the room, which is two doors down another hallway and on the left-hand side. Brit is hunched over a body, investigating the cadaver's stab wounds.

Rocco's right, the body is more disgusting than how we found Tang Meadow. A naked and bald male in his mid-thirties lies on the floor. The guy is muscular with a pretty handsome face. His chest looks sliced down its center from numerous stab wounds. Blood covers the floor, the body's torso, and the surrounding walls. Organs and bone are viewed. I think I'm about to vomit when Rocco immediately yanks me out of the room and into the hallway.

I'm hugged and my back is rubbed. I place my head on my lover's muscular shoulder, prevent myself from throwing up, and whisper, "Who is he?"

"Nolan Cutler."

"Who's that?"

"Tang's assistant. They worked side by side for the last three years."

"Do you think Dane Duncock is responsible for that mess in there?"

Rocco squeezes me close to his torso; I can feel his heart beat against my chest. "I'm not sure."

"Did you question Dane about Tang Meadow?"

"I couldn't find Dane to question him. I received a mysterious call on my cell phone from a woman. She gave me a tip that someone was murdered inside The Skin Artist."

"Who made the call?"

"My father's men are working on that. I'll have an answer in less than an hour. Honestly, I think it's one of the tenants who lives upstairs. Maybe they heard some ruckus, screaming, and whatnot."

"The smell is atrocious," I confess, pushing away from my boyfriend. "When do you think this happened?"

"Brit says it happened last night."

"The killer was looking for Tang and knocked off his assistant. Didn't they?"

"Maybe. I'm not sure."

"We need to find Dane and learn a few more details about him."

"You need to get home because you're looking really pale. I shouldn't have asked you to come here."

"What will Brit do with the body?"

"Again," Rocco states, "I have no idea. That has nothing to do with me."

# # # # #

Rocco walks me out of The Skin Artist and to his Hummer. I pull away from him and say, "I can drive. I'll take the BMW home and you meet me there."

"You sure you can drive?" he asks, always caring about me, worried about my safety with the most appealing concern.

"I can." Feeling woozy after seeing Nolan's mutilated torso, I climb into the BMW. After starting the vehicle's engine, I pop it into reverse, begin to back up and ...

Bang!

I hit Rocco's Hummer a second time; this time harder than first.

Rocco is ready to cry on the sidewalk. He raises his palms up to his temples and shares a look of shock with me.

Quickly, before he decides to kill me, I shift the BMW into drive, pull out of the parking spot, blow him a kiss, wave goodbye, and make my escape to home.

# # # # #

Rocco returns to the beach house approximately three hours after I do; obviously he was busy working the homicide cases. I half believe he is going to rip me a new asshole for the damage caused to his Hummer. He's pretty cool, though, plus he loves me, and decides not to murder me.

Locked in his arms, pressed against his chest, he whispers, "I should spank you for denting my Hummer today."

I giggle, teasing him.

"It's not funny." He swings me in his hulking arms and lifts me off the foyer's floor with his massive biceps. "I have to get it repaired now."

"I'll write you out a check." This is so easy to say lately. What would I do without Felicia's twenty million dollars? Thank Jesus the woman willed me her fortune or my ass would be in possible debt and completely broke.

"You have to be more careful, Derek. Your driving skills are horrible."

"Do you love your Hummer more than you love me?"

He places me back on the floor and vehemently shakes his head. "That's not what I'm saying at all."

"That's exactly what it sounds like," I pout and put on a show, just for the attention. I like to be a drama queen sometimes, but who doesn't?

"Stop with the cute lips. Don't be sad. I was just thinking of your safety." He brushes blond curls away from my eyes and dots my nose with a finger. "I'm not mad at you. I love you. Don't forget that."

"Speaking of love … I have something to show you." I pull him upstairs and into our bedroom. On the bed is Mr. Chaz's new DVD,

Man-Break. I pick the movie, pass it to him and tease, "I hope you fuck me while we watch this together."

He hands the DVD back to me after a quick glance and asks, "Isn't that your ex on the front?"

It is. Rocco doesn't miss a trick. Mr. Chaz and I used to live in the same apartment building last year. *Man-Break* just so happens to be his fourth raunchy flick in less than five months. Worth is obviously keeping his husband naked and busy in front of the XXX camera.

"We're not fucking while we watch your hot and hairy ex on a DVD."

I laugh, hiding the DVD away; I'll watch it alone some other time, curious to see what hot little twink the once-architect slams his dog into. "You know I was just kidding you, right?"

"Sometimes I have to wonder."

"Trust me … I'll make it all better." I move up to my future husband and strip his shirt off. My tongue finds his hairy nipples and navel, which sends him into an immediate state of unspoken bliss. Fingers begin to unbutton his jeans, slip inside his boxer-briefs, and explore his tools. My appendages wrap gently around his plump pole and provide it with a gentle squeeze. Feeling naughty, I pull away from his right nipple and whisper, "You're going to have to fuck me for backing into your Hummer. Don't you think I need reprimanded?"

"I was thinking that all along," he groans, enjoying my handy tour in his cotton.

Straying lips find his other nipple. My mouth opens and I dart my tongue out, licking its mound of erect flesh. Horny for him, I inhale his strong scent of sweat and citrus soap. I drag my tongue along his rippled and furry belly, inside his navel's divot, and to the top of his jeans where my hand wants to toy with his tools.

"Pull my jeans down and blow me," he instructs in a whisper. "You know I like that."

Indeed I do. Fingertips release buttons. The denim covering his center is pushed down to his ankles. Rocco still sports his white Calvins, and my tongue travels to places where few men – according to his confessions of past sexual adventures – have traveled to before. My slippery appendage rolls over his diagonal rod that is temporarily hidden by the natural fabric. Carefully, I place the covered spike against my lips and kiss it with likeness.

Above me, he runs his palms through my blond hair. The Mafia man shares a murmur with me and follows it with: "Take it out and play with it, Derek."

Truth is I love his cock: its eight inches of length and mushroom-capped head; the thick purple-blue veins running along its tubular structure; the way it easily slides down the back of my throat; and the way it squirts inside my mouth or on a cheek during his heated orgasms. Pleasure is a first priority at this very intimate moment. Fingertips discover the rim on his boxer-briefs and pull the cotton down. Rocco's massive shaft is exposed, already dripping with pre-ooze. Hungry for some goo, I lap up the succulent and sticky liquid from the mast's head and swallow it down.

"Do it, Derek … Put it in your mouth and suck me off." He pushes his body against my face, rushing our moment of cozy bliss. A grunt escapes his beautiful mouth and he tops it off with: "I want to fuck your face."

I pull the cotton briefs down to his knees and unexpectedly have his hard pipe smack me in my right cheek. A light sound of shock escapes me, now a giggle, and I end up with the thumper's head inside my mouth and begin to gently roll the end of my tongue around its circumference.

My lover clamps his palms on the back of my head and pushes my throat over his cock. Both of us grunt, but for different and gratifying reasons. My boyfriend decides to take matters in his own hands and plugs my body with his equipment, holds me against his fuzzy navel and cut abs, and almost causes me to suffocate.

I must confess: I like to be in the submissive role sometimes. My hands find the mobster's sculpted hips and hang on as my head swings to and fro on his beef. Saliva builds within the cavern of my mouth and leaks from its corners because of our heated friction.

"Fucking you," he moans, swinging his head and neck back, arching his spine.

I gag on his protein and lose oxygen. My nostrils gape and close in search of air. I wheeze and grumble and make animal-like noises on my knees, busy with his rod in my throat. More saliva leaks from my collapsed lips and tears begin to fall out of my eyes and roll down and over my reddish and burning cheeks.

"Fucking you," he chants yet another time, working against me. His hips thrust forward, pull away, and push into my face again. Fingernails dig into my skull and his hairy balls swing into my chin with a rhythm of their own.

# # # # #

What transpires between us next is not uncommon in our shared relationship. Rocco loves it when I release my mouth from his dick, spin him around, tell him to spread his legs, and to bend over.

"Lick my ass," he begs. "Shove your tongue inside ... The deeper, the better."

And so this is accomplished. I pry his smooth bottom open with my fingers, admire his pink-tight core, decide to spit into the man-sliver, and run a fingertip against its warm and wet sliver, and drive him erotically mad. I delve a finger up to its knuckle inside for a few seconds, twist the appendage to the right, and eventually pull the digit out.

My tongue now replaces the finger, which causes the mobster to grumble in front of me, half-bent over with his palms planted on his knees. He searches for air, gasping uncontrollably. Now he begins to rock to and fro, enjoys his erotic ride as he backs into my face, pulls away, and backs into my pretty boy good looks again.

I lick and lap his hole in a hungry-driven manner. My tongue darts in and out of his cave in a feisty way, and continues this action for the next ten minutes or more.

"Derek ... Christ, Derek," he rambles, overjoyed with our heated link.

The shameless moment between us only becomes more vibrant. I release my right hand from his taut rump and reach around his thick thigh. The hand finds his burning shaft and begins to tug on it with a steady motion.

He pants, "Make me shoot on the floor ... Trust me, it's not going to take much more."

My sliver of busy tongue meets his tight center again as fingers work on the extra skin that covers his cock. I slurp and gag, lap and suck. My palm gyrates up and down on his post, milking his flesh.

He heavily breathes, trembling in front of me. A few masculine grunts escape his mouth. He attempts to fuck my hand, swings to and fro, but every time he does his ass pulls away from mouth and his pleasure is lost. So he decides to stand still and warns, "I'm going to spray my load."

The bad boy doesn't lie to me. In fact, with just a few more strokes applied to his flag, his breathing becomes more intense and he vibrates with a fresh orgasm. Growls fill the modern bedroom as his firm hose washes down the floor. Strings of gunk fly down to his feet and cover his toes. More droplets decorate the ruby-colored Berber and his shins. The strong stink of post-sex fills the room with thick perspiration.

When I rise from my mouthy adventure, he spins around. We intimately lock faces and chests together. The mobster broadly smiles, thrilled with our unexpected sex antics, and informs rather affectionately, "I'll fill the bathroom tub up with some bubbles, light a few candles, pour us some champagne, and ... finish you off."

I tease him and bite his lip. Afterward, I decide to play with him and say, "You wouldn't dare."

"Try me," he heavily breathes, holding me against his heated skin.

"You're on," I reply, and follow him to our shared bathroom for an evening of fun in suds and more heated sex with his unbelievable rocking body.

CHAPTER SIX –
DIRTY DEEDS

We have unsettling hangovers the next morning from drinking too much the night before. Rocco and I both sleep in, snuggled together in our bed, hidden from the February light.

It's maybe the first time since he's been home that he doesn't dream of Zulan Cane. Rocco is still and quiet throughout the night at my side, unharmed and free of the wicked jungle dream that consists of a bad black man, voodoo, diamond smuggling, and South African violence.

I wake first, grab a shower, eat a banana, drink some pineapple juice, take two aspirin for my headache, and decide to accept my mother's call on the back patio, out of ear's reach from Rocco's sleepy time.

Barbara yells into the phone, "Good morning, baby!"

"Jesus, Mother, stop with the screaming. I put in a late night with Rocco. Why are you so happy, anyway?"

"I won the lottery yesterday. Two thousand dollars. Melvin bought me a ticket and it was a winner." The excitement in her voice is overwhelming. Barbara never wins anything, even herpes if she tried.

"That's great news. Melvin can pay me for his parking tickets now."

The day is beautiful, if I may say so: not a cloud in the sky, blue and perfect, no wind, and on the warmer side for the beginning of February. I snug my cotton robe around my middle and listen to her somber and almost reserved voice ask, "Why would he do that, honey?"

"I paid off his parking tickets and would like my money back."

"Oh darling … this isn't his money. This is my money. I plan not to share it with anyone."

True, it is her money. A very good point. How dare I spend Barbara's money for her; God knows Melvin will accomplish this feat on his own. "What are you going to do with it?"

"Gamble in Tampa. They have the best slots."

"Gamble?" I question, rolling my eyes. I should know better for asking such a stupid fucking question. Shame on me.

Barbara loves to gamble. Bingo. Daily numbers. Horse racing. Basket auctions at local high schools. Lottery tickets from all the convenience stores in Flamingo Cove. Any method she can find to gamble, she does. Never does she win, except for last night, which sort of surprises maybe the both of us.

"I'm leaving in an hour. This is why I'm calling."

"Why?" I inquire, unsure of where this conversation is going.

"Boob needs to go out. I plan to spend more than twelve hours in Tampa and really don't want to leave him alone for that long."

Boob is Barbara's short-haired black Cockapoo. A mean little wiry shit that bites and growls, and absolutely hates me. The dog and I have a sketchy history. Upon our first meet and greet, he decided to try to use my left ankle as dinner. I wasn't tolerating his unkindness and acted rather villainous by choking him. Barbara stepped in and broke the two of us apart. None of us have forgotten the ordeal, especially Boob.

"Can't Melvin take care of Boob?" I ask, wanting to keep my distance from the evil pooch.

"Melvin is driving me to Tampa. You have to take care of poor Boob."

Honestly, I'd like to murder Boob. Don't get me wrong, I like dogs, particularly larger dogs with calm tempers. Boob is nothing but a spoiled beast from hell, a snippy-snapper with more attitude and teeth than Paris Hilton. Fuck!

"I can't take care of Boob, Mother. Rocco and I have plans today."

She's quiet, obviously thinking of a way to blackmail me. Silence is an introduction to such trouble. If anyone knows how to work me, it's mother. Before I can utter a single word, ending our conversation, she asks, "You don't want me to tell Rocco that you stopped by the police department to see Garrett Haute, do you?"

Fuck again! Barbara can be vicious, just like Boob. The two are a match made in heaven. Both are feisty, bitchy, and quite intolerable. Grrrr.

"Of course not." I sound weak and deflated. The last thing I want to do is piss Rocco off because of a minor, explainable, and innocent visit to see my ex-cock buddy from high school.

I can see her sneer with delight and happiness on her end of the call: white-huge teeth glowing, upturned and thick whore-red lips, eyes wide with interest, perhaps knowing she has won this battle between us. Calmly, she replies, "I didn't think so."

"Mother, this isn't fair."

Gruffly, she responds, "Life isn't fair, baby boy. Get over it. Boob will need to be put out at six this evening. His canned food will be on the counter. He will also want some fresh water. And don't disappoint either of us."

She hangs up before I can say anything more or vehemently protest, which ruffles my feathers. As I press the END button on my cell phone, I decide to give her credit for one thing and one thing only: Barbara always gets what she wants. Good for her.

# # # # #

Not even ten minutes later Rocco decides that we have to find Dane Duncock. We climb into his Hummer, head north, end up in Swashton Bay, pull up in front of a place called The Manatee Motel, and scope out the joint.

"This place is a dump," I share my opinion, telling the truth. The Manatee Motel is a long, J-shaped, two-floor structure with a few broken windows and rusted railings. Doors hang off their hinges and drug dealers loiter in the parking lot. Think projects in the city; the absolute worse place you would ever want to live.

"Jay-D and Con are here," Rocco says as he discreetly looks to our right in the parking area.

Two massive African-American guys share a powder drug in a stolen BMW M3 Turbo the color of midnight black. Neither scope us out. In fact, we kind of look like we belong in the parking lot because of Rocco's Hummer.

"How do you know those guys?" I inquire, brushing up on my street knowledge.

"Gang bangers. This is their territory so we can't fuck with them. They will blow us away without even thinking about it."

I'm nervous as hell, unsure of what we are doing at the motel. "Do you know for a fact that Dane is here?"

"Nope."

"Who told you he might be here?"

"My father."

Boss Malonni knows his shit. If he thinks Dane Duncock is here, the man is; I won't ever question him.

To our advantage, Jay-D and Con drive away. This gives Rocco and me time to plan our escape from his Hummer and search out Dane.

We still don't know where Dane is, though. The guy could be anywhere. I ask Rocco, "Which room is he in?"

"That one," he shares, pointing at Room 211 on the second floor, near a wrought-iron flight of rickety stairs. "It's the only room with a closed door and a blanket covering the window."

Rocco's right; bless his queer soul for being so observant and smart.

"You ready to bolt up there and risk being in danger?" he turns his attention to me and asks.

"Risk what?"

"Your life. Dane could have a shitload of guns holed up there and we wouldn't know it."

"Every day is a risk with you, rocket man. I think I learned that on our first date," I respond, climb out of the Hummer, and immediately head to Room 211.

"Where are you going?" he asks, hopping out of the metal beast and dashing up to my side.

"I have work to do, dude. Someone has to question Dane about Tang's murder. I'm the guy to do it."

We head up the wrought-iron steps. I go first and Rocco brings up the rear, which I kind of like, since this is where he enjoys spending a lot of his free time when we're naked and together.

Behind me, he informs, "I got your ass."

"Thank God ... That's why I'll marry you, if you ever ask me to."

Since becoming involved with him, I now know it's necessary to pack heat. Today I'm carrying a .357 Magnum revolver in mint condition; Rocco's father gave it to me as a Christmas present. Bless his Mafia-loving soul. Truth is I don't know if I'll have to use it, but it's better to be safe than sorry, right?

My sexy sidekick sports his favorite handgun, a Beretta 90two with a 15 magazine capacity. The thing is a beauty and shoots with a smoothness that leaves his heart flutter with joy.

"Be careful, Derek. Act smart when we get inside the room."

"Will do, Scooby Doo," I reply, make my way to the top of the stairs, and end my travels in front of the bright red wooden door of Room 211.

My boyfriend has a look in his eyes that says he wants to break down the door and barge inside, which I think is a big mistake. Sometimes it's best to be a gentleman, even when you're dealing with bad guys. Before he has the opportunity to ruin our day, I tap three times on the door, cause my voice to raise a few octaves like a queen's, and say, "Room service, darlin'."

My boyfriend gives me a stare that says: I didn't know you had it in you, Darla. Nicely executed.

I provide a smartass grin, delighted with my impersonation of a female housekeeper, put my ear up to the wooden door, and begin to eavesdrop on Dane inside the room.

Rocco's forehead touches my forehead in the cutest way. Both of us hear the same sounds: two male voices heavily grunt, huff for breath, and sporadically moan. A young man's voice calls out, "Fuck me hard! ... Shove your cock into me, Dane!"

A sneer of surprise covers my face and I somewhat blush. Rocco does everything to hold back a string of laughter. Both of us look at each other with shock and shake our heads.

Of course we should leave the duo to their sex-gig and go on our merry ways. My lover's mobster side kicks in, though. The next thing I know, he turns the room's rusted door knob, pushes the door open, and begins our unexpected entrance.

What I witness is rather scathing inside the room: Dane has an eighteen-year-old boy tied up to the bed with leather straps. The boy has short brown hair, deep blue eyes, a scruffy goatee on his chin, and pork chop-shaped sideburns. Metal clips are attached to his strawberry-colored nipples. Some type of red ball-gag that was once wedged inside his tender looking mouth dangles near his chin and neck. The boy-thing on the bed has tiny sprigs of curly brown hair between his strawberry-colored nipples, no muscle tone whatsoever, and sports a seven-inch uncut flag between his legs, which showcases a bubble of pre-ooze at its tip. Dane just happens to be fixed in place between the boy's fully spread legs. His nine-inch pounder is solid, veined, and very much ready to be shoved into his lover's pink and rather loose bottom.

Dane is a beauty on the bed; porn-star material without a single ounce of fat. He has red curly hair, expressive green eyes, a muscular torso, bulging biceps, and a six-pointed star tattoo on his right shoulder.

Truth is I know very little about the tattoo artist. The information I have on the entrepreneur is rather unhelpful. He has an identical twin, Mario Duncock, who is married with a baby on the way. Dane lives at 67291 Shotner Street in Tampa Bay, has a gambling problem, and now owns and operate his own tattoo palace called The Ink House.

Things I should know about Dane: How badly did he and Tang tear down their business relationship? Does Dane despise Tang? And, is the man willing to commit murder over the nasty breakup of their business? Perhaps this is why Rocco and I are inside Room 211 at this very second, attempting to learn a little more about Dane Duncock and his mysterious ways.

Dane jumps off the bed and stands ass-naked with his arms up, surrendering. He yells at the top of his voice, "What the fuck is going on here?" His nine-inch spike still has protection on it and points straight up, touching his tight navel. The guy is built like a model: V-triangle patch of red curly cues of hair between his legs, perfectly man-scaped balls, ladder-like chest, pert pecs and nipples, and biceps that a wrestler wouldn't complain about.

The room is a shithole with emerald-green shag carpet, dilapidated furniture, a broken mirror, cracks in the pastel-green painted walls, and water spots on the ceiling from a recent rainstorm. The rank smell of urine, semen, and pot lingers about the confines, causing me to choke on my own spit.

Rocco shares, "We just want to ask you a few questions, my friend." He points his Beretta at Dane and provides a rather sexy and cocky grin.

The naked boy on the bed is wide-eyed with fear. His once-firm cock is now completely deflated, comma-shaped between his legs. Thick sweat lathers his toneless chest, sticklike arms, and legs. Saliva dribbles out of his semi-parted lips.

Standing in front me, my charming cohort waves his gun at Dane and asks, "What happened to Tang Meadow?" Damn does he sound sexy, rugged, and beefy all the way; I'd rip his clothes off and hump him in the hotel room if we were alone.

"Someone poked him." Dane looks terrified. Truth is he's terrified and looks like he's going to drop a load right on the shag carpet. "I don't know who it was."

"You were business partners with Tang, right?" Rocco asks.

Dane nods his head. In doing so, his firm cock bounces against his tight and rippled torso. "We owned the The Ink Den for three years."

"Which ruined your relationship with Tang?" Rocco shifts his view to the boy on the bed, who still looks petrified, white as paper on the sheets, and continues to be tied up with the leather straps.

"Let me just say we made better lovers than business partners."

"Because Tang was skimming money off the top, right?" I have to hand it to my lover, his questioning rocks. He gets to the point and doesn't hold back; good for him.

"Something like that," Dane finally lowers his arms to his sides. If he had access to a handgun right now, he'd take Rocco and me out with no remorse whatsoever. The only weapon he sports is the nine-inch tool between his legs, which looks ready to fire its load at any second.

"He was stealing from you, Dane. Everyone in Flamingo Cove knows it was no secret. You got pissed, backed out of the shop deal, and decided to murder Tang on my beach."

Damn, Rocco's good. His spill sounds believable. I will surely honor him with a tongue-kiss and blowjob as payment, following this unannounced interrogation.

Dane shakes his head, realizing his position as weaponless and a suspicious liar. "I was the one skimming from the business. I shafted him out of thousands."

"Because you like your drugs?"

"Meth works. Some of us have vices. Meth just happens to be mine."

"Meth and boys," Rocco confirms, and turns his view to the bound and naked eighteen-year-old on the bed. "Nice combo." His attention now quickly turns to Dane again and he asks in a rather rugged tone, "Did Tang owe you money?"

Dane shakes his head. "I probably owe him some."

"If you didn't kill him, who did?"

"The fag does some bad business. He's fucked over a number of guys. The list is pretty long. Anyone could have offed him."

"You have names on the list?"

Dane is quiet for a second … two seconds … three seconds. He looks to the boy on the bed and now back to us.

Rocco loses his patience and fires off a bullet at Dane's feet. The bad boy jumps to his right in fear. His boner bounces up and down in its plastic condom, snapping against his torso. The boy on the bed squeals like a little pig, terrified.

I sort of chuckle because of the scene, loving the entertainment.

Dane's nicely built chest rises and falls, producing carbon dioxide. He blurts, "Just one I can think of."

"Who is it? Tell me and I won't hurt you," my boyfriend rattles off, sounding serious and menacing, which sort of turns me on. Even I wouldn't want to fuck with him at the moment.

"Croon."

Rocco waves his gun at the redhead's chest and asks, "Who is Croon?"

Dane looks as if he's about to cry. Tears well up in his eyes and his lips begin to quiver. "Buli Croon."

"Who is Buli Croon?"

"If you're smart, he's someone you need to stay away from."

"Why do you say that?"

"Croon has a bad temper. He's not nice like me."

"Why does he have a bad temper?" Rocco asks.

"He's fucked up in the head. Too many drugs and a mass of anger."

"Meth?"

"And other drugs."

"Was Tang into drugs?"

Dane shakes his head. "Never. Hated them. Another reason why we weren't good for each other."

"Croon have anything against Tang?"

"Maybe. Not sure."

"Croon knock off Tang?"

"Could have. Don't know."

"You're a man of few words, aren't you?" Rocco asks, pointing his Beretta at Dane's erect junk.

Dane nods his head, still silent and unmoving.

"You have a nice cock, though," Rocco says, turns around, escorts me out of Room 211, obviously happy with our visit and the information he has obtained.

CHAPTER SEVEN –
DANGEROUS BITCHES

Rocco leaves Flamingo Cove for the next three days. His father has him working in Miami, probably on a mission to knock off a bad guy or abduct someone's wife, holding her ransom. The mob is known for these trivial and brutal matters, accomplishing daily goals. I guess I've become used to the mob's naughty escapades in the past months, succumbing to illegal doings.

Honestly, I respect the Malonni family. Each member has taken me into their arms, kissed me on my cheeks, and welcomed me into their organization. Uncle Joey calls me on a regular basis to find out if I need anything accomplished. Mickey, the oldest of the six Malonni boys, always sends me text messages to see if I'm safe. Middle brothers, Franco and Nico, unexpectedly visit the beach house and check up on me. Younger brothers, Enzo and Michelangelo, are often seen in my vicinity, obviously watching over me. Bella, Uncle Joey's wife of forty-eight years, always visits the beach house, bringing Italian casseroles in her hands. Other wives adore me and share lunch dates with me: Esperanza, Izabella, Minolta, Bree, and Lucia. These Mafia wives have taken me under their wings, wined and dined me, honored me into their little group of dangerous bitches, and have made me one of their own. Bottom line: I am loved by the Malonni family, and none of them can wait until Rocco finally decides to marry me. Every one of them cares for my needs as if I'm a baby penguin and part of their austere flock.

Rocco's trip to Miami allows me enough time to gather some valuable information on Buli Croon. Because Fisk Deveraux has a history with drugs, curricular activities of buying and selling, I decide to call him about Croon. If anyone knows the man, my friend Fisk does.

According to Walter Landing, Fisk's significant other, Fisk is in Lima, Peru studying a new drug for malaria. I know he has a cell phone with international capabilities, since I paid for it with just a sliver of

Felicia Horodowski's twenty million dollars. I dial his number, wait for it to ring, listen to a stranger say, "Hola!" with exuberant cheer, and become dumbfounded. Half of me wonders if Fisk has found a Peruvian boyfriend on his drug study for malaria. Is he cheating on Walter in Peru? Not that I am surprised if he is, since Fisk has always been sexually unstoppable, surely willing to find a sexy male somebody to shove his dog into. Does Walter suspect an affair? I'm quite sure he does since he's been acting a bit bitchy. Truth is the situation isn't any of my business, but my sniffing nose smells infidelity from afar. But honestly, I'm not really sure.

I hear rustling noises, silence, and now Fisk on his phone. Out of breath, he says, "Hello?"

"Fisk … it's Derek." The connection is very bad between us, scratchy and almost inaudible.

My friend asks, "What's going on, Derek?"

"Is that your new man who said hello to me?"

"Just a friend. Walter has nothing to worry about."

"How is the studying going?"

Fisk has a lift in his voice, seeming happy. "The culture here fascinates me. Malaria is serious in these parts and the new drug that is currently being studied by six of us will help these people." He pauses for just a second, clears his throat, and asks, "I miss my mystery writer. How is he?"

"Walter is fine, and he misses you too."

"You're taking care of him, I presume?"

"To the best of my ability."

"He means the world to me. I wished he were here in Peru with me. Tell him to hop a flight and get his ass down here."

"Walter has his own things to do, I'm sure. Before you know it, the two of you will be back in each other's arms.

We chat for the next few minutes regarding my health, Rocco's return from Africa, and the details about the nasty murders of Tang

Meadow and his assistant, Nolan Carter. Eventually I inquire, "Do you know a Buli Croon up here?"

He thinks about it for a second, two seconds, three seconds. "He's trouble. Why do you ask?"

"I'm mixed up with him a bit."

He sort of laughs, but not in a good way. "Trust me, you don't want to be doing that. The man has the capability of eating men up and spitting them out. He doesn't have a heart."

I tell him all the scathing details about Tang Meadow and his assistant being murdered. "I think Croon has something to do with it."

"He could. The guy is into illegal drugs, a sex ring with underage boys, and harvesting body parts."

"Body parts?" I ask, surprised to hear this.

"Yeah. Croon's a hunter. He searches out his victims for their body parts. His sufferers wake up without kidneys, dicks, and whatnots. Croon is known for removing organs himself and selling them to doctors in Prague."

"Shit," I whisper, stunned to hear this creepy truth. "I think he may have murdered Tang and his assistant."

"Croon has the potential. I'm talking devil man. Someone who doesn't give a shit about life. He has the strength and smarts. So, whatever you do … just be careful."

Before ending our call, I quickly ask, "What about Dane Duncock? Do you think he has the potential to kill the tattoo artist and his assistant?"

"Not a chance. Dane is a pussycat. He seems rough around the edges, but honestly … the guy's a little teddy bear. Squeeze him and he giggles." He sounds confident, without any question whatsoever in his voice.

"How do you know this?"

The world traveler provides a boyish laugh and admits, "He and I had a fling a few years ago. We did some drugs together. We fucked around. He might have stolen some cash from his business partner, but that doesn't mean he has the ability to kill Tang or anyone else. He's just not that angry or evil. Dane lives for his boys, meth, and other drugs. Murder is not on his to-do list."

I take a few mental notes, filing away Fisk's information about Dane and Croon. Eventually he tells me he has to get back to his professor (the Peruvian man who said hello to me a few minutes ago) and adds goodbye. I blow him a kiss through the cell phone, tell him that Walter is in good hands, and to be safe. Fisk agrees, whispers his farewell, and ends our call.

# # # # #

2069 Peninsula Way sits approximately three blocks away from the Gulf. Barbara's house is one floor, all white stucco, and concealed by massive palm fronds. I borrow Rocco's onyx Hummer while he visits Miami and park it in my mother's concrete drive. Her house key is on a Justin Bieber key chain, which I pull out of my Rufskin shorts's front pocket and use.

The day is in the high seventies for early February and no shirts are required. I walk up to Barbara's wrought-iron front door, use the Bieber key in the Kwik lock, and find myself inside.

The place is decorated in Spanish tile and accented with bright blues and yellows. Terracotta pots house indoor palms, jade plants, and prickly cacti. Echeveria succulents decorate the foyer and connected mud room. Barbara has Valencia floor rugs displayed on the pink pastel walls and very little furniture. A wall-size aquarium accommodates three Cuban green anoles, Barbara's favorite creature on the planet, besides her bitchy pooch, Boob, a pesky little shit of a Cockapoo that needs to die. The lizards lounge under their heat lamps among green foliage and stare at me with their beady and judgmental eyes.

Boob finally makes his aggressive appearance. He bolts out of Barbara's bedroom, scampers down the hall toward me, growls at the top of his canine voice, shows his teeth, and begins to bark. Approximately three feet away from me, the pooch immediately leaps off the tile floor, flies toward my motionless position in the foyer, and lunges at my visible neck, going for my jugular like Cujo.

A girlish yelp exits my mouth. My palms go for the little terror's furry sides. Fingers and nails dig into its black fur and muscle. Boob is held in midair, growling and snapping at me in a ferocious behavior. He lets out a few barks, attempts to move left and right in my firm grip, and tries to set himself free, continuing his expected attack

I say to the dog in a rather snippety manner, "I am not your mother. If you don't let me feed and water your furry ass you'll die. God knows when she'll be back, so the two of us have to get along."

Boob tries to leap out of my grip and go for my nose with his snappers. Only inches away from my face, his little mouth opens and he shows off his dagger-like teeth. In a matter of seconds, as he tries to bite off some of my flesh for a snack, his muzzle snaps closed, millimeters from my left cheek.

Discouraged with his rude behavior, I tell him, "That's it. I'm putting you in your room." In truth, I just want to shake the little bastard and show him who's boss. I'm not aggressive with animals, though, and understand that they have emotions and rights, just like humans. So instead of locking him under my left armpit and squeezing his hairy head with ease, popping his eyes out, I decide to walk him back the hallway, make a left into Barbara's bedroom, drop the little crazy bastard on the bed that he shares with my mother, and quickly bolt out of the room in hopes that the furry terror will not follow me, ready to eat one of my heels, thighs, or ass.

Fortunately, this plan works. The only thing that goes off-kilter is the obnoxious thud heard once I close the bedroom's door. Boob obviously throws his weight against the hard plane of wood, hoping to bash through it like a super dog, and seek vengeance for his failed captivity. In doing so, little yelps exit his demonic body and fill the quiet house. The door is apparently too strong for his hairy weight and limitless power, which he eventually comprehends. Boob gives up after twenty seconds, jumps on Barbara's bed, circles three times next to her two fluffy pillows, and decides to take a nap.

I feed and water the fuzzy prick, process exactly what is expected of me, and carry out the visit in a reasonable amount of time. Half of me wants to add some anti-freeze to Boob's water, poisoning the beast, but Barbara loves the Cockapoo, treating the pooch as if the hairy prick were her own son.

Following my farming task, I decide to gather mother's mail from the front stoop and place it on her kitchen counter. Once this is accomplished, I am just about ready to release Boob from his bedroom prison and leave. In doing so, while walking back the hallway, someone appears behind me, cocks a gun at the back of my head, and warns, "Mr. Reed, we need to talk."

# # # # #

The voice sounds Russian, arrogant, astute, and definitely badass. Feeling numb and flustered, but cautious and alert, I politely decide to ask, "Can I turn around and see who is about to kill me?"

"Please do," the Russian informs.

Slowly, I spin around on my heels and look into the barrel of a .9mm. Behind the weapon is an attractive black man: six foot tall, misty-green eyes, wide lips, a four-inch scar along his right cheek, dreadlocks down the middle of his back, and one gold tooth in his ridiculous smile. He looks like a black pirate in one of those Johnny Depp movies, not like the typical Russian mobster.

I've learned years ago that flattery will get you places, so I say to Big Lips, "You're gorgeous. Totally my type. You have a boyfriend?"

He vehemently shakes his head and replies, "No, but you do."

Everyone knows Rocco, but I'm the only one who gets the one on one naked gig with him. Lucky me. I lie again, and try to squirm my way out of this ugly situation: "Unfortunately, I am. But just for the record, if I were single, you could have me."

Big Lips is not at all pleased with the idea of dating, kissing, licking, or fucking me. He waves the barrel of his .9mm at my pretty boy face and informs, "Stay away from Dane Duncock and Mr. Croon. They got nothing to do with you."

"I tend to disagree with you regarding that statement. A body was found on my beach. Another body was found inside The Skin Artist. Dane and Croon are apparent suspects regarding both murders."

"Let police handle it," Big Lips clearly states. "You shouldn't be involved. You end up plugged if you find yourself in their business. I'm sure you don't want problem on your hands."

He has just admitted that Dane and Croon are part of the two murders. What a dumbass. Some men will spill their guts without even trying. I guess it's how the world ticks, right? Now, I ask, "Who do you work for?"

"Who you think I work for?"

"Some asshole like Croon."

"If you want me work for Croon, then I work for Croon."

"You're not denying that you don't work for him," I say, sounding gruff and to the point.

"Watch what you say. I wicked mean when upset."

"Are you a dangerous bitch, sweetheart?'

He nods his head and growls at me, "I kill you so easy."

I tell him, "Listen, you're a bad guy, and I'm a bad guy. Why don't we just sit down in my mother's living room, have a drink, and work through this like two adult men?"

Big Lips's response catches me off guard. He keeps his gun aimed at my face, steps closer to me, reaches for my navel, and pulls the rim of my Rufskin away from my torso. He now looks down at the goods inside my shorts, smiles, and chants, "Nice stuff you got. I think I have better idea for us."

Crap. This unscheduled meeting with the black Russian goon is not going where I want it to. The last thing I want to do is fuck around with him. Some guys are so pushy, though, and ridiculous. I back away from him with caution, closer to Boob in mother's bedroom, shake my head, and insist, "Rocco will kill you if you lay a single finger on me. He's known for offing men like you."

Big Lips is nasty to the core. Eating my tool and pounding my bottom against one of the hallway walls is the only thing he has on his derelict mind. He says in a matter of fact tone, "Rocco is pussy. I'll take him any day. Trust me, I can rock his world with my cock."

"You might regret saying that. Tell me who you work for." I continue to back away from him, one step at a time. Danger lurks within mother's house and I have to be careful, on guard, and make sure that Big Lips doesn't accommodate his way with my skin.

The goon still has his gun aimed at my face. Both of us are on task, ready for whatever is going to happen next. He says, "I work for self."

"I don't believe you for a second."

"Your nose always in wrong ass, do you know that?"

Better in the wrong ass opposed to other places, right? "Honestly, I'm not into that kinky stuff, my friend. I'm pretty boring in the sack."

"I talking about the bodies and who you think killed them. That none of your business. Keep nose out of it. Spend some of your millions. Take long trip. I don't want you to get hurt." He swings his gun at my face to the left and right like a flag, grins at me, and accidentally pops off a shot.

The bullet flies into the wall behind me, which wakes up Boob from his nap in the bedroom behind me. In truth, I almost drop a load in the hallway. Now is not the time for such an ugly event, though. I have to save my ass from this goon and his undeniable cock-hunger. If not, I will be thrown against the wall or hallway floor and become his sexual toy for the next fifteen minutes, or longer. This action doesn't transpire, though. Instead, I stand next to Barbara's bedroom door, quickly reach out, give its knob a little turn, provide it with a gentle push, call out, "Here doggy, doggy," and Boob does the rest

Boob is a fucking monster dog from hell that just happens to be a little racist and hates black Russians who work for bad guys, particularly those types with scars and gold teeth and big lips. He yaps and jumps off the bed, bolts out of the bedroom, and fires past me like lightning. All in a matter of seconds, the raging Cockapoo from hell leaps from the hallway floor and lands on the goon's face. Boob growls and bites at the man's nose, eyes, lips, ears, and neck. Blood splashes against the hallway's floor and walls.

Barbara's pooch is unstoppable and seems to be on an adrenaline rush. He causes Big Lips to lose his balance and tumble backward. The mass of black man falls down in the hallway. In doing so, he cracks the back of his skull on a marble table's leg. Blood gushes out of his brain and forms a puddle around his head and shoulders. He passes out cold, falling limp under Boob's furry fury.

Before Boob causes anymore damage to the goon's face, ripping off an ear, his nose or lips, I rush toward the mutt, quickly snatch his fifteen pounds up with two hands, and rush him into mother's bedroom, where he will be kept as a prisoner for the next hour. During this process, Boob no longer barks or growls at me; maybe we now have respect for each other, turning into great friends, I'm not really sure.

Next, I stand above Big Lip's body and study the damage. What a mess. The goon is surely dead, unmoving on the floor. The pool of blood around his skull and shoulders is quite large, and increasing in size by the seconds. Boob, I see, really messed the bad ass up. One eye hangs out of a socket. Part of his nose is bitten off – Boob probably ate it – and the man's left ear is complete gone; Boob, I imagine, woofed it down during his brazen attack. "Damn," I whisper, disbelieving the sight at hand, and realize that the dog is just like my mother: brutally dangerous, anger-driven, and quite impulsive.

I check for a wallet on the guy but he doesn't carry any. Oh well, whatever.

Rocco has taught me to call either Brit or Dragon when things like this occur. Dragon's number is listed in my phone. I ring him up, tell him the situation, and listen to him inform me that he and Brit will be at mother's house in a matter of minutes. He also adds, "Don't touch the body. Keep away from it. Brit and I will handle everything."

The second call I make is to Roberta Collins, Barbara's housekeeper and errand runner. The woman is seventy-years-old, a complete angel, thick around her Irish waist, and one of my mother's best friends. I tell her that Boob had a little accident at my mother's, and ask her kindly if she will clean it up in a few hours.

Roberta agrees, delighted to help me. She asks in her cracking, old lady voice, "Is Boob alright? Your mother would go off the deep end if he isn't."

"Boob is rather happy at the moment," I reply, rolling my eyes.

"I'll be by after dinner. I have to take Manny to the doctors." Manny is Roberta's main squeeze for the last thirty years; bless their souls.

Our conversation ends with goodbyes. Again, I look down at Big Lips's body. This time I say, "You poor bastard. You should have known about Boob the killer dog. Shame on you."

I have no intention of sticking around while Dragon and Brit do their thing – wrap the body in plastic, load it in one of their Escalade's, and drive off with it, disposing it somewhere in the city where it won't be found – so I decide to leave. Before I know it, I'm in Rocco's onyx Hummer and cruise back to the beach house, unharmed and safe ... but only for a very short period of time, since my world among the mob seems chaotic and quite intense lately.

CHAPTER EIGHT –
CROON THE GOON

Walter is at the beach house, awaiting my arrival. He's on the back patio, sitting in the shade with a Long Island Iced Tea. He thumbs through the latest release of *Under Gear*, which sits on his lap. I imagine the daddy figure in my life grows hard beneath the catalogue, which discretely covers his aged and used goods.

I help myself to his Long Island, taking a whopper of a sip.

The mystery writer doesn't yell at me; he adores the attention. Instead, he tells me to sit down, closes the catalogue, directs all of his attention to me, and says in a somber manner, "I think Fisk is having an affair on me with his Peruvian scientist."

"Why do you say that?" I take the catalogue from the mystery writer, begin to skim through it, check out the semi-naked and uber-steamy hot dudes on its glossy pages, and decide it's a bad idea, knowing I will become hard if I continue. Instead, I close the catalogue and pass it back to the old man.

"Every time I call him, a young man answers in Spanish."

"His supervisor."

My friend nods his head. "The scientist." Now he adds, "Their laughing is insidious. They sound like they are hiding something from me. I don't like that very much."

I fervidly shake my head and reply, "That's wrong. Fisk is not having an affair with the Peruvian scientist. He loves you with all of his heart and he misses you. You're the only man for him. The two of you will soon get married and live happily ever after."

"I don't like him down there," he admits. "And why is that Peruvian guy answering Fisk's phone? That makes no sense to me whatsoever. In fact, I find it rather annoying. Only boyfriends or lovers will answer a phone like that."

Honestly, I don't have the answer to his question. I also find it uncanny that Fisk's supervisor/scientist friend is answering Fisk's phone. How bizarre. To comfort Walter the best way possible, I say, "It's all innocent play. Fisk knows not to cross a line when it comes to your relationship, even if he's very sexual. He's a good man who loves you. You're worrying over nothing. The man is down there to get a job done. I hear that he's doing wonders regarding his duties."

"Fisk will fuck anything he gets close to. His has a history of being easy with men. I know this about him. If this scientist is remotely cute in the littlest way, Fisk will be over him, inside him, and God only knows what else the two will do when they become naked."

"I don't think they have that type of relationship. Fisk has you. He's down there studying a new drug for malaria. I'm sure he doesn't even have the time to fuck around with his Peruvian boss."

Walter's obviously stressed regarding the topic. Quickly, he finishes his Long Island off and immediately requires a new one.

As I fetch my mystery writing friend a fresh cocktail at the outside bar area, I call to him, "Walter, do you know anything at all about Buli Croon?"

He scans a memory of Croon between his temples. Eventually he chuckles and shares, "The man has the smallest dick ever. I'm talking mini-cock all the way. I think I fucked him in 1986 at a Wham! concert in Fort Lauderdale when I was a cop. What a waste of my time that was. I don't even think I came."

I let out a chuckle and carry the writer's beverage to him, which he takes from me. "Do you have anything more on him?" Now I find a seat across from the popular author and become comfortable.

"I don't. Our time together was very short and not at all exciting. It was just a date or two. Croon moved to Flamingo Cove. I moved to Coconut Key. We've never bumped into each other throughout the years. Both of us have different lives. Why do you ask, darling?"

I fill Walter in on everything I know about Croon, which leads me into the topic of Dane. "The man seems like a weasel, but I'm just not sure why."

He surprises me by saying, "Sweetie, Dane is a compulsive liar. He will do anything in his power to fuck you, or whomever, out of anything that he wants. His character is dark and menacing. On the outside he is sugar, but his insides are quite sour. I suggest you keep a close eye out for him. You can't trust that man. No one ever has. You turn around and he will surely stab you in the back ... or have his dick up your ass."

I put the most obvious question on the table: "How do you know Dane."

My author friend is apprehensive at first about answering my question. Hurriedly, he takes a smooth sip of his Long Island, sighs heavily, and replies, "Let's just say that some writers have a downfall in their careers and a certain drug can pull them out of it."

"You used meth at one time?" I ask, honestly not surprised at all. The daddy figure is decades old and rather experienced in different areas. He lived through the Stonewall riots in 1969, the AIDS epidemic in the 1980s, and the life and times of Freddy Mercury. Of course he took meth at one point in his career, what a silly question.

"Something similar to it. Right at Dane's side. We too were lovers, but only for a very short period of time. I was the Daddy and he was my Boy. Dane was very young at the time. Sometimes we played Master and Servant. I can't remember if he was even eighteen or not." He doesn't bat an eye when he says this. In fact, he sounds rather proud of his history and the many lovers he has cared for.

"Can you give me any more information about him?"

He finishes off his second Long Island, places the empty glass down on the patio table in front of him, and shares, "That was moons ago, long before he was business partners with Tang Meadow, and long before Tang ended up dead on your beach. My history with both Dane and Croon is very dated. I'm sorry I can't help you, Derek."

"Don't be sorry, Walter. Just listening to you talk about your past is exciting. Thank you for sharing."

He blows me an invisible kiss, which I catch and place against my mouth. Both of us drink a few too many Long Islands together, eventually pass out in our chairs, and snooze the night away.

# # # # #

The following night a bunch of us guys decide to hang at Pallyo, a local gay bar on Pelican Way in downtown Flamingo Cove. Brit, Dragon, Mantabaun Choaa, Walter, and I all bombard the two bartenders, wanting drinks. The bartenders are twenty-two-year-old brothers who live in an apartment on Stinger Street, which is just a few blocks away from the bar. Both look exactly like Taylor Lautner, which allows them to obtain quite the tips during their eight-hour shifts. Rumor has it that they are incestuous lovers, boinking each other on a regular basis in the privacy of their shared apartment; no one has yet to prove if such hearsay is true, but that doesn't mean the fags of Pallyo aren't trying.

Tonight is drag queen competition night at the bar. A string of queens strut their shit on a catwalk for approximately two minutes. Each is critiqued by ten judges in three categories: beauty, creative attire, and grace. The winner gets a two-person trip to Puerto Rico. The losers get their wigs pulled off, but each is granted a free drink of choice from the bar.

The lookalikes are very good this evening: Cher, Madonna, Lady Gaga, Beyonce, Katy Perry, Fergie, Marilyn Monroe, Liza Minnelli, and Taylor Swift. Other contestants include a red-headed bombshell with DDD-size breasts, two cheerleaders, a naughty school girl from a private school, a nun, and a candy striper. All the men/women do the catwalk, strutting their gorgeous bodies. One removes rose petals from a wicker basket and throws them into the audience. Katy Parry blows bubbles into the hooting and hollering fag-gatherers. A Dorothy look-alike from The Wizard of Oz carries a wand that ejects glitter into the crowd. Lady Gaga is dressed in all-black from head to toe and carries two whips. Madonna strips out of her cowboy outfit and shows off her boobs, faux nipples and all. The nun carries a stripper pole on the catwalk with her and sports a sign that reads: JESUS LOVES WHORES.

Cute boys, beefy jocks, greasy city mechanics, flavorful gigolos, spent tricks, and worked over daddies watch the gig. All seem to enjoy the evening to the fullest. Herds of city men and boys in the crowd whistle and yell. One drunken sailor rushes the stage, but the bouncer –

a guy who just happens to look like a Colt porn star – steps in and hauls his ass out of the bar, probably beating the shit out of the fag on the sidewalk.

By ten o'clock in the evening, Fergie wins the competition. She is crowned with a glittery tiara, handed a bouquet of roses, and given a bottle of very expensive champagne. The MC announces that her two trip tickets to Puerto Rico will arrive in her mail box approximately three weeks from tonight.

Fergie is placed on a number of queers' shoulders and slowly carried around the bar. On her throne of porcelain twinks, meaty jocks, and bulky construction workers, she waves like a princess, glowing with a smile. She blows the all-male audience kisses, continues to wave like Kate Middleton, and eventually is returned to the narrow catwalk where she is handed the MC's microphone, ready to thank the crowd.

Lady Gaga is very displeased this evening, and perhaps feels that she should have won the drag queen competition. On her own accord, manic and in a state of rage, Gaga turns ugly and rushes the stage. In a matter of seconds she stands in front of Fergie with her whips, blocking the woman/man from the awestruck audience. Gaga rips the tiara off the woman's head and tosses it into the crowd; a twenty-year-old queen catches the bedazzled accessory and puts it on his head, wearing it for the rest of the evening with glamorous pride. Gaga now removes the bottle of champagne from Fergie's right hand and tosses it to the catwalk's black floor where it explodes; the patrons are doused in the bubbles and shards of glass, but no one is hurt. The roses Fergie holds are torn to shreds by Gaga. Petals and thornless stems fly into the audience and decorate a number of beefcakes. And last, but certainly not least, Gaga rips the winner's wig off and tosses it over her head into a group of dashing Army men, none of which catch it out of mere sport.

Fergie honestly doesn't know how to react to Gaga's attack and begins to cry.

The crowd turns manic in just a few seconds, outraged by Gaga's mean temper. Brit, Dragon, Mantabaun Choaa, Walter, and I all begin to boo and hiss. T-shirts are ripped off of suntanned bodies and thrown at Gaga. DJ Dizzy Speed blasts "Big Girls Don't Cry" on the overhead speakers. The crowd cheers with delight, knowing it's a Fergie hit. Crazies in the audience begin to empty their glasses of beer and cocktails, dousing Gaga on the stage, hoping she exits the catwalk. Security ends the bedlam, removing Gaga from Fergie's side. The drag queen is taken behind the stage and rushed outside in fear that the patrons will rip her to shreds with their catlike claws and menacing tempers.

The scene is over, and quite quickly. The bar turns happy once again. The stage is cleaned up by STAFF. Champagne shards of glass are removed from the floor and disposed of. Drunk patrons begin to dance. Boys kiss in dark corners. Drug dealers pass out uppers in the shape of little pink and red unicorns. Fergie turns out to be a hero/heroine. And the night progresses with fag-joy, billowing into the city.

# # # # #

I can't believe I'm the only one who sees Croon at Pallyo. Perhaps Brit, Dragon, Mantabaun Choaa, and Walter are all a little too buzzed from drinking. I spot Croon next to the bar. He orders a beer from one of the Lautner twins and makes eye contact with me. Does the guy maybe recognize me? I really don't know. Something is definitely mysterious regarding the man, though. Before receiving his beer and after seeing me in the crowd, he decides to leave the bar. Croon walks through the partying men, to the front door, and exits Pallyo, all in less than a minute.

I give Croon credit: he's sexy as hell, a meaty heartthrob for all the right reasons. The man sports rugged looking jaws, a nicely manicured goatee, coconut brown buzz cut, broad shoulders, freshly shaven chest, nipple bars, rolled abs over his stomach, barbed-wire tats around his biceps, fall-into amber-colored eyes, a six-two frame that weighs no more than 195 pounds, and snug jeans, which show off his globular ass and an all-you-can-eat buffet between his strapping legs. I place him at forty-three or a little older, a scholar of the street, bad from the inside out, obviously rough around the edges, but resembling something totally delicious.

Discreetly, I find a spot for my beer and follow Croon out of the bar and down Pelican Way. He's easy to spot since he's so tall and bare-chested. Croon digs keys out of the front pocket of his painted-on denim, finds his mint Mercedes GL 450 in a nearby parking spot, climbs inside, starts its engine, and drives off.

I'm unseen behind him, climb into Rocco's Hummer, and follow Croon. God only knows where he's going, but I want to find out. Three cars back, I watch his whore-red Mercedes drive through downtown Flamingo Cove. Croon is tough to follow, but I manage. He heads east, drives alongside the city's looping highway, and obeys all the rules of the road. I try to get his Mercedes's license plate number, but I refuse to close in on him and blow my cover. The last thing I need is for him to come after my ass and blow me away with a high-powered rifle or other weapon; Rocco would not be too pleased.

Croon makes a right onto Iguana Way, a left onto Bay Drive, and drives north for ten miles, entering the outskirts of the city. This part of the city is called The Reach, a classless section with dilapidated buildings, broken down junk cars lining the streets, and ominous bums as its inhabitants. The Reach is a bad boy's paradise to take cover in. Here, behind and beneath its ugly exterior, is where numerous goons reside in their grungy holes. Think of it as an underworld of hell for anarchists. Hideaways for the obscurely dangerous. Homes for the city's worst murderers, rapists, thieves, and queer madmen. A zone for the devil's angels.

Croon the goon parks his Mercedes GL 450 behind a row of dumpsters and under a string of foliage-concealing oaks on Malin Street. He climbs out of the metal beast, locks it, sets its alarm, and walks three blocks through The Reach, heading north.

From Rocco's Hummer, I watch him grab a cup of coffee in an all-night convenience store with steel bars welded over its glass windows. Two guards dressed in civilian clothes man the shit hole. He exits the store approximately two minutes later with the coffee. He walks for three more blocks, makes a left on Gulf Square Road, and ends his journey at a ten-floor apartment building that looks as if it has barely survived inner city crimes.

I park the Hummer and rush to follow Croon. In less than a minute I'm at the mouth of the uninhabitable building and enter. Once inside, I hear him climb the stairs to the right; I'm sure the two elevators probably haven't worked for the last seven years or more. Quietly, I follow the bad boy up the shit-stained stairs to the fifth floor.

Croon is gone. I can't see him anywhere in the empty and dark hallway. Three apartment doors sit to the left. Four sit to the right. I hear a baby cry and a mother yell behind one door. Two guys argue behind another door. And two queers have sex behind a third door; one of the men literally howls with XXX-satisfaction. The aroma that floats about the hallway is of shit, urine, semen, and alcohol. A lingering cloud of marijuana wafts by my flared nostrils, providing me with a contact buzz.

I'm just about to turn around and back down the stairwell when I see a dark blue blur or mass move at my far right, near the end of the hall. My attention moves in the blur's direction and I get a pretty clear view of Croon's back: splayed muscle that tapers into a succulent V, two tattoos of Christ on the cross near each shoulder blade, and a thick layer of man-sweat. He uses a key on the metal and windowless door from his key ring, opens the door, and vanishes inside.

Again, I follow the bad guy: quietly, discreetly, without having any fear whatsoever. Truth is I should be scared shitless. Croon can have a hidden gun next to his cock, snug in his cotton briefs. He can easily pull it out and Swiss cheese me with bullets, if he wants to. I'm not as careful as I should be and Rocco would be very disappointed regarding my labor; shame on me.

I reach the metal door in a matter of seconds, find it unlocked, turn its brass knob, pull it open, and step inside. A second stairwell opens at the end of the gray hallway. There are thirty steps here that rise straight up and seem too narrow. The stairs open to a room with boxes, vintage furniture, and other miscellaneous items. I believe it to be a concealed and private storage unit on the sixth floor. The room is semi-dark, smells like marijuana and …

Croon steps out from behind a walnut wardrobe. He swings something in his right arm at my head. I quickly jump to the right, missing his blow. The item in his hand is a hammer, which he possibly discovered in the room for his use. We make eye contact and he provides the shittiest grin with me that says he's about to kill me.

When the second blow occurs, I'm not as fortunate. Croon nails me in my right shoulder and I fall to the floor. Pain skies through my neck and arm. A ripping headache instantly forms between my temples. The hit practically knocks me out cold. As I reach for my .357

Magnum, planning on using a bullet or two on him, the goon bolts past me, through the door at the top of the narrow stairs, and vanishes into the night.

CHAPTER NINE –
TOUCHY FEELY
SEX TOY

Long story short: I wake to a thunderous boom prior to dawn and think the world is exploding by a falling meteor. Honestly, I have no idea where I am. My mouth is dry and my vision is blurred. Horrendous pain skis through my right shoulder and my neck. I sit up, see a stuffed owl in front of me, two giant tables, boxes of paper, and a walnut wardrobe. It hits me where I am now: on the sixth floor somewhere in The Reach section of the city. I was following Croon and he ended up doing a doozey on me.

I smell rubber burning, oil, and gasoline. Something loud sounds like its crackling. Fire trucks blare in the distance. A second boom is heard, which causes me to jump. Now I smell smoke and know there's a fire nearby. A natural instinct of survival kicks into my system and I stand. My exit from the storage room is rather clumsy. I maladroitly stampede down the thirty narrow steps, reach the metal door at the bottom, swing it open, and step onto the fifth floor of the decaying shithole of an apartment building. Granted, Croon can be waiting outside the door for me, ready for a surprise attack, very willed to kill me with his bare hands, but he isn't here. Again, the hallway is empty. This time there are no human voices or altercations. Quickly, I find the second set of stairs and begin my final exit, travel southward inside the building, search out the street and early morning darkness, and whatever else awaits me.

The two booming sounds just happen to be Rocco's Hummer exploding, which is now on fire. Fire trucks are everywhere. Two homeless people are near one of them, gawking at the sky-reaching flames and catastrophe at hand. Flamingo Cove cops arrive at the scene, including Garrett Haute. The street is a hustle and bustle of complete chaos as the Hummer burns and patrolmen barricade the area.

I don't know what to do. It's not every day that my form of transportation is sabotaged by Croon. I merely stand on the sidewalk and stare at the red, yellow, and orange flames rise two stories high. My heart races and feels as if it will explode within the layers of my chest. I think I'm in some big shit trouble. Everything about the moment screams of bedlam.

To my utter surprise, Dragon and Brit appear on location. Both are in their street clothes and walk toward the scene. Dragon moves up to me and warns, "I suggest you head back to the beach house. We've got this covered. You have nothing to worry about."

I quickly fire off, "How did you know I was here?"

Dragon smiles and confirms, "All of Rocco's vehicles have tracking devices. We always know where you're at."

I should have known. Why do I seem so surprised? I mean, seriously, Rocco works for the toughest mobster in Florida, a certain handsome somebody who just happens to be his father. Of course the Hummer was bugged with a tracking device.

Three blocks away from the fire, I call a cab. I'm picked up approximately eight minutes later, climb into the back of the jiz-smelling cab, and try to relax as the cabbie drives me back to the beach house.

One mile later, my cell phone rings. I expect it to be Brit or Dragon, confirming my safety. Neither is on the line. Instead, Rocco calmly asks into my left ear, "Are you hurt?"

It's nice to know that he still cares for me, especially since I just murdered his Hummer by following Croon. Bless his queer soul. His mobster ways have yet to turn his heart completely black and scandalous. His call proves that maybe he does love me, and will possibly prompt him to ask me to marry him soon, which I will surely accept.

I respond, "Very safe. Dragon and Brit are on it."

"What happened? Why were you in The Reach?" He sounds concerned, almost frightened. Maybe he was afraid of losing me, thinking I was in the Hummer when Croon decided to torch it.

I slowly share the details of my evening with him: from having drinks at Pallyo clear up through following Croon to The Reach. The only thing I leave out is how long I was passed out in the storage room on the sixth floor; I still don't have the answer to this question. Maybe an hour. Maybe two hours. I haven't a clue.

"So Buli Croon is behind this?" Rocco asks, sounding serious, profoundly thinking.

"Yes. I don't doubt it one bit. He almost killed me with a hammer."

"You think he killed Tang and Nolan Cutler?"

"Who?" I ask, still a little frazzled by my evening's events.

"Tang's assistant at The Skin Artist. Nolan Cutler."

"I don't know who else could have offed the two of them to tell you the truth, Rocco. Croon is certainly not a nice guy. In my opinion, he is not above murder."

"We have to keep a close eye on him. I'm sure he knows where the diamonds are." He clears his throat, sniffles, and says, "You're currently in lock-down until I get back into town, lover. I don't want you to try and kill yourself again."

"You're reprimanding me?"

"Only for your safety, guy."

I utter with conviction, "I can take care of myself. Give me some credit."

"Never. You're my man and I don't want anyone to hurt you. I'm putting Vest on you until I get back."

Shit, Vest adores me, a little too much. He's Garrett Haute to the nth degree. I'm talking sex-hungry to the fullest, unable to keep his paws off me, and his cock. I've tried to explain this to Rocco on numerous occasions, but the mobster just doesn't get it. Rocco feels that Vest is one of his superior men, ranking above Dragon and Brit. The two go back fifteen years as street kids and practically consider each other brothers. To deter Vest being my bodyguard for the next day or two, I say to Rocco, "Give me Dragon. I feel more comfortable with him."

"No can do," he shares, probably shaking his head on his end of the line. "Dragon is on the diamond case. Vest will look after you."

Shit! Vest is all I need right now. He'll be all over my skin, wanting to fuck me every other minute. Now, I have a really big problem. Again, I try to convince Rocco to put Dragon on me, or even Brit, but my boyfriend doesn't want to hear it. He rather snaps in a bad boy manner, "Listen to me. Vest is on you. I don't want to discuss it any longer."

I roll my eyes and shake my head. Abruptly, I say, "Fine," and click the OFF button on my cellular. If this is what Rocco wants, this is what he'll get; not that I agree. Vest is hard to fend off, though. The guy is model-gorgeous with a six-foot frame, cocoa-colored skin, and yummy features. The last thing I want to happen is to be caught in an uncompromised position with Vest, risking my relationship with Rocco Malonni, putting our love for each other on the line.

Rocco calls my cell phone back, which I ignore. This is probably not the smartest move on my part, but it buys me some time to at least calm down. In the next five minutes, he calls me seven times; I don't take any of the calls. And when the taxi arrives, picking me up and eventually toting me back to the beach house, Rocco texts me the sweetest words: I GET YOU. I'LL PUT DRAGON ON IT. LOVE ME.

# # # # #

Later this early, early morning I find the beach house trashed from top to bottom. All the rooms are in a state of disarray. Furniture is tumbled over, collectable knickknacks are broken, books are tossed here and there, kitchen closet doors are open, and some of the dishes lie in slivers on the marble floor. Our bedroom is possibly in the worst condition: clothes are strewn about the room; nightstands and dressers are upturned; signed paintings are sabotaged, crumpled on the floor; our bed is a heap of foam and feathers; two windows are broken and ...

I stand in the middle of the room and prevent myself from crying. It looks as if a hurricane has swept through the beach house, leaving a pathway of destruction behind. Truth is I don't know who sabotaged the place. It could have been one of Croon's men, Dane Duncock, or some other unknown party. Whoever it was, Rocco will surely get even. This is one of my boyfriend's mottos: You piss him off and he'll make your life twice as bad.

I don't know why I call Mantabaun, but do. He picks up on the second ring and says in a groggy manner, "Yes, Mr. Reed?"

"Where are you?" I sound huffy and disrespectful, totally on edge.

"With a friend. The two of us are under his sheets. I was sleeping."

Of course. The houseboy left Pallyo with a guy; shame on me for disturbing him. I should have guessed. Bluntly, I ask, "When were you here at the beach house last?"

"Hours ago. Last evening. Why, Mr. Reed?"

"Are you aware that the house has been ransacked?"

"Oh my," Mantabaun replies in a shocked whisper, sounding surprised at my news.

"Can you come home immediately?" I don't know why I ask him this, but maybe he can help me put the beach house back in order.

"I can, Mr. Reed ... of course. I'm on my way."

# # # # #

My second call is to Rocco. He immediately picks up and says in his bad boy and sexy way, "You missed me, didn't you? I know you want some of my dick in your mouth or ass."

Granted, the situation at hand is pretty serious, but my boyfriend sounds hot and alluring. If only we had time to have phone sex right now, I would. Honestly, a heated session of heavy panting and dirty talk is out of the question, since the beach house has been plundered overnight. In response to his cordial invite, I seriously say, "Rocco, we have a problem."

"Another one?" he asks, the charm in his voice vanishes with such ease.

"The beach house is turned upside down. Every room looks like a bomb went off in it."

The mobster thinks exactly the way I think – sometimes – and asks, "Where is the houseboy?"

"As usual ... with a friend. He was here last night. He's on his way back to the beach house now."

My lover is silent for a second ... two seconds ... three seconds. I picture him rubbing his jaw in deep thought, furrowing his left eyebrow. Eventually he says, "I have to send Vest over. Dragon and Brit are tied up at the moment with the Hummer. Vest will know what to do when he gets there."

I heavily sigh, sounding like a princess, and inquire, "Can't you send someone else?"

"Why? Vest likes you. He considers you one of his friends."

"That's my problem. He likes me a little too much, if you know what I mean. Send Poco or Lance or Ringo or Duce. Leave Vest out of this."

"Vest is harmless. He just likes to flirt with you."

"Rocco, the man pinches my nipples and plays with my ears. I'm like a toy for him. When he gets the chance, he goes for my goods, providing them with a tug. I'm sure you don't approve of that."

My boyfriend ignores me and foolishly laughs. Following his laughter, he rattles off, "Listen, he'll be there in a half hour. Let me call my father and see if I can fly back to Flamingo Cove. This sounds important and I feel I should be there."

I concur, telling him I love him, and that ... I'll deal with Vest.

He ends our call with: "Love you, babe. Hang in there until I get back."

# # # # #

Approximately twenty minutes later, Alejandro "Vest" Vesto arrives at the beach house. The man sports an adorable smile from ear to ear, is drop dead beautiful in his Cuban skin, and welcomes me into his muscular arms for a friendly cock-against-cock hug.

I decline the hug, telling him I have a bug and feel ill.

"So sad, Derek. You know I enjoy your hugs." He looks lovable, similar to a puppy dog that needs a good home. His pale-blue eyes shimmer with erotic bliss and his lips turn into a seductive pout that just about make me hard.

Of course I cannot keep my gay-gaze off his steamy hot bod. Vest rarely wears shirts, like today, and his chest is ripped from navel to neck. Plates of naturally tanned Cuban skin glow in the morning sunbeams that shine in through the kitchen window. His nipples are rock-hard, just like his sculpted abs. Beneath his navel is a narrow strip of black hair that falls into his Lasc reversible print shorts, which outline his eight inches of deflated hose. Helplessly, I lick my lips, and find our moment uncomfortable in the kitchen, but erotically cleansing.

"I'll let you kiss me if you want."

"That's a death sentence," I inform rather clearly. "Rocco with have your balls in a nutcracker if you go that route."

He chuckles, teases one of his nipples with two fingertips, and obviously attempts to corrupt me with his fiery hot body and masculine play.

I turn away from him and head to my catastrophic bedroom, hoping I don't lead him astray and cause him to believe that we are going to become frisky.

Fortunately, Vest doesn't follow me. He stays in the kitchen, helping himself to a bottle of chilled water from the fridge.

Once in the bedroom, I tunnel for a clean pair of New Balance sport briefs and find myself in the bathroom, climbing in the shower.

Perhaps Vest is a man who knows his boundaries. To my surprise, he doesn't find his way into the shower with me. Nor does he wait for me to exit the shower after I shampoo my blond hair and soap up my flesh. Instead, he is a pure gentleman, still occupied in the kitchen upon my return, perhaps observing my wishes of being plutonic with him for the very first in our relationship.

Vest says, "That was a quick change," doing a once-over of my sexy-ripped body.

It was a quick change. I now sport a yellow tank snug against my firm torso, vintage cargos around my middle, and Bed Stu sandals. I ignore his comment, though, and share, "Dragon and Brit can handle this mess here ... I have to go and look after my mother's pooch. I suggest you ride with me because you're only going to follow me, anyway."

"We can take my Mustang," he says. "I'll drive."

"Suit yourself, big guy. Let's not waste another second."

# # # # #

Vest tries to play with my left inner thing with his right palm as he drives us to my mother's place. I shoo his frisky palm away and insist, "Contain it, buddy. I can't let you use my skin in any way. Rocco and I are getting married someday. Respect that, please."

The Cuban comprehends my explanation and applies his hand to the Mustang's steering wheel. He replies, "That's too bad. I've always been hard for you, Derek. Frankly, I've always wanted to be your boyfriend. If Rocco changes his mind about marrying you, I'll be glad to fill in for him as your husband. Your sexiness is on fire. I can't tell how many times you've made me hard."

"That's flattering. Thanks for the available opportunity. I'll keep you posted."

Ten minutes later, we end up at 2069 Peninsula Way. Barbara's house looks vacant from the outside. After Vest and I climb out of his Mustang, walk up the sandstone walkway, and eventually enter the house, I sense something uncanny and eerie within my mind and chest.

One, Boob usually attempts to attack me upon every entrance; today he is nowhere to be found inside mother's palatial home. Two, one of the window screens is loose inside the kitchen; it blows to and fro in the warm summer wind. Three, fresh blood is seen on the white tile kitchen floor, floral walls, oak cabinets, and Formica countertops; footprints and doggy paw prints decorate the Spanish tile. The kitchen looks like someone was brutally massacred, butchered next to the Summit stove and Kenmore refrigerator.

Vest doesn't waste any time and asks, "What the fuck happened in here?"

"Jesus," I whisper, feeling my heart fall to my knees. Granted, Barbara and I usually never get along, but we don't hate each other to the fullest potential, and certainly wouldn't want anything bad to happen to the other person. Our relationship is based on tolerance, acceptance, and any remaining emotion we can positively muster for the other involved.

"Where's your mother?" he asks, staring at what looks like a murder scene, minus the body.

"Tampa Bay. She's gambling again."

He tries to snuggle up behind me, offering me a hug; his package of dick just so happens to rub against my bottom, which I pull away from.

I say over my right shoulder to him, "I'm calling her now before I start to panic." Quickly, I find my cellular, punch in her number, hear her phone ring three times in my ear, and now her voice say, "Good morning, baby doll."

Unable to hold my composure together because of the scene at hand, I blurt, "Mother, what's going on? Where are you?" Truth is I don't want to tell her that Boob is missing, possibly dognapped or murdered by a crazy person.

She whimpers, "Boob is with me at his vet's. A seagull flew into the kitchen and decided to attack him and ... everything in that room is ruined now."

Actually it's not. The place just needs some soap and water to clean up with, and the screen in the kitchen needs repaired. I ask, "I thought you were in Tampa?"

"I lost all of my money and came home early. Melvin is with me. Boob's left ear is mutilated. The damn seagull tried to eat it."

I try and hold back my laughter, but a few huffs of enjoyment escape my mouth.

Of course Barbara notices my giggling and asks, "Are you laughing about this?"

"Absolutely not," I lie, which I should know better about.

She hangs up with a prominent gasp, abruptly ending our call.

I kind of feel bad, turn around, eye up Vest, and say, "You want to give me a hand in cleaning this mess up?"

As expected, Vest grabs my goods, provides them with a little hug and tug, and supplies, "I love to clean up messes with my mouth, Derek … if you know what I mean."

I roll my eyes, pull away from him, and say, "Let's get started. I have other things to accomplish today besides being your sex toy."

"Such a pity," he declares, frowning.

I ignore the man and go in search of a bucket, Clorox, and mop, ready for the exhausting chore at hand.

CHAPTER TEN –
A VERY BIG BANANA

Good news: Rocco is safe at home and we have incredible sex for six straight hours; the beach house is turned right side up; Boob is only missing half of his left ear.

Bad news: The four million dollars' worth of diamonds is still missing; Tang and Nolan's murders are not solved; no one in Flamingo Cove knows who ransacked the beach house; Croon is still on the run.

Good news: Rocco has a private meeting with Dane Duncock and finds out that he has nothing to do with the missing diamonds and two murders. Granted, this meeting is probably held in an abandoned warehouse in The Reach with three of Rocco's men, loaded weapons, and just as many vulgarities. My boyfriend always gets what he wants out of men, whether by his good looks (as in my case) or by brutal force; the mobster always wins.

Bad news: Vest gets drunk and hits on me again, inadvertently calls my cell phone and asks me if I would like to suck his knob. Rocco laughs about the invitation and I'm ready to slug him one, even if he can kick my ass.

Good news: Walter Landing has a book signing for *Bottom Tales* at Simone's Books in Arubadae, a sister city to Flamingo Cove. I'm hired to be Walter's assistant. My duties include: standing over him while he signs novels for his mostly male gay fans, fetching him green iced tea with slices of lemon, and whatever else he demands from me to fulfill his petty needs.

Bad news: On my way to assist Walter at his signing, driving Rocco's sporty 182i BMW I get pulled over by a Flamingo Cove patrolman and ...

Shit! It's Garrett Haute. What the fuck does he want, anyway? He stops me on Isle Way, turns on his brights, and saunters his sexy goods up to my open window. He removes his G&B sunglasses and slides them into a nearby pocket on his shirt. The first thing out of his handsome mouth is: "You know you were going ten miles over the speed limit?"

I retort rather rudely, "You know Melvin Caspi's parking tickets have yet to be cleared, right?"

"Touché," Garrett admits. "I like a guy with attitude, especially when he has his shorts positioned down at his ankles."

"You know I wasn't going ten miles over the speed limit, Garrett. Why don't you step into my office so we can take care of some business?" I pat the seat next to me.

"I think that's a very wise idea," he announces, reaches for the goods between his uniform-covered legs, and jostles them with his right palm.

In a matter of seconds, Officer Garrett Haute walks around the BMW, opens the passenger door, slips in beside me, and says, "I've been dying for a blowjob from you." Before I can respond, he rises his cop hips, unzips his goods, and pulls out his semi-swollen hog for some show and tell.

I admit rather uncomfortably, without intentionally hurting Rocco Malonni in any way whatsoever, that Garrett's cock is actually one of the most attractive I have ever seen. The tool is perfectly cut, veined, and ten inches tall. It's a rod that one can easily crave, taste, or ride. Something viewed on a Jake Cruise amateur porn star, always ready for action.

He tugs on his meat and prompts pre-bubbles of spew to surface at its tip. He huffs and puffs, turns his attention to me, and shares, "You can get your mouth down here anytime you want. I'm ready when you are."

"It ain't happening, man," I say. "Rocco or Whitney would murder you if I sucked or handled your cock. And to tell you the truth, I wouldn't blame them."

He begs, "Give me a two-finger stroke, dude … I'm dying to connect with you."

I sigh heavily, roll my eyes, and keep my hands and mouth to myself. "Hide it away, Garrett. I'm not giving into you or your needs. I'm a taken man."

The cop doesn't hide his goods away, though. Instead, he ogles me behind the steering wheel, strokes his shaft up and down in a heated manner, and moans with a tempo of heady groans.

Here I am on the side of Isle Way with my ex-tug buddy seated in the passenger seat, watching him play with his monkey. Honestly, I'm not even turned on by the faggot's chore; I've seen him do his hand-deed so many times before that I am now numb to the action and completely unaffected. If it were Rocco next to me, though, I'd be all over his shit, begging him to fuck me with his meaty shaft inside the BMW. Rocco's not anywhere around, though, and Garrett is certainly not his replacement.

"Suck me," he whispers. "Do it, pal, for old time's sake. Put my dick in your mouth." His right hand moves steadily up and down on his junk as his breathing intensifies. Both of us know that he's getting closer to his all-out spew-fest.

I try to deter his frantic handjob and ask, "When do you plan on voiding Melvin's tickets?"

"As soon as you suck me off, man," he whimpers, pumping his fist as he rises off the seat and falls back into its curved leather.

"No can do," I say. "You said you would take care of it. You gave me your word. I gave you a thousand bucks to get it done. What the fuck, Garrett?"

"Blow me," he chortles, strokes his thumper, grits his teeth, and has a numbing look about his face that reinforces the idea that he is just about to erupt some cock-churn.

I confess rather moderately, "I cannot suck you off … I'm getting married. Rocco is the man of my dreams and I'm not about to ruin it with him."

Suddenly, Garrett comes. He parts his legs and murmurs with self-pleasure. His left hand is positioned between his uniformed-covered thighs, ready to cup his sticky sap. The hot cop lets out a grunt … two grunts … three grunts, bucks his hips upward, and releases a pool of white cream from his hose, catching the ooze in his left palm, cupping the goop like a Tupperware bowl.

"You want to eat it?" he asks.

I chuckle, "No thanks. I'm good. I've had a lot of liquid protein these days. There's no reason to have yours."

He moves his left palm up to his mouth and smears the thick goo against his pretty boy face.

"Jesus, Garrett, have some manners about eating your own spunk," I suggest, shaking my head in surprise because of his ravenous action.

I note that his car-fun ends rather quickly. He sucks up his goop from his palm, licks his reddish lips, cleans every drop of it up with skill, and eventually turns to me with a sticky-looking smile. He says, "You should have had some of this. I swear it's the yummiest stuff on the planet."

Again, I roll my eyes, disbelieving his comment. "Are you going to handle the tickets for me?"

"Not until you put out, buddy. That's the deal."

I try to plead with him, "You know I can't do that. Give me a break."

"Your loss, pal," he shares. In a matter of seconds he zips up his goods, puts his sunglasses back on his face, and exits the BMW. The cop is back in his cruiser in less than a minute and eventually speeds off. Hereafter, he leaves me in a blurred state of confusion and irritation.

# # # # #

Simone's Books in Arubadae is an independent bookstore owned and operated by Cecilia Simone, a gorgeous drag queen who just happens to look like Sharon Osbourne. Cecilia was once Sylvester Simonetti, a bad boy who used to work for Rocco's father in the early eighties. Sylvester was a headhunter before retiring from the Mafia, decided to change his look and gender, and thereafter, Cecilia was born.

At the front door of the business, next to the bay window, Walter is seated at a wooden desk with two Waterman pens, a stack of his hardback novel *Bottom Tales*, and his pride ruined. No one is in the store to buy his book. In fact, the place is wall-to-wall empty. Even Cecilia has left, running next door for an afternoon coffee with just a pinch of sugar and a few drops of skim milk.

"You look depleted, Walter. What can I do to help?" I sit on the edge of his desk, thumb through a copy of his tales, and feel horrible for him. The last thing I want to witness is the mystery writer turning into a crybaby; I will do everything in my power to prevent this puzzling and high maintenance creature a bad day.

"Buy a few copies of my book, darling. I will be glad to pay you back. Feel pity for me," he complains, almost sobbing. The wrinkles around his eyes seem deeper today and his lips are chapped. A pallid hue settles over his face, which causes him to almost look like he's suffering from seasickness.

What I feel pity for is the way he is dressed today. The writer sports a chick-yellow chiffon blouse, matching sunhat, Ray-Ban sunglasses, and a bangle bracelet on his left wrist. If I don't know any better, I can say that he is in a drag competition with Cecilia. Walter doesn't do drag, though ... until today, which I highly recommend that he not accomplish anymore.

Because I am sometimes rude and not on the best of behavior, I ignore his comment about buying two or three of his hardbacks, and inquire, "Why are you dressed like Big Bird?"

He stands up, spins around, and asks, "What, you don't like?"

I shake my head and reply, "I'm afraid not. It's all just a little too canary for me. You look like a very big banana, Walter."

He removes his sunglasses and hat, places them on a nearby chair, brushes fingers through the remains of his aging hair, and challenges me, "I worked hours on this look all morning, Derek. How dare you insult me."

"With all the love in my heart for you, Mr. Landing ... you look hideous. No wonder no one is coming into Simone's to purchase your book. They are surely afraid of being terrorized by a middle-aged man dressed as a giant banana."

He sort of shares a muffled laugh, waves his right hand at me, and sits back down in his chair. "Okay, I get it. So I overdid it a touch. I was feeling happy in yellow until you came along."

"I'm sorry, Walter ... A friend has a duty to share such criticism and cruelties. I do hope you would bring it to my attention if I were having a bad outfit day."

"I don't want to talk about this any longer," he lashes out. "Just drop it. Besides, we have more important matters to discuss."

I lean over the desk, note his serious tone, and immediately change the topic for both our interests. Now, I inquire, "What kind of important matters?"

He finds a silver flask in his front, right pocket on the yellow blouse that he flamboyantly sports, twists it open, takes a swig, offers me one, which I decline, twists the lid back on the narrow and stainless-steel flask, and eventually hides it away.

"Whiskey?" I ask, knowing it's his absolute favorite, and weakness, smelling it on his breath.

"Of course. I wouldn't think of drinking anything else at a signing. My readers demand nothing less from me."

I unintentionally crinkle an eyebrow and suggest in a rather brisk tone, "Tell me about these important matters." If anyone has information on the two murders, Walter does, since he thinks mysterious deaths all the time. He gets around Flamingo Cove and Flamingo Bay with much flamboyancy and digs up residents' dirt. Citizens of the county seem to flock to him because he is considered the local celebrity, although he probably uses such idealistic natures against them on paper.

He whispers, "Dane Duncock was in here just a half hour. The bastard had no intention of buying one of my books."

I'm all ears, absorbing his information. "And what did Dane have to say?"

"Croon is your man."

100

Obviously Walter doesn't know about my adventures in The Reach. Perhaps I've failed to call and inform him about following Croon, and ending up with a torched Hummer. Humbly, I inquire, "Why would Croon murder Tang and his assistant?"

"These guys are all connected in one way or another. Business is business and things sometimes get out of control, which I'm sure you're familiar with since you date Rocco Malonni."

I take no insult or injury regarding his true comment. Rocco comes from a loving and caring family. His father, Antonio "Boss" Malonni is one of the sweetest men on the planet, if you're on his good side, which I fortunately am. Boss is a dove, a powerful man who happens to have much devotion to his family, and me.

"Dane says Croon did the hits. The two used to work together a few years ago in a fish packing company."

"Why did Croon do it, if he did?"

"I asked Dane that, but he didn't have an answer for me."

"Did you learn anything about the missing diamonds?" I ask. Surly, someone knows something about the vanished goods; crooked men cannot keep secrets among bad boys, I've learned, it's what keeps them in business, of course.

Unfortunately, Walter shakes his head. "I haven't heard a thing about the diamonds. If I learn anything at all, Derek, you'll be the first to know."

"I appreciate that," I rattle off and study the time on my right wrist: 2:34 PM.

# # # # #

"Duncock did mention one other bit of information you might just be interested in knowing," Walter says with a twinkle in his right eye and a semi-smile, catching me completely off guard.

"Are you holding back?" I ask, know he's teasing me, and feeds me little by little of his discovered facts.

"Dane mentioned another party involved in the two murders."

I raise my right eyebrow with interest and ask, "What other party?"

Walter scratches his chin and says, "Balls Banco."

I stand and shake my head. Persistently I share, "Balls is one of Rocco's father's allies. He works for Chain Chin. Chain would never have one of his men betray my future father-in-law."

Walter defends himself by raising his voice a tone, and says, "I'm only telling you what Dane shared with me. Don't shoot the messenger, darling."

"You're regrettably being fed the wrong information. Balls would never be involved with a crime that affects Rocco's father. The man has better morals than that. If Boss finds out about this, which he will, Balls is ruined. Boss will surely start a war with Chain over the matter."

He inquires, "How does the murder of Tang Meadow affect Boss Malonni?"

"The body showed up on Rocco's beach. That's a reasonable connection. Who wants to be involuntarily involved like that? No one."

"So you're saying that someone was sending Boss a message?"

I don't have to even think about this and reply, "Exactly. Someone is fucking with Boss through Rocco and me. Maybe they've used Balls and Chain Chin to do that. This could be some serious shit, Walter."

He retrieves his flask from his blouse again and takes a sip. Following this act, he questions, "Where are the glittery gems, Mr. Sherlock? Who has them? And tell me how, and if, the diamonds are connected to the two murders."

Confidence is a key trait in my personality and I say, "I'm sure everything is connected. I'm still working it, though."

"Is your bed buddy, Rocco, helping you?"

"He'll be home today. The two of us will work through this together. The man is very supportive regarding my needs." I wink at Walter, glad to be at his side and share this discussion with him. If anyone can give me advice, it's the mystery writer.

He smiles, glows with a semi-buzz from his whiskey, and murmurs, "You're a magical couple in love. How sweet. I'm sure a mystery will come out of it on paper for me."

I don't know if the writer is being sarcastic or not. In truth, I don't want to stick around the bookstore and find out. I need more information about Balls Banco, Chain Chin, the two murders, and the missing diamonds. Again, I look down at my watch: 2:43 PM.

The author notices my time-studying and asks, "Do you have to run, sweetheart?"

"I do. There are things to do and people to see."

"Of course. I'm very pleased to know that you're staying busy. Give me a kiss before you go."

I provide a soft one to his right cheek.

He giggles following my cheek-kiss, and adds, "Fill me in on anything you learn."

"I will surely do that," I reply.

"And give a hug to Rocco from me. Make sure it's bear-big. A man like Rocco doesn't like those twinkish boy hugs, but you already know that."

"Of course. Rocco loves his bear hugs, particularly from best-selling mystery writers," I answer, pull away from him, and continue with my day.

CHAPTER ELEVEN –
MAN-HEAT

Once back at the beach house, I convince Dragon to investigate the e-mail sent from Tang before the skin artist was murdered.

Dragon plays around on the Gateway for an hour or more while Mantabaun tidies up. Brit takes fingerprints to determine exactly who broke into the beach house. And Rocco phones, lighting up my world with a full smile.

I decide to take my boyfriend's call outside. The day is obnoxiously beautiful again: baby blue skies, light wind, a moderate temperature for early February. Seagulls inhabit the Gulf, overcoming the disastrous oil spill a few years ago. Stone crabs scurry and click over the sun-covered beach.

He says, "How's my babe doing?"

"Missing you. Things have been crazy since you left." Truth is Rocco's voice is comforting to hear; a blessing of sorts in my day.

"You can't miss me a second longer. My flight is early and I'm waiting here at the county airport for you to pick me up."

"That's good news," I supply, beaming with a smile, feeling all warm and fuzzy inside, really missing him.

"How soon can you get here?"

I think about this for a second … two seconds … three seconds. The thought of Rocco's hot Italian body mixing with my naked body surfaces inside my mind, and within my shorts. A burst of sexual energy jolts my goods to life; my dick actually bounces with interest to have a hump and bump with the man, since I truly miss him. To clarify this notion, I tell him, "Better yet, meet me at The Rune Inn. I'll be there in an hour."

"Why not the beach house?" he legitimately asks, concern locked in his sexy-deep voice.

"Too much is going on here. Dragon. Brit. Mantabaun. They are all doing whatever. The Rune will work out better for us."

"Is this a booty call?"

I sort of provide a masculine giggle and say, "You bet your sweet ass it is."

"So I should be wearing nothing at The Rune when you find me?"

"Only if you want me to make some mind-numbing naughty with you."

"I'll see you in an hour," he happily agrees and abruptly ends our call.

# # # # #

The Rune Inn sits on Palisades Drive near the county airport, next to the Gulf. Think ten stories high, casino on the first floor, three restaurants, and two theatres. The place is colossal in size, a great addition to Flamingo County.

After learning Rocco's room at the front desk, wooing a twenty-year-old Justin Timberlake look-a-like, I discover my future husband in Room 1012, a suite overlooking the Gulf.

Although the suite is quite glamorous with its Louise XIV motif, I am more interested in Rocco's nakedness on the king-size bed. My lover sits on the center of the bed with a full-size mast between his pulsing legs, gripping the tool with his right hand.

While ripping my clothes off, I take in his Prince Charming looks, devouring every morsel of his olive-colored skin with my needy eyes: fur-lined chest, puckered navel among tight looking abs, perky nipples, muscular thighs and biceps, a smile to die for, and a twinkle in his boyish eyes that clearly states that he wants to be a dirty boy with me.

"Did you get started without me?" I inquire, moving up to the bed with a full boner between my legs.

He visually takes me in, adoring my skin: smooth and ripped chest, man-scaped triangle patch of blond hair above my upright wanker, droopy balls hanging between my hairless thighs. "I wanted to make sure I was ready for you."

I climb on the bed, nuzzle my head between his legs, and take in his brusque smell of man-sweat with just a hint of urine, which is a total turn-on for me. Shocking him, I nuzzle my chin against his hairy balls, take a stronger whiff to become intoxicated and dizzy a touch, provide his sack with a gentle lick, pull away, and share, "Woof!"

Rocco chortles above me, "Get it started, dude, or I'm going to cream all over myself."

And so this is done. I lick and lap and kiss his balls, pleasuring my man. My mouth consumes one orb, now the other, and I groan with bliss, always glad to be in the mobster's naked company.

He whispers, "Damn, you've got it going on." Rocco now reaches between his legs and applies one palm to the back my head. In doing so, the man of my naughty dreams directs my attention to his rump and …

I provide his tight hole with a little lap, suck, and kiss; Rocco moans on the bed, blown away by the action. Helplessly, I peel his ass apart and dart my tongue inside, quickly pull away, and continue this heated action for the next few minutes.

He goes numb beneath me, murmuring my name. The goon begins to pull on my blond curls with his right hand, obeying his hunger for my mouth tour. The sexy lug opens his thighs even wider and allows me more access for his anal titillation.

Together we connect with sweat, saliva, and pre-bubbles of semen. My man is unable to hold a portion of his load in. His rocket dribbles out four droplets of ooze without even being caressed. The juice drips to his sultry skin and decorates his fuzzy navel. A whimper escapes his mouth with a tender groan of deep satisfaction.

My tongue is still busy on his rump, licking and lapping at his affectionate tightness. I draw the slippery piece of tool against his pink center, shyly pull away, and continue this act of man-bliss for the next seven … nine … eleven minutes. Helplessly I reach up with my right hand and wrap my palm and fingers around his erection. Greedy to touch every square inch of his sultry skin, I begin to manipulate his pole and gently tug on its excess skin in a north and south current.

The Mafia man is locked in a state of unconditional eroticism. He murmurs my name, dizzy and lethargic, under my spell. The guy seems completely captivated by my hand and tongue motions, gurgling in a state of man-heat. Of course he is almost ready to come.

My own shaft leaks a few drops of man-syrup on the bed's sheets. Elation is discovered for me as I play with my lover's bottom and rod, pivoting him into a condition of no return. A current of unstoppable jubilation careens throughout my core and I become delighted with this naked connection.

Selfishly, he explodes, unable to keep his sticky load inside his chiseled system any longer. A gruff sound escapes his blood-colored lips, two hip-thrusts, and a spray of ooze garnishes his furry abs, puckered navel, and my playful fingers. Two more groans exit the mobster's mouth and another string of jiz oozes from his flesh-spigot.

Now spent, limp on the bed, the mob man glows on the sheets as I pull away from his skin. A nearby cotton towel is found and I wipe off my face. Hungry for his gooey load, I kneel between his muscular legs, lower my head to his abs, and begin to lap up his sticky, bittersweet cream.

He mutters beneath me, "Take it all … Eat it all up, Derek."

I listen and gobble up his goods, dramatically suck the tip of his cock, and make sure that every gooey string of his load is in my system. Drop after drop of his seed enters my core and coats my insides, exactly where I want it to be.

Our sexual communication doesn't end here, though, even if I believe it should. Rocco is concerned about my needs and instructs, "Climb onto my cock, I want to show you a good time."

# # # # #

I first find a pump bottle of lube on the sheets to his right and lather up his still-stiff cock. Another dab of the lube is applied to my bottom with one of my fingertips. In a matter of seconds I'm cocked over Rocco's naked torso, kneel over his rammer, and let the tip of its lubed head meet my bottom.

I gasp with wanted pain as the first inch of his dog enters my behind. Slowly I lower myself onto the shaft, inch by inch, and press my palms over my lover's solid and sweaty pecs. Calmly, I whisper, "Take it slow. Don't hurt me."

"Never would I hurt you, Derek ... You know that."

I slide over yet another inch of his upright stick, pleasuring my tight hole. My weight haphazardly consumes his remaining inches. I am split up the middle, gasp for breath, and feel saturated pain consume my organs.

Rocco is persistent with his action and rams my hub in a rapid manner. He pulls away, bolts inside me again, releases his spear, and continues this motion for the next few minutes.

Riding his meat, I flourish with a yearning ache. Up and down I react, jab myself with his device, pant above him, and feel exultation zoom vividly through my torso, which prompts every nerve ending on my body to feel hyper-sensitive.

Beneath me, smiling from ear to ear, glowing with a sense of man-connected-to-man satisfaction, he says, "I'm going to jack you off, man ... Get ready for the time of your life."

"I'm ready. Give it to me, guy."

As promised, he manipulates my log. His right hand works my dick in a speedy up and down motion. Beneath me, vibrant with his hip thrusts, he coaches, "Don't hold it in. Shoot it all over me."

Endless amounts of pain continue to ski throughout my interior. Moans of enlightenment echo within the inn's room. Uncontrollably I twist the Mafia man's nipples, one at a time ... both at the same time ... continuously.

More humps happen to my rump. Rocco is not as gentle as he can be with my bottom; not that I mind, since I tend to enjoy his rough work. A smile of overflowing elation surfaces at the edges of his mouth and he shares a boyish smile. His eyes are glazed with thick satisfaction. His shoulders and biceps are covered in a light sweat from his action beneath me. Once, and only once, does he whisper, "Fucking you," which I find alluring, exactly what I want to hear. His right grip moves the excess skin of my tool in a north and south motion, unstoppable with its current. Sweat by our flesh touching is used as lubricant. And bliss is found. No longer can I keep my load pent. A flood of euphoria surfaces within every pore on my body, and I announce rather implicitly, "Coming, Rocco," providing a warning to what is about to happen between us.

Spew ejaculates from my hose, twirling against my thruster's chest. His pecs and chin are covered in the sticky mess. A string of the white and sticky glue flies against his lips and he abruptly, rather hungrily, licks it away. More of the man-liquid collects against his cheeks and his nose, which he wipes away with his free hand, sucking his fingers clean.

To my utter surprise, he continues to jam his cock inside my center, hectically sliding the piece of meat in and out. The man's eyes close and he begins to grit his teeth. Rocco's cheeks turn a blistery red. The cords that line his neck become stringent and pulse along his flesh.

"You're coming again," I whimper, enjoying the last seconds of my own orgasm.

"Too late to pull out," he chants, overzealous with his heated action. Now he fires his load inside my rump, thrusts his hips against my middle one last time, and ultimately releases his second load.

In a matter of seconds our orgasms seize. Unconditionally we meet as one, sealed together as a couple in lust and love. Here, on this bed inside The Rune Inn, we are unbroken at the moment, sealed together by our man-explosions ... our cohesive passion revealed yet again.

Windblown, post-sexed, heaving for breath, I fall overtop the mobster and kiss his neck. Our bare nipples touch and my rod presses against his ripped stomach.

Also spent, he is still firm in my ass and becomes breathless, emptied of his seed yet again, proving that he is the man of my dreams. My Prince Charming. My superstar. A mythical god I will obviously love and relish forever.

# # # # #

Following our shared romp, snuggled beside him, tucked in the crook of his naked arm, sticky and breathing heavily, I whisper, "You came twice. That's amazing how you can do that."

He huffs and puffs for oxygen, possibly dizzy and incoherent. The badass chants in a state of ultimate satisfaction, "You're fucking hot, Derek. You drive me mad with your sex. Everything about you is perfect."

"I give it my best."

"That you do, man. If you only knew how much I care for you."

Minutes later, we shower together, scrubbing each other down with a bar of ash-scented soap. After exiting the shower and drying off, we scurry back to the bed and cuddle again in each other's arms. Quietly, we agree to fall asleep for just a nap, close our eyes, and drift into united sleep – cherished happiness discovered between us.

# # # # #

Mr. Right at my side dreams of Zulan Cane again. He mumbles things in his sleep: jungle, run, diamonds, murder ...

"Rocco," I place a palm on his right hip and stir him awake. "Rocco, you're dreaming again."

He sits up, removed from the dream. Sweat clings to his torso. The man pants beside me like a dog. His chest heaves in and out.

I say, "Zulan visited again."

My lover nods his head. "He tried to murder me."

"You're safe here with me," I reply and graze fingers against his chin.

"Thank you," he whispers, snuggles against me, and falls back to sleep in less than six minutes.

111

I hold and protect him from the wicked Voodoo practicing warlord in South Africa. Together we sleep silently, aligned, and without dreams.

# # # # #

When do we wake up? An hour later? Two hours? Seven hours? It's dark out and nighttime is present. Rocco rises from the king-size bed and nudges me awake with one of his gentle and caring palms.

When I finally open my eyes, he's face to face with me and stares into my eyes. He brushes my blond curls away from my face and whispers, "Rise and shine, prince."

"What time is it?"

"Almost nine o'clock."

"That's absurd. Did we really sleep most of the afternoon and evening away?"

"Afraid so." He brushes fingers against one of my cheeks, kisses the tip of my nose, and whispers, "You look like a little boy when you first wake up."

"I probably smell like a truck driver, though, don't I?"

"I like that too."

I sit up in the bed, stretch and yawn, and admit, "I'm starving. Should we get room service?"

He says, "I've got that already taken care of. Dinner is on its way up."

"Always on the ball, aren't you, lover?"

"I try to be," he replies, sitting next to me on the bed. One of his fingertips purposely finds a nipple on my chest and begins to roll around it, allowing flesh to meet flesh.

"Stop that. You're going to make me hard again."

"I was hoping you would say that. Want to do another round with me?"

I shake my head and admit, "I'm too hungry. Maybe later."

Honestly, I'm sexually depleted at the moment. My beefcake of a lover has pleased me to the nth degree. For once in my life, I actually feel completely satisfied.

"Too bad. I was hoping you would want to fuck me."

I raise an eyebrow with possible interest, but this action is soon deterred by his cell phone, which rings twice.

As expected, he finds his cellular, flips it open, and takes the call.

# # # # #

What I hear, or believe I hear, putting the pieces of Rocco's one-sided conversation together entails: Rocco speaks to his father; an emergency has occurred; Dragon and Brit left the beach house earlier today; they are both at the beach house again; Rocco is to be careful.

When Rocco hangs up his cell phone, I immediately ask, "What was that about?"

"Mantabaun is dead."

A shocked gasp escapes me and I share wide eyes of concern with my bad boy lover. "What are you talking about?"

He moves up to the bed, sits down beside me, and shares, "His body was found on the beach. Pretty much in the same vicinity where Tang's body was found. Mantabaun was stabbed a few times. Bled to death. My father is having it looked into. He suggested we not interrupt what is unfolding at the beach house."

"My God," I whisper. "I wasn't too keen on Mantabaun, but no one deserves to be murdered."

"I know. It's all a surprise to me, too."

Again, we become comfortable on the bed. He holds me in his arms and we try to absorb as much of his father's information as we possibly can. In truth, I don't know when I close my eyes and fall asleep against his solid and masculine chest, but do, obviously exhausted by his news, and stressed to learn that a third murder has been committed; this one closer to us than the previous two.

CHAPTER TWELVE – DRAGON DUDE

I shower the next morning while Rocco sleeps, dress in the same clothes as the day before, decide I'm hungry, and go in search of a bagel and cream cheese somewhere in The Rune. My travels take me down to the casino where a bunch of blue-haired tourists put quarters in one-armed bandits and try to win big. I'm surprised exactly how many gambling ladies there are polluting the seats at such an early hour. One stops me as I pass her while heading toward the breakfast buffet. She clings her clawed palm to my thigh, edges it to my dick, and chants whimsically over her right shoulder, "Bring me luck, baby. Let me rub your cock for some luck."

Quickly, I pull away from her clawing grip and bolt toward the buffet, which sits at the south entrance of The Rune, directly behind the strings of slot machines.

Five minutes later I stand at a seventy-foot long breakfast buffet and fill a Styrofoam container with breakfast provisions: a variety of fruit slices, honey-smoked bacon, buttered 12-grain toast, scrambled eggs, two slices of French toast drizzled with cinnamon-enhanced syrup, and a bagel with cream cheese. I'm just about to head back upstairs and supply Rocco with his morning meal when my view catches Buli Croon. He stands near one of the old ladies at a slot machine and eyes me from head to toe.

I take him in like a visual disease, ready to vomit, yet still surprised he is at The Rune, possibly monitoring our every move.

Croon turns and begins to book out of the casino.

I drop my breakfast treats on a nearby table and zoom after him. Granted, this is one of the most foolish things I accomplish on my own, but what the hell; I certainly have nothing better to do. Speedily, I chase him through the blue-haired old ladies and their one-armed bandits. Croon jumps over a security railing and I follow behind. Two casino security guys are after both our asses now, bringing up the rear of this impromptu perusal.

Buli Croon flies out of the casino, through valet parking, across Palisades Drive and into a jungle of Floridian foliage.

Planes fly overhead, taking off and landing at the nearby county airport. Some are massive steel structures with two hundred-plus passengers. Others are small charter planes with just a few passengers, hopping from one southern city to the next. Honestly, I ignore the traffic overhead and follow Croon into the jungle.

Surprisingly, I lose the casino's security. The two vanish behind me, heading back to their jobs and the remaining hours of their shifts. Not that I really think the amateur team can catch me, of course. I'm not weak, unafraid of them, and certainly can take them down at any price, if necessary.

My legs are strong and I travel behind Croon at a Herculean speed. Think vampire on the loose. A werewolf from one of those teen novels with too many words. Someone with superhuman powers perhaps.

Frankly, I'm just running, following Croon at top speed through a bunch of palms, ferns, Spanish moss, and a variety of shrubbery. Soon, my lungs and legs will give out and I'll be up shit creek. Then what I am going to do? Nothing, I believe. Absolutely nothing.

Croon is an animal in the thick jungle, faster than me. His speed is twice the velocity of my own. There is no way he can be mortal. Honestly. Or, maybe he's just an experienced athlete; one who has obtained prizes in the fifty-yard dash or ten kilometer. Crazily, he zigzags through the flora, becomes lost, and outruns me. Croon vanishes before my eyes, bolting away, free again.

I stop running, positioned somewhere inside the small jungle. My heart races and my mind begins to spin. My chest rises and falls in pain. Half of me believes I'm about to suffer from a heart attack, but I don't. Everything seems fine after I catch my breath. I'm only winded, lacking oxygen. I'm okay. Really, I am.

# # # # #

Once back in Room 1012, I find Rocco awake. He sits up in the king-size bed, rubs a fist in his right eye, and asks, "You're sweating everywhere. Where have you been?"

I tell him about Croon and my jungle run.

"He's watching us closely," Rocco admits. "Something serious is going on."

I still huff and puff for air, and reply, "I think he's the killer."

He shakes his head. "We don't know that for sure."

"We'll find some evidence to prove it. I want to nail him to the wall."

"Thatta boy," he responds, smiling from ear to ear. "That's my Mafia man talking now ... and it's sexy as hell." He pats the empty spot next to him on the bed, ready for some body contact.

I shake my head. "No sex for you."

He pouts. "Why not? What did I do wrong?"

"Haven't you had enough?"

"A Malonni can never have enough sex." He pulls back the sheet and exposes his semi-hard rock between his legs. Playfully he taps his cock's head with two fingertips and says, "Come to papa and show him a good time."

I roll my eyes, grinning from ear to ear. In a matter of seconds, I strip out of my clothes, find myself against his naked body, and decide to use my boyfriend's delicious man-hide for my heated pleasure.

# # # # #

Home again. The place is tidied up pretty well; Dragon and Brit must have worked their asses off to get the abode so immaculate. Unfortunately, Rocco and I notice that valuable items are missing from the beach house: his rare copy of Mario Puzo's The Godfather, two paintings, a Wedgwood bowl, a Japanese vase, two crystal figurines, our LG flat-screen from the living room, Rocco's iPad, and my prized Hello Kitty stuffed animal, which sits on the sofa.

Rocco is pissed and swears, "Motherfucker! ... What the shit is going on?" He slams his right palm on one of the kitchen's countertop, which shakes; I don't think I've ever seen him so angry.

"Call Brit or Dragon ... They might know something about this." I try to soothe him, which is next to impossible since he has the temper of Zeus.

He heeds my advice and calls Dragon. The Asian-American is on his way to the beach house, always at Rocco's disposal.

A half hour later Dragon arrives in his Avalanche. Some blond man with piercing blue eyes and diamonds in his earlobes sits in the passenger seat. I presume the stranger is Dragon's afternoon date. Maybe the two are celebrating Valentine's Day early.

Rocco and Dragon have a beer in the study. I choose to pass on any alcohol since it's not even two o'clock in the afternoon. Both sit in high-backed chairs among shelves of leather books. Rocco asks Dragon, "What do you know about my missing belongings?"

"You're father had the items removed to be fingerprinted." Dragon is always professional and never cracks a smile. The poor thing has the sense of humor of a rock; I hope his blond date or afternoon cohort gets him to smile because no one else can seem to get the job done.

"My father?" the mob man asks, befuddled.

Dragon nods his head. "Yes. He's the one who signs my paychecks; this is why I listen to him."

Rocco rolls his eyes. "Leave it to my father."

Enough about the missing items from the beach house. Dragon needs to feed Rocco and me in on the details of Mantabaun's murder. I ask Dragon, "When was Mantabaun murdered?"

"Approximately eight o'clock last night."

"Were their footprints in the sand?"

Dragon shakes his head. "Not that Brit and I saw. We were all over the beach and discovered no clues."

My boyfriend rudely says, "Obviously you two weren't looking hard enough."

I scowl at him, providing daggers. My attention is now drawn back to Dragon, who seems to be enjoying his beer. I ask, "How many times was Mantabaun stabbed?"

"Four."

"All in the same area?"

"His lungs."

"And he bled to death?"

"Yes."

"Was he wearing anything?"

"Do you mean clothes or a gun?"

"Our houseboy didn't carry a gun. I'm talking clothes."

Dragon shakes his head.

"Were his wrists and ankles tied?"

Again, Dragon shakes his head.

"No clues of any kind were spotted?"

My future husband rolls his eyes; I feel like slapping him.

Dragon whispers, "I'm afraid not."

"It sounds like a dead end," I reply.

Once again, being professional and on task, Dragon shares, "Boss is having professionals look into it. I'm sure they'll discover a glitch of some sort to help us."

"I thought you and Brit were professionals?" Rocco bursts.

"Rocco!" I yell at him, outraged by his behavior. Can't he just keep his mouth shut sometimes? "Apologize to Dragon. You're treating him like the murderer."

My sidekick shrugs his shoulders and admits, "If the shoe fits."

I snap my fingers on my right hand, point at my lover, and briskly say, "Knock it off. You owe Dragon an apology. Now, do it!"

The Mafia man listens to me. He probably knows that I won't bend over for his sexual needs if he doesn't apologize. Now, tell me who wears the pants in our relationship after being together for almost six months?

Dragon accepts my lover's apology, quiet and reserved, unaffected by Rocco's outburst and my demand.

"Can we move on from here?" I inquire, ready to proceed with my questions for Dragon.

"What's the point?" my lover hisses, obviously disgusted with my minor interrogation.

I clear my throat and politely ask, "Rocco ... sweetie, can you give me a moment alone with Dragon?"

"Fuck yeah!" the mobster exclaims, rises from his reading chair, and exits the study. He vanishes into another room of the beach house with his beer in tow, perhaps happy to remove himself from our presence.

I decide to deal with my boyfriend later. For now, I have just a few more questions for Dragon while I have him under my care. "One," I begin, "where were you while Mantabaun was being murdered?"

Dragon sort of blushes. His face turns a rose red hue, which is darling. Possibly feeling embarrassed, he admits, "I was with Zach this morning ... in his bed and arms."

"Who is Zach?"

"The guy in the Avalanche. My boyfriend. Zach Merlot."

"And where was Brit?" I ask, serious as the plague.

"With your future father-in-law in Miami. Boss requested his services."

This is not a big surprise for me. Antonio "Boss" Malonni III is always requesting someone's services in his circle of hit men. Truth is he usually abducts his employees or relatives when he needs them. Frankly, I'm surprised Dragon doesn't share a detailed story regarding such a concern.

"What did Boss want with Brit?"

"I don't know."

Of course Dragon doesn't know. No one knows what Boss does or who he has secret meetings with. Hence, the job description of a practicing godfather. No one has a right to know his business.

"You think the three murders are connected?" I ask Dragon, watching him take a drink of his beer.

"I do. I'm really not sure how, but ... yes. They have to be."

"Any guesses referring to who just might be involved?"

He shakes his head, quiet as ever.

I like him and would probably date the man if I didn't currently have Rocco. He's handsome, intelligent, and dedicated to his job. The only problem I really have with the Asian-American is how quiet he is, always so reserved and almost timid. The silent type are always deviously calm and patient, which is why Boss has probably hired him to join his team.

I cut to the chase regarding Mantabaun's death and ask, "Dragon, if you did know something about these murders, would you tell me?"

As expected, he shakes his head yet again.

"Because Rocco's father is working on the three killings?"

"Exactly."

"Shit," I whisper. "Subconsciously I knew that. Sorry for wasting your time."

"It wasn't a waste," he admits and politely excuses himself from my presence because his cellular rings the national anthem and he has to take the call.

Less than a minute later, I find Rocco in our bedroom. He lies on the bed with his beer and stares at the ceiling. I move up to the bed, sit down next to him, brush a hand over his adorable head, and ask, "What's gotten into you? You were pretty sharp with Dragon."

He begins to peel the label off his Rolling Rock and replies, "This is too close to home. Someone I love is going to get hurt if we don't figure these murders out. I really liked Mantabaun ... even if you had an altercation with him."

I nod my head. How can't I relate to him? Half of me is pleased to know that he's worried about our safety, and the rest of his family. The other half fears he'll take these murders upon himself and recklessly become the center of the killer's attention, putting a target on his back. Granted, Rocco does have a heart, even if he seems to be a hardcore dick sometimes. Honestly, he doesn't mean any harm, is just a boy inside, and darling to the core. I get him, though, comprehending exactly what he's saying about the people around us being in danger: his father, brothers, their wives, his nieces and nephews, and ... me.

"This will all work out," I provide, lean into his mouth with my face, and apply a kiss to his reddish and beer-smelling lips.

"Don't bullshit me," he challenges.

"Can't bullshit a bullshitter, right?"

"Exactly."

# # # # #

This night, sleeping and tucked against Rocco's naked arms, his firm shaft pressed to my right hip, I dream of meeting him for the first time at Sabone's Restaurant on Pilsner Street. The dream is warm and fuzzy, perhaps everything a dream should be. We argue in the dream, almost throw fists at each other, and ...

He wakes screaming Zulan Cane's name.

It's a long night as I rock him in my arms and tell him, "Everything's fine. I'm here. You're safe. No one is going to hurt you."

# # # # #

Over breakfast, watching WFBF, local news Channel 11, Rocco and I learn that The Skin Artist burns to the ground. A pup of a blond journalist suggests arson was involved. Fire Chief Neil DeMark believes gasoline may have started the blaze. A further investigation will ensue.

"Croon is at it again," I tell Rocco after sipping my morning coffee.

"How do you know it's him?"

"Gut feeling."

"You rely on those?"

"What else do I have to rely on?"

"Good point, lover. You're not just a pretty face."

CHAPTER THIRTEEN – BALLS TO THE WALL

Valentine's Day comes with a hellacious rainstorm. Rocco decides to take the day off from his Mafia gigs to spend the entire day with me; one of my Valentine's Day presents. He has a list of our planned day on the kitchen counter that reads:

Wake up and fuck (I top).

Eat breakfast at Liz's Fine Eats.

Fuck in a public place, preferably in an office somewhere (I bottom).

Shop for springtime shirts and shoes.

Fuck in the BMW (jerk-off session is mandatory).

Enjoy lunch at Panama Isle's.

Tour Flamingo Bay Museum.

Fuck in the bathroom at the museum (I top).

Take a walk in Palma Park.

Fuck in the park (I bottom).

Eat dinner at Restole's Italian Cuisine.

Return to beach house and fuck (blowjobs).

After reviewing the list, I say to him, "There's a lot of fucking that's going to happen between us today. What's up with that?"

"You have a problem with my agenda?" His eyebrows raise and he mischievously grins like a little boy, adorable as ever.

"So you've decided to have my body for the most romantic day of the year?"

"Trust me, I have no complaints about that. If it were up to me, which it isn't, we'd spend the entire day together in bed, naked, and under the sheets. My dick is dying to be in your ass, pal. I don't even have to think twice about it."

"You're so naughty today ... I love it, babe. And I'm crazy in love with you." I move up to him, collapse our bodies together in a hug that fags will pay good money to watch, kiss his chin, an olive-colored cheek, and finally his mouth, which is succulent and tastes sweet.

He quickly pulls away from me and says, "I'll check the first line off the list."

"Who says we're going to fuck?"

"You turning me down, pal? No one turns me down. My family runs all of southern Florida. A smart guy never tells any of us no."

I sort of giggle, find his cashmere sweater with my hands, pull it up and over his head, and decide to play with his smooth skin for the next hour, perhaps even longer, seducing the man I love and want to spend the rest of my life with him, under his Mafia spell.

# # # # #

Approximately two hours later, Liz's Fine Eats is jam-packed with patron; the waiting line is out the door, and we decide to eat breakfast somewhere else. Not that I care, since I'm still spending the day with my man. On the way to The Cassidy Inn, which is known for their pineapple fritters, Dragon calls me on my cell.

Rocco heads east in his speedy 182i BMW, which is really my baby, and rushes through the falling rain. It's a twenty-minute drive to the inn, so I have enough time to take Dragon's call. "What's going on, Dragon?"

"I did a track on the e-mail from Tang." He sounds sure and confident, which is a blessing.

"And what did you find out?"

"The e-mail wasn't from Tang."

"Who was it from?"

"You sitting down?"

"I am ... Tell me who it was from." I sound a bit impatient and rude, but this is serious. Three bodies are connected to Rocco and me, and we have to deduce exactly who murdered the trio. If not, we're in deep shit and number one suspects regarding the crimes.

"Mantabaun."

I almost drop the cell phone to the convertible's foot well. "How is that possible?"

"Anything is possible on the Internet. You just have to be clever."

"You think my houseboy was that clever?" I sound condescending, but what the hell. The issue at hand is murder. Who in their right mind wouldn't be condescending?

"I do," Dragon replies. "He was trying to confess something to you by portraying Tang. It was the only way he possibly felt he could communicate with you. Maybe he didn't want to be a target regarding the killer. If you think about it, he was clever to send the e-mail like he did."

"Unbelievable," I whisper, consuming Dragon's information. "So Mantabaun knew something that he didn't feel comfortable telling me in person and found a way to send an e-mail to me by using Tang's identity?"

"Exactly. It's nice to know you're listening to me."

"That's fucking clever," I chant.

Rocco looks across the space between us with furrowed brows, obviously trying to piece together what Dragon is sharing with me, but also driving at the same time.

"Did you learn anything else?" I ask Dragon.

"Not as of yet. When I do, you'll know about it."

"Thanks, man," I reply, end the call, and draw my attention back to my valentine.

For the next few minutes I tell Rocco what Dragon uncovered.

Still driving, Rocco asks, "What do you think our houseboy was covering up?"

I reply, "Maybe he knew that Tang and his assistant were going to be murdered."

"And maybe he knew the diamonds would be stolen from our beach house."

"That's a good possibility."

Rocco swerves the BMW around a pothole, jars our bodies to the right, gathers his composure behind the wheel, and says, "No matter what, he was involved."

"I concur. I'm not even questioning that at this point. Mantabaun was sneaky. I liked him, but could never trust him."

The Mafia man at my left nods his head, puts his left turning signal on, begins to slow down the convertible, and makes a left on Bannerman Road. Approximately one mile later we pull into The Cassidy Inn, park, and spend the next hour filling our bellies with pineapple fritters and Nicaraguan coffee.

# # # # #

Although our Valentine's Day agenda explains that we are to have wild sex in a public place, and shop for springtime shirts following brunch, Cupid decides to mix things up for us, which is probably expected. My boyfriend changes our plans, and on the spur of the moment, we make the drive into downtown Flamingo Cove to investigate the discovered and cluttered room of junk in The Reach.

I should object, but don't. What the hell? I'm always up for a rugged afternoon of Mafia kick-ass, especially if it's with the hottest mobster on the planet who has a heated love-crush on my doable rump.

The BMW is like a submarine, floating through the downpour with its roof up. State-size puddles splash up and over the flaming red vehicle. Lightning zigzags across the bruised heavens. Thunder causes havoc overhead, which is boisterous and angry. Rain gushes down and over my passenger window. This does not prevent me from spotting Balls Banco. The man isn't hard to miss since he's the size of a walrus.

When Rocco stops at a red light on Fountain and Murray inside The Reach, I see Balls lumber into Ruff's Tobacco Shop to my right.

Balls certainly is not attempting a Jenny Craig nutrition plan these days. Instead, he looks fifty pounds heavier than the last time my vision consumed his meaty waistline. If he gets any fatter, he's going to have his own zip code, or possibly explode.

"It's him," I tell Rocco, pointing out the window. "Park the car." The light is still red, I realize, but whatever.

My partner turns to me and asks, "Who is it?"

"Balls Banco. I see him in Ruff's. He's huge. The man is a walking heart attack that's just waiting to happen."

The light turns green and my boyfriend quickly slides the 182i BMW between a Ford Focus and dilapidated Ranger. Within seconds, we jump out of the convertible and into the pelting rain. My current jack-buddy leads the way, making sure I'm right on his ass, which I'm sure he likes.

Concealed by an old phone booth, Rocco and I stand outside of Ruff's and wait for Balls. The downpour is heavy, loud, and unstoppable. Noisy thunder rakes across the sky like a snow shovel on cement. Part of the city lights up with streaks of playful lightning, which is blinding.

I ask over my lover's shoulder, "What's the plan, Mr. Perfect?"

"We follow Balls to his car and do the old climb-in-the-backseat routine."

"You sound like you've done it a million times."

He grunts with laughter. "Maybe not a million, but plenty. Follow my lead and you won't get hurt."

A Hispanic leach works the counter at Ruff's. He has Jesus and Mary tattoos along his arms and around his neck, which all look quite demonic. He smokes a cigar, filling the place up with unhealthy clouds. Two teeth are missing from his mouth. His ears are decorated with bronze pentagons that hang from their lobes.

We watch Balls purchase a pack of tobacco and rolled papers. Money is exchanged with no gunfire. Eventually, Balls leaves the store, steps into the rain, and returns to his black Lincoln, which is parked two cars up the street.

As planned, Balls climbs into his Lincoln, barely fitting behind the wheel because he's as big as an Army tank. Rocco and I bolt to the back door on the passenger side, swing the door open, and quickly jump inside.

Balls knows some shit is about to hit the fan and attempts to bolt. Rocco is street smart and quick, ready for immediate surprises at all times, no matter what the situation entails. What transpires next occurs all in a matter of seconds: Rocco leashes his right palm around what little hair Balls has left on his skull and pulls the fat man's head back; my boyfriend's Glock is removed from his side and aimed at Balls's right temple; Rocco immediately clicks the safety to the OFF position on his weapon and informs, "You move your fat ass an inch and I'll blow your fucking head off."

I snuggle up beside Rocco, enjoying this action-packed evening to the fullest. Honestly, when I see him in his tough-man mobster mode, I kind of sport a boner and find his powerful antics a total turn-on.

"What do you want with me, Rocco?" Balls inquires, recognizing the hottest Mafia man in the city behind him.

"I have a few questions for you ... Nothing else."

"What kind of questions?"

My brutish boyfriend has the list of questions memorized and begins with: "You still work for Chain Chan?"

Ruthlessly, Balls replies, "I work for myself."

"You know anything about Buli Croon, freak?"

"I know he's an asshole like you, motherfucker."

Rocco does not take light to this comment and its rude label. He digs the Glock's cold muzzle into Balls's temple with force, grits his teeth, and growls, "He set The Skin Artist on fire?"

Balls is pretty tough, unflinching in his seat, which is typical bad boy behavior according to *The Bad Boy Handbook: Flamingo Cove Edition 2013*. "That's a good bingo."

"Does he have something to do with knocking off Tang, Tang's assistant, and my houseboy?"

"Croon's behind everything. I'm sure the asshole is connected one way or another."

Rocco pulls Balls's hair a little more. Surprisingly, Balls does not flinch, obviously he's used to having the shit beat out of him because of his street job. Rocco asks, "How's he fucking connected, freak?"

"I didn't say he was."

Mischievously and skillfully, my boyfriend taps the tip of his gun to Balls's temple and responds, "Don't bullshit me, goon. You won't get hurt if you play by my rules. I've killed men before and you're not special enough to live. I can promise you that."

I have to hand it to my sexy companion, he surely gets his point across. Perhaps Balls knows he's in a sticky situation, destined to see heaven today if he doesn't abide by my boyfriend's agenda. Balls simply blurts, "Izzy Ramon ... That's who you need to talk to."

Rocco pauses, thinks for a second, spins the name around in his skull, and whispers, "What's he have to do with me?"

"He works with Croon. The two are cousins and connected at the hip. Rumor has it he took out Tang."

"What about Tang's assistant and my houseboy? Who popped them?"

"Don't know and don't fucking care. It's none of my goddamn business."

Again, Rocco taps the gun against Boss's skull. He asks in a rather brutish tone, overpowering the goon, "You don't know ... or you just don't want to tell me?"

Our victim attempts to shake his head but he really can't because he's too fat. The man mumbles, "I don't know."

"Why did Izzy take out Tang?"

"I don't know that either."

"You know who blew up my Hummer?"

"That I know," Balls groans with just the slightest wave in his voice. He looks like mush in the front seat, motionless and a big blob of seamen.

"Who?"

"Croon. He likes to catch things on fire. Give him an accelerant and he goes nuts with it."

"And who trashed my beach house?" Rocco doesn't mention the four million dollars' worth of diamonds missing, but maybe he should. Perhaps he believes that if he finds who poked Tang's assistant and our houseboy, he'll learn where the stolen diamonds are.

"I think it was Croon."

"You think?" my lover sounds bitter, rough to the core, without any sense of compassion.

"Yeah ... I think. I don't know for sure."

"Was it Izzy Ramon?"

"No. Izzy don't do no shit like that? He's fucking crazy, but not that crazy."

Balls's grammar kills me. Who needs a serial killer in the city when Balls butchers me with his urban chat.

"Was it you? You look as if you can do shit like that?" Rocco asks.

"Wasn't me. I got bigger and better things to do." Balls attempts to shake his head, but he really can't.

"Does Izzy work for you?"

"Fuck no. Of course not. That's a stupid fucking question. Izzy can't be trusted."

"You work for Izzy?"

"Wouldn't dare. He's trouble. Grade-A dangerous. Izzy's like the devil. He breathes on you and you'll catch on fire."

"You lying to me?" Rocco lets out a devious laugh that suggests Balls is a master at being coy.

"I'm an angel. Angels don't lie. You bump me off here and now and I go to heaven. No stops. Heaven, here I come."

Rocco hears enough. He pops Balls in the side of the head with his gun. Balls makes a hog-like grunt and instantly passes out behind the steering wheel.

My lover now directs his attention at me and says, "Let's get out of here."

"What about Balls?"

"Fuck him."

I swear, I have the biggest erection. There's nothing better to witness than Rocco in high-impacted, testosterone-boosted macho man mode. Hell, I can probably spew a load right in my low-cut boxer-briefs if the truth be known because of his gung-ho aggressive shit. Seeing my future husband in his bad boy manner is a total cock-hardening experience for me; something I crave, enjoy, and wish would happen more often.

Hmmm … Maybe he can use such naughtiness in the bedroom with me … That would be rather stimulating, wouldn't it?

# # # # #

We never do get to investigate the upstairs room of junk in The Reach. Rocco has other things on his mind. We drive the two hours north to the small city called Watergulf to find Izzy Ramon.

On the drive, I ask Rocco, "How do you know Izzy? I saw you pause back there with Balls and …"

"You shouldn't know some things," he interjects.

I turn in my seat and give him a dirty look: pursed lips, slanted brows, and direct eyes. Scolding him, I say, "No secrets, Rocco. You'd better tell me now. If you don't, I'll only find out on my own. Don't even tempt me."

"Forget about it. It will only piss you off. Both of us don't need that, which you're very much aware of."

"Is Izzy an ex-boyfriend of yours?" He is. I just know it. Intuition kicks into my system and ... Izzy Ramon was once my lover's lover. Rocco can't hide anything from me. The longer you spend with someone the less they can keep from you. I know this for a fact, and Rocco also knows this.

I wait patiently for him to reply to my question, but he never does. His lips are sealed, though. Motherfucker!

# # # # #

Watergulf is Key West with a shitload of more money. The houses are titanic and everyone drives a Bentley. No one with less than fifty million dollars lives in this neighborhood: brokers, best-selling novelists, commercial artists, oil tycoons, casino owners, expensive lawyers, and brain surgeons.

Izzy's abode is a sky-reaching palace next the ocean. The entire property is gated, secured by a staff of twenty men, and reeks of cold hard cash. Hundred dollar bills grow on the palms like coconuts. The clouds above the mansion are shaped like dollar signs. Think Richie Rich plus one hundred billion dollars more.

We learn from Bunny, Izzy's housemaid, that the goon isn't at home.

Bunny is really Benard Tanner, a transsexual who works for Izzy. Bunny is blond with big boobs, no penis, wide red lips, and is about as ditzy as a cartoon character. The woman is Jessica Rabbit all the way with much more sass and va-voooom.

Rocco and I are not invited inside. Instead, we have to stand on the front veranda while Bunny stands at the open door and asks us what we want.

My sidekick says, "I need to talk to Izzy." He sounds like real Mafia: hardcore tough, seriously straight, and armor-plated. There's no way he can be more sexy, I swear.

Bunny is Izzy's lover, isn't he/shit/it? I know this. I sense it. Bunny brushes two fingers again my lover's left cheek, provides a flirtatious smile, and chants, "Izzy misses you. It's a shame he's not here. I'm sure he would like to suck on your Italian cock while I watched."

Rocco pulls away from Bunny's fingers and blushes because of her comment. "Tell him I stopped by and I'm looking for him."

"To break his heart again?" Bunny chants, grinning from ear to ear. "How typical of you, Mr. Malonni. Crack his heart twice, why don't you? A serial heartbreaking criminal like you should be behind bars."

I make some severe eye contact with Rocco that implies death, sigh heavily, and turn my attention back to Bunny, who says, "I'll tell Izzy you're looking for his cock again. I'm sure you miss it. And I'm sure he misses your face in his ass, darling."

Rocco's voice cracks, "Fine. Just tell him I was here."

Bunny agrees, wishes us a good day, spins around, lets out an obnoxious and unladylike fart, and eventually heads back into her palace, sashaying away.

I'm left with Rocco on the expansive verandah and ask, "What the fuck was that all about?" The look I give him is exactly what he expects: pissy, judgmental, and perplexed. The man has a lot of explaining to do regarding Bunny's information and his secret past with Izzy Ramon.

Rocco says in an aggressive manner, "No questions right now. Get the fuck in the car."

"You're going to eventually have to tell me the story behind Izzy Ramon, Rocco. You can't keep it from me forever. You do know this, right?" I sound absolutely miserable and bitchy, but he has it coming.

Mr. Goon heads to the BMW, climbs inside, waits for me, and we make the extended drive back to Flamingo Cove in silence, which is one of the longest rides of my life.

# # # # #

I admit, today has not been so grand and award winning for it being Valentine's Day. One good thing surfaces within my mind (and

135

heart): I've spent every second of it with Rocco Malonni, even if he was once lovers with a man named Izzy Ramon.

Following the trials with Balls and Bunny, Rocco and I find ourselves back at the beach house. Here, confined in our shared bedroom, he presents a tiny box wrapped in throbbing hearts, long arrows, and boyish cupids. A small and glittery red bow sits on top that screams for me to unwrap the festive delight.

I glow with excitement, taking the box from him. "For me?"

"Always for you," he whispers with a ruggedly cute smile, perhaps pleased that we are done with the silent treatment and no longer pissed at each other.

Hurriedly, I pull off the glittery bow, remove the wrapping, and discover a white box. How exciting! My heart races and the back of my hands begin to sweat. Steady boyfriends are so amazing to have.

"Open it," he demands in a light tone. "I think you're going to love it."

Slowly, I pull the lid off the white box and … "Oh, Rocco … This is beautiful."

Inside the box is a one-inch onyx pendant hanging off a rawhide necklace. The gem is somewhat shaped like a Colt .45, but only if you look at it close enough.

"Do you like it?"

"I love it," I explain, lifting the necklace out of the box and placing it around my neck.

He helps me latch the necklace at the back of my neck and confesses, "I found it in South Africa for you. A native has a tiny shop in Springbok and … I was thinking of you when I saw it."

Following his help, we kiss with hunger. Lips connect as well as cocks. Our arms wrap around each other. When I finally decide to pull out of the kiss, I stare deeply into his dark purple eyes and confess, "I have something for you, too."

"You don't?"

"Oh, but I do."

"What's that?"

Intoxicated by his strong man-scent of sweat, I pull his tee up and over his head, devour his corded neck with kisses, and follow it up with my lips as they brush over his right nipple. Falling on my knees, my mouth meets his navel, decides to head southward to a place I have visited often; a place where men connect in lust, driven by passion, infinite desires, and man-joy. And here, using my mouth and throat, I offer my personal gift to him on the hearts and arrows holiday – good for me, us.

CHAPTER FOURTEEN – IZZY, IN BED

As expected, I do a little bit of homework on Izzy Ramon. The need to find out how's he connected to my boyfriend is relentless. To accomplish such details, I have a private meeting with Tex Dardin, a personal assistant to Izzy.

I meet Tex at an underground fuck bar called Butchopolis. The place is known for burly guys in leather and dominant tops in search of submissive bottoms. Leather daddies are always welcome and blond-haired twinks sometimes arrive out of pure curiosity. College jocks are far too clean-cut for the place. And butch men wrestle naked with long shafts in the back room on Champion mats. The winner of each match decides who to escort into a fuck room and have the time of their sexual lives with. I know if you don't want to get laid or roughed up at the place, you don't go to Butchopolis. Bottom line: the place is naughty, dirty, and hardcore rough. Stay away, princesses!

I'm not at the bar to be laid or roughed up. But I do want to discuss Izzy in full with Tex. Sometimes you have to make a sacrifice to learn things about a person, particularly Izzy Ramon.

Tex is not a cowboy, which is sort of ironic. Instead, he's a light-skinned African-American drug dealer with light blue eyes, handsome crew cut, beautiful facial features, and an IQ of 190. The guy is thirty-three-years-old and stands at six-two, is thin as a lightning bolt, declares himself the smartest gangster in the tri-state area, and the best personal assistant that Izzy has ever had.

We shake hands; his grip is solid and refined. He doesn't accomplish any funny stuff with his thumbs or fingers like other gangsters I know. Tex asks if I'm carrying any heat and I pat my right hip and reply, "A revolver, which I don't intend to use. How about you?"

"Two forty-fives."

"You going to use one?"

"Neither."

"How nice of you."

As a vintage Depeche Mode song plays on overhead speakers, we order drinks from a gray-haired daddy behind the bar. Tex orders a double martini and I order a light beer. Our drinks are served in a matter of seconds; good service is so hard to find – kudos to Butchopolis.

We drink our beverages and stare at a few half-naked Harley guys. Eventually, I say, "Tell me about Izzy Ramon."

"What do you want to know about him?"

"How long have you worked for him?"

"Ten years. Maybe longer."

I cut the small talk and ask, "How does he know Croon?"

"Everyone knows Croon. You tell me one Mafia guy who doesn't know Croon and I'll give you a million bucks."

I shake my head and reply, "I have more money than I know what to do with. Thanks for the opportunity, though."

To my surprise, Tex admits, "Izzy works with Balls Banco. The two pretty much rule The Reach."

"They work for Croon?"

"Everyone works for Croon in their own way."

"Izzy in good with Croon?"

"If Izzy wasn't in good with Croon, he'd be dead. Anyone who fucks with Croon will end up dead."

"Like Tang Meadow?" I ask, getting to my point.

"Yeah. Just like Tang."

"And his assistant?"

Tex shakes his head. "I don't think so. Tang's assistant was just in the way. It sometimes happens."

"What about my houseboy?"

"What about your houseboy?"

"He was murdered on my beach … exactly where Tang was knocked off."

"That's a pity. Mantabaun was a nice guy. I liked his cock."

"He was a pretty good houseboy."

"My condolences."

"You think Mantabaun was in the way or …"

Tex interjects me with: "Do you know that your houseboy worked for Croon?"

I'm blown away by this news, possibly believing that the guy is lying to me. "What do you mean?"

He smiles at me, takes a sip of his drink, swallows the sip down, and adds, "Your houseboy worked for Croon for almost three years. He was Croon's sidearm, if you want to know the truth."

I believe him. Tex is a good source for information. Rarely lies. Smooth at his job. A keeper, and possibly someone to trust. No wonder he works for Balls and Izzy.

"Back to Izzy," Tex said.

"What about Izzy?"

"Why are you asking me about Izzy when Rocco dated him for like nine months?"

I almost fall off my bar stool in surprise regarding this information, even though it's expected.

Tex sort of chortles and says, "Tell me you knew that."

I shake my head. "Rocco doesn't talk about his ex-boyfriends. Maybe I knew it, but didn't really want to admit it to myself."

The drug dealer grunts with pleasure beside me, broadly smiles, and shares, "Trust me, Derek, Rocco and Izzy were more than boyfriends."

I'm all ears, take a pretty hearty sip of my beer, and inquire, "Give me the scoop. I want to hear it all."

So Tex Dardin spends the next forty minutes telling me the following facts: Rocco and Izzy met at an AIDS fundraiser in Key West; the two hit it off fairly well; they went missing for a week, hiding in San Francisco on a "love" escapade; for the next year they dated, received the title "boyfriends" and Rocco asked Izzy to marry him.

I know that Rocco was never married, though. His father never mentioned it to me, as well as his slew of brothers and their chatty wives. This prompts me to ask Tex, "Why did they break up?"

Tex says, "Izzy fell for an artist. Rocco was pretty devastated. Boss Malonni was about to knock Izzy off, deciding to chop the poor bastard into little pieces. Rocco stopped his father from killing Izzy, claiming he still loved the man, and always would."

"Then what happened?"

"It didn't work out between Izzy and the artist. Izzy wanted Rocco back and the sexy Mafia man wouldn't have him. Rocco broke my employer's heart. It was like murder for Izzy."

"And then what?" I inquire, fully interested in Tex's spill.

"Nothing happened next. Izzy went his way and Rocco started his life over."

"They weren't friends with benefits?"

"Of course not. Rocco severed his lust, love, or whatever he had with Izzy. It was doomsday to the hilt for their relationship."

"Most interesting," I supply, absorbing Tex's information, but not really knowing how much it's worth. Again, I ask, "You think Izzy murdered Tang and Mantabaun?"

"I don't. Croon would do something like that, but not Izzy."

"Why do you say that?"

"Izzy stays away from Rocco because he knows the man can have him erased in a matter of seconds. Your boyfriend has a lot of power in southern Florida. Izzy won't risk that. Croon, on the other hand, doesn't give a fuck about anyone but himself. Murder is not beneath him."

I finish my beer, consuming all of Tex's comments.

Tex finishes his drink.

Side by side, we talk about how hot we think Easton Corbin is, the country music singer and ...

#

Maybe I'm part cat because curiosity continually kills me, of course. Rocco's past lovers have always been a mystery to me; a topic he never discusses with me. To seek out one, explore his world a little, and maybe uncover a fact or prolific detail regarding my boyfriend's history, seems like an afternoon of fun. Why not? What do I have to lose?

The drive to Watergulf is actually a good time. Walter Landing has *Bottom Tales* on CD and I listen to a few chapters. Once in the driveway at Izzy's palatial mansion, I find myself at its hulking front doors, ring the bell, and wait patiently for an unannounced visit.

To my surprise, Bunny, Izzy's housemaid/lover/whatever, does not show at the door to let me inside. Of course I'm a man to take matters into my own hands and find my intrusive way inside. Because the front doors are locked, I skirt around the massive edifice through an east garden consisting of pawpaws, flax lilies, sage, and powderpuffs. Here, I find a tiny side patio with two wrought-iron chairs and a table, potted plants, and unlocked French doors.

Yes, I find myself inside the mansion on my own accord, enjoying the smell of freshly baked cinnamon rolls in an all-white kitchen out of the pages of *Martha Stewart's Living*. The room is immaculate with alabaster countertops, a matching floor, and Jenn-Air appliances.

Because I hear muddled murmurs of masculine struggling from an above room I discover the narrow stairs at the rear of the kitchen and decide to take them. Beforehand, I remove my Pradas, carry them at my side, and quietly work my way to the second floor.

Once on the next level of the obnoxiously-size house, the garbled murmuring becomes much louder. To no avail, I follow the noises down an expansive and shadowy hallway and pass a number of guest bedrooms in various themes and colors, all of which are interlaced with private bathrooms.

To my surprise, in the last room on the right side of the stretched hallway, I come upon a sight so rare, but feasibly enjoyable. Here, I discreetly spy on the man of the house fully naked on his California King-size bed, handling his tool of seven steeping inches.

Izzy Ramon doesn't see me, which I am happy for. The last thing I need to happen is to be discovered trespassing on his private party, accruing a list of law-breaking deeds upon this happenstance adventure.

In truth, the twenty-something man on the bed is utterly beautiful. I calculate his height at six foot, his weight at 180 pounds, and admire his ripped and suntanned torso. Izzy has blond hair and blue eyes and …

Fuck me sideways. The man looks just like me. My twin. A mirror image of Derek Reed – me! I realize quite bluntly that Rocco likes one type of guy: men around my age and with my dashing pretty boy looks. Although this discovery on the bed is shocking, and the fact that Rocco has replaced Izzy in his life with me, what surprises me most about Rocco's former boyfriend is the width of his cock. The slab of meat is no less than two inches wide and quite the handful for the drug dealer on the bed.

Of course, Izzy is at work on his stiff timber. As one hand toys with a nipple, his other hand rises and falls on the seven inches of knob between his legs. The drug dealer pants heavily and his solid chest is sweat-lathered as it inflates and deflates. He squints his eyes, breathes chaotically, and thrusts his hips upward, into his fist.

The jackoff scene is undoubtedly the hottest. Indecipherable moans escape Izzy as he rotates his wide shaft up and down. Again, he raises his hips, and just as timely, falls to the bed. Bubbles of perspiration collect over his forehead, wide shoulders, and muscled thighs. A hearty gasp is heard, a moan, and more hip-thrusts occur.

I'm stinging hard under my chinos. Droplets of ooze leak into the cotton, moistening my balls. In truth, it looks as if I'm watching myself on the bed, toying with my goods, and getting myself off. More truth: I like what I see, enjoying Izzy at his laborious alone-time.

In a matter of seconds, he lets out a steady moan, immediately stops jacking his meat, and holds its base. Three long arcs of white juice splat against his suntanned torso. His tight navel is filled with the goop and his solid abs and fist-size pecs are drizzled. A fourth arc of sap glazes his chin and neck. One final gasp is heard and he falls limp on the bed, catching his breath.

I'm about to sneak away when he turns his head in my direction and spots me at the door. Rocco's ex quickly asks, "Were you entertained?"

I stop dead in my tracks, embarrassed by my actions and …

"Derek Reed, I know it's you. Come in. Don't be afraid, my darling look-alike."

I become wide-eyed and still, panicky and ready to plan my escape in a manner of seconds.

# # # # #

"Derek, at last we meet," Izzy says. "Don't be shy and come in here."

As I enter his navy-blue bedroom with chiffon pillows and a few of Picasso's Blue period paintings on the walls, I observe the man and his chest-mess. A nearby towel on the bed is retrieved and the bubbles of spew are casually wiped away. Politely, he covers up his erect and wide Johnny with the white cotton towel, and watches me stand at the foot of his bed.

"My God, we look exactly alike. Perhaps we have the same mother or father that we don't know about."

I choose not to reply, edgy and unsure of my purpose in the drug dealer's presence.

"You're the spitting image of me," he says, summing up my features from head to toe. "My twin. A replica of me. My brother."

"I'm sorry I interrupted," I confess, uncertain of how to respond to his comments, possibly blushing from ear to ear because of our uncanny similarities.

He waves a hand in my direction and says, "There's no need to apologize. I knew you were there all along. In fact, I felt that I was giving you a personal show."

A box of Marlboros sit on a nightstand, which Rocco's ex rescues. He slides one of the cigarettes out, lights it with a Zippo lighter, and begins to smoke, filling the room with a gray-blue cloud. Following this act, he says, "I know it's a horrible habit, but what can I say? Cigs are my absolute vice. They keep me away from drugs and alcohol."

"I don't mind," escapes me. Why do I feel embarrassed, misplaced, and possibly introverted at this very moment? My goal is to learn a little bit about Rocco's past. Nothing more. Nothing less. I shouldn't feel incessantly awkward. I presume Rocco knows everything about my past loves, obtaining certain details from my friends. Having this private meeting with Izzy possibly balances the weights between Rocco and me a bit. This rationale does not take away my nervousness, though. In fact, my throat turns dry and my hands begin to shake.

"You're here about Rocco, I deduce. Correct?"

"I am."

"And what is it that you want to know about the mobster?"

"I just wanted to see you in person."

He stretches his arms out like Jesus on the cross and says, "Here I am." He yawns and adds, "You talked to Tex, didn't you?"

"I did."

"And you learned that Rocco broke my fucking heart, right?"

I nod my head, fearing for my life for some peculiar reason.

"What did you expect to see today?" he asks, grinning from ear to ear, portraying the Alpha male regarding the both of us.

"I expected someone different. I didn't think you'd look exactly like me."

He takes another drag on his cigarette and blows smoke into the room. "How so?"

"Someone who has his own image. Not a replica of me."

"I'll give Rocco credit regarding men, he's very consistent."

"It's true."

146

He squints his blue-blue eyes, puckers his lips with concern, and eventually questions, "You're here about Tang and Mantabaun's murders, aren't you?"

"I am."

"And you think I'm connected to those murders, right?"

"I do." I nod my head and feel my lungs become contaminated with his cigarette smoke.

Truth is he could have a handgun in the nightstand next to his bed. Easily, he can retrieve the tool from its wooden home, pull it out, and blast bullets into my body. My presence is risky, of course, but Rocco has taught me to be brave, stay on task, and fight my battles with integrity.

"If you have any information about the murders, I would appreciate it, Izzy."

"Croon is your man," he confesses, unimpressed with my visit now.

"Everyone is telling me that."

"You should investigate him. Or maybe you're too busy taking Rocco's cock up your ass." His words are sharp and a bit scathing. He has more interest in the cigarette that hangs out of his mouth opposed to me, which I really don't have a problem with.

"I haven't," I admit. "No, that's not true. I have. Croon is very hard to question."

Izzy tilts his blond-pretty head back and provides a laugh that sounds like my own. Once his laughter ends, he confesses, "You're very naïve, Derek. And, you're far too nice to be connected to the mob. I say get out while you can. Rocco hurts men. He's a heartbreaker. You don't want him to break you, do you?"

I shake my head and reply, "I don't want that."

"Find Croon and ask him about the murders, my look-alike man. Expect him to lie. Expect him to be a bitch. Pry into his life and business, and then you'll learn that he is very much behind the murders."

Believing him, fully satisfied with this information, I prepare to leave.

After telling the man thank you for his help and turning away from the bed, he calls out my name. I spin around inside the doorframe and say, "Yes?"

"Do you love him?" he asks, his voice being a whisper, faint and almost tiresome.

"Rocco?"

"Yes, Rocco. Do you love the man?"

"I do. With all my heart. Why do ask?"

He takes another puff of his cancer stick, blows a cloud of smoke into the room, and confesses, "I wasn't in love with him. I wanted to be, but couldn't change my feelings for him, although I continuously tried. It's why I found the artist, whom I very much fell in love with, but he didn't want me." Again, he inhales on his Marlboro, exhales, and admits, "Let Rocco know that from me. I never wanted us to hurt, but … I needed to find someone to love. I'm sure he already knows that, though."

I nod my head, silent to the core, unable to respond. Honestly, I expect Izzy Ramon to be the biggest dick on the planet, and pop a few bullets into my exposed torso. What I learn is the opposite, though. He cared about Rocco at one time, deeply and with much regard, but never loved him. Today, he still possibly feels some guilt for the affair that he started with the artist behind his back, inevitably ending his relationship with the mobster. Frankly, I learn that Izzy is a nice guy with a heart and soul hidden under his skin. Some bad guys are like this, I guess, and Rocco, similar to Izzy Ramon, just happens to be one of them … or so I believe.

CHAPTER FIFTEEN – MAN-CHASE

I leave Izzy's room, satisfied with my visit. Behind me, Rocco's ex loses it and suddenly calls out, "You're not going anywhere, asshole!" He fires off two shots at my head from a Haggle .9mm. The bullets puncture the wall in front of me; obviously Rocco falls for sexy-hot gay guys who can't hit their targets and have bipolar personalities.

What the fuck is happening? I mean, seriously, what's happening? Izzy was an angel a few seconds ago. Now, he's fucking mad for some reason. What's up with this? How crazy is the guy? And why didn't he take his happy pills this morning? Is this sudden change in his mood why Rocco didn't take him back as a lover after he did the diddle with the artist? I imagine so. How elementary, of course.

I bolt down the hallway at a superhuman speed.

Izzy Ramon screams at the top of his lungs as if it is the end of the world, "You motherfucker! … Don't run away from me! … Come back here, asshole!"

I almost trip over my own feet while fleeing. My heart races and my temperature rises. Every muscle inside my body immediately loosens up and I turn into an Olympic runner with super-human power, strength, and charisma.

Although I think I'm fast, Izzy is a jet behind me. He flies out of his bedroom and chases after me. Again, he fires off a shot at me, which zooms past my right ear and smashes a Japanese vase on a four-foot high pedestal at the end of the hallway. Ceramic pieces of the Ming dynasty shatter and spiral in all directions. Quickly, I make an immediate right, find the stairwell, and begin my heedless decline.

Naked Izzy is right behind me. Somehow the psycho catches up to me. Another shot is fired and almost splits my skull into two equal pieces. The bullet careens past my left ear this time and lodges into the wall. He screams at his highest pitch, "You cocksucker! I'm going to fucking kill you! Don't run too far because I can catch you, dick-eater!"

I jump down three steps, four steps, and three more steps, leaping. Before I know it, I'm in the kitchen and he's on my ass, ready to fuck me up.

In a matter of seconds, his naked body lands on top of my back like a tick and pushes me to the kitchen's marble floor. My nose meets the flat surface and an immediate head-rocking jolt of pain twists between my temples. I think my nose is broken, but it's not. I roll over and attempt to push him off my bulk, but the guy is like a Skitter in *Falling Skies* and he's all over me, pissed out of his crazy mind. Eventually, I get the cock-licking bastard off me with a heavy push. Rocco's ex-boyfriend flies backward, which enables me enough time to face him and plan my next move.

"You took Rocco from me." He grins overtop me like a lunatic, positioned on his knees. Our bodies are locked together, but who cares since the .9mm is pointed at the center of my forehead. So much for the nice guy I just shared a decent conversation with upstairs.

"Don't shoot me," I plead, ready to piss myself.

"Of course I'm going to shoot you, faggot." He gawks at me with wide eyes and resembles The Joker.

Fuck! Izzy Ramon is off his rocker. Why did I come up here on my own? What was I thinking? The guy is totally messed up in the head, possibly a schizophrenic or suffering from more than one personality. I really don't know what his diagnosis is since I'm not a psychiatrist, but the guy is definitely a victim of some mega-mental shit. Drugs are needed and a good therapist. The crazy motherfucker needs some balance in his life.

"You need to die, Derek Reed," he whispers, crawls overtop my skin, presses the barrel of the .9mm at my skull, and begins to twist it with some heavy-duty force. "Thought you were going to get away from me, didn't you, queer?"

Indeed I did. But the crazy just happens to be a fast runner, wrestler, and gangster. Clothed or naked, he's a championship bolter. Suffering from the worst headache in my life, I calmly say, "Izzy, let's talk about this like rational men. We're not children. A positive outcome can be reached, of course."

"Fuck that," he provides with a demonic stare. "It's time to blow your brains all over my kitchen floor. Bunny can clean up the fucking mess in a cute pair of Victoria's Secret panties and nothing more."

"Izzy ..."

The gun clicks once ... twice ... three times, misfiring. Disgusted, he lets out an unpleasant grunt and tosses the .9mm against one of the kitchen cabinets. Now, he screams at the top of his lungs, pissed like a wet cat. He looks and sounds depleted. A breakdown of sorts is starting to happen that neither of us completely understand. Izzy is mentally losing it right in front of me, misplacing his mental marbles.

I think piss leaks between my legs because I'm frightened. It's not the first time a goon has tried to pop a lead load into my skull and spill my gray matter everywhere. Granted, the goons have to work at it, and so far they have failed, which means I'm a contender. If I don't respond in the next few seconds to him, the fucker will attack me. The psycho has the potential to kill me with his bare hands, but only if he really wants to. Defending myself, I ball my right fist into something powerful and lunge it at the bad boy's right jaw. Seconds later, I make contact with his face, cause his mouth to bleed, feel a tooth break under a few knuckles, and mush hereafter. Good for me.

He makes a ridiculous umph sound and reaches for his mouth with his left palm. Blood gushes out between his split lips and decorates his fingers. Now, his right hand forms a compact ball and swings against the side of my head. Surprisingly, he nails my right eye; even gays can fight, especially crazy ones.

I have about enough of his crap and use both of my fists on his similar face. Punches swing against his pretty boy lips, pinkish cheeks, blue-blue eyes, and smooth forehead. The asshole bruises and begins to bloody right before my stare. Anger surfaces in a full dose and I yell at him, "No wonder you're not with Rocco, you stupid piece of shit!"

Two punches bash into his right jaw. Another punch pounds him in his left eye and causes his head to fly backward. In doing so, the drug dealer starts to bleed from his nose and tears begin to fall out of his left eye. He yelps as I continue swinging my fists. Honestly, I'm a real fan of Chuck Palahniuk's *Fight Club* and find the strength to sit up and decide to bash my balled fists at his face numerous times. Both meet his chin and cheeks, knocking loose teeth out of his mouth, which fall into his lap. I'm Rocky Balboa to the nth degree. I'm a motherfucking butterfly who stings like a pissed off bee.

Izzy releases a gasp and hiss like air exiting an inflated balloon. Cherry-red blood rolls out of the corners of his mouth like a vampire and his eyes produce tears at their corners. The look he shares with me says he's going to kill me when, and if, he has the chance. For now, Rocco's ex-bad boy with his mental disability becomes a slump on the kitchen floor and bathes in his own blood.

Honestly, I don't know if the crazy fucker passes out or not, but I'm surely not going to stick around to find out. Instead, I rise from my seated position, feel a number of disjointed aches and pains ski through my core from our man-on-man battle, and walk away from the scene, leaving the fuckhead's mansion and its slumped-over owner behind.

# # # # #

Frankly, I never really thought I'd turn out to be connected to the mob. Errand running was my gig for years. If you wanted lunch, I was the guy to fetch it for your hungry tummy. If you needed a package delivered to the other side of Flamingo Cove, I certainly didn't have a problem handling the situation. If you were out of groceries, I not only wrote a list for you, I fetched the provisions from the store, delivered them to your apartment, and even put them away for your lazy ass. This is what I used to do until I met Rocco Malonni and his Mafia family. Now, I pack heat when I have to, throw fists like Sugar Ray Leonard, and use vulgarities that would cause my own mother to faint. I know all about drugs, dirty money, stolen diamonds, and almost every end of the goon business. If you want to know about hustlers, I'm your guy. If you need a Colt .45, I can arrange it for you. If you want your biggest enemy to have a broken arm, I can either do it myself or carry out the job through someone I know. If you desire something illegal to be smuggled into the country, I can certainly get it done. No, I am not an errand boy anymore. My life has twisted into something rather queerly astounding. I'm now a millionaire who just happens to be in the mob because of my hot boyfriend. I beat up crazy cats like Izzy Ramon, try to solve murders, and never … never piss off my goon family for fear of being knocked off.

Izzy is not down for the count in the kitchen. Go figure. Motherfuckers are hard to keep down, right? Instead, he stands up, limps after me through his lavishly decorated mansion, bleeds all over himself and the floor, and follows me through the massive front doors. Behind me, I hear the psycho yell, "I'm not done with you yet, queen! You can ride but you can't hide!"

Hurriedly, I climb into my BMW, start its engine, and zoom away. I head for Key Water Road, which leads to the highway, and begin the two-hour drive back to Flamingo Cove, Rocco, and the beach house – safe at last.

I'm not even a mile on the highway when I see a white Escalade behind me. A naked Izzy is perched behind its wheel, grinning like a madman.

"Christ," I whisper, knowing I'm in deep shit now.

The loon makes eye contact with me that informs: You messed with the wrong guy, McFaggot. He now gives me the bird and alert eyes. In a matter of seconds, his front bumper meets my back bumper and I jolt forward in the BMW from its fruitful impact.

"Fuck!" I yell, keeping both hands on the steering wheel, preventing a fatal wreck by jamming the speedy car into a guardrail or ditch.

Three vehicles are ahead of me: two Hondas and a small pickup. Only crazy Izzy is behind me. The sneer on his face is ludicrous, disheartening, and menacing. I can't believe my current lover, and future husband, actually had the gull to be engaged to such a wacko. Honestly, I thought Rocco had more sense. Perhaps he was just interested in Izzy's model-nice looks, or the width of his cock; I'll never know.

Rocco's ex definitely means business and wants to hurt me. Again, he gives me the finger, waving it from left to right so I don't miss it.

I decide to floor the BMW, attempting to rocket away. The BMW has power, a V6 engine, but Izzy's Escalade must have more. He hits my back bumper again and rocks me forward at eighty-nine miles per hour. I almost lose control and fear that the vehicle will begin to tumble over numerous times on the highway like a cumbersome cardboard box in a feisty wind. This doesn't happen, though. All's good behind my wheel. I keep the racer racing and my eyes on the prize, which is freedom from the crazy behind me.

I think about stamping on the BMW's brake and letting the Escalade ram into its metal ass. In truth, I'm afraid that his vehicle will roll over the BMW and crush me to death. Or, I will completely lose control of my ride and spin chaotically into a Jersey barrier that separates the lane from the oncoming traffic.

Izzy is so out of his fucking mind that he holds a Remington M887 Nitromag out of his driver's side window and pops off a shot at my back, left tire.

"Holy fuck!" exits my mouth in fear, deciding he must keep the weapon in his Escalade for such emergencies.

The shot nails the tire and I feel the convertible rock to and fro with haphazard motion. Immediately, I remove my right foot from the accelerator and begin to slow the metal beast down. I hear a battering drum sound, metal grinding against asphalt highway, and smell burning rubber.

Izzy somehow pumps the rifle and fires off a second shot, which totally misses the BMW since the car weaves back and forth on the highway due to its flat tire.

I decide to steer the vehicle to the side of the highway in fear of killing myself. I can maybe run into the nearby woods and escape his rage. Slowly, I swerve the BMW to the right, come to a stop on the highway's flank, turn off the ignition, pull a Colt Defender out of the glove compartment, exit the car by its passenger door, leap over the aluminum-colored guardrail, and fly into the nearby jungle.

Psycho Izzy is right on my ass. He hurriedly parks his Escalade behind my BMW, quickly climbs out of it, jumps over the guardrail, zooms after me with his wide dick swinging between his muscular legs. The bipolar fag is still naked and screams like a warrior at the top of his flaming lungs, "You can run, Derek, but you can't hide!"

The jungle area is dense with buttonbush and swamp titi trees. Ming ferns and umbrella plants litter the ground. I leap over and through the foliage. My legs carry me around some thick undergrowth.

154

Collapsed against my chest is the Colt Defender, loaded and ready to fire. Since he's right behind me, I fire off a few shots at him over my right shoulder, missing the villain's dashing body.

He heartily laughs through the deep jungle. And like any goon that is half-decent at his job, his Remington is loaded and he pops a shot off at me, which totally misses me by a mile. Following his blow, he yells, "You can't get away from me, ass-muncher!"

What transpires next in the jungle is something of a miracle, I presume. My feet tangle in a swamp titi root on the surface of the ground and I go flying head-first and scream like a girl. My forehead cracks against a second root and insurmountable pain skies throughout my skull, ricocheting between my pulsing temples.

He catches up with me and leans over my still body. Quickly, he removes the Colt from my hand, aims it at my skull, turns me onto my back, points the Colt between my eyes, and says, "You're a fast little fag-rabbit, but not fast enough."

With intensified breathing, I see two of Izzy instead of one. Helpless under his control, I say, "You're fucking mad."

The loon lifts his head back and begins to laugh in a vigorous way, which kind of creeps me out.

"Little fag-rabbit is caught. The chase is over, Derek." He presses the barrel of my Colt between my eyes and digs it into my skull, apparently ready to blow me away.

The miracle occurs within the next few seconds. Just as he is about to pull the trigger and pop my head open like a nut, Dragon and Brit save my ass. Brit appears out of nowhere inside the jungle and ends up on Izzy's right side. He quickly snatches my Colt and Izzy's Remington out of the crazy's hands and bashes the drug dealer/pimp in his right temple with the handgun's butt.

Izzy falls backward in pain, screaming at the top of his lungs. Blood pours out of his skull from the mishap and …

Dragon stands over Izzy with his own handgun pointed at the man's chest. He warns, "Don't even think about fucking moving, asshole. I will plug you so fast with ammo, you won't even know what hit you."

Absorbing Dragon's comments, my contender lifts his hands, surrendering. He says, "You guys are good. I fucking hate you ... but you're still good."

Brit pulls out a pair of handcuffs from the back of his belt. He clips one of the cuffs on Izzy's right wrist and causes the goon to scream and yell like a baby. Brutally, Brit begins to pull the bad boy through the jungle, back to the Escalade; Brit will inevitably return both to their proper residence, following a little one-one-one of rough manhandling.

Dragon helps me up; always being a polite young man. He asks if I'm alright.

"I could be better."

"We need to get you home and cleaned up, Derek."

Before we walk back to his Ford Sport Trac, Dragon eyes me up and down. He informs, "Your temple is bleeding."

"It's nothing a little bandage won't help."

While escorting me out of the jungle, he jokes, "I love a man who is masculine and butch."

"Don't tell Rocco that, or he'll kick your ass."

"It will be our little secret."

When I climb into his Sport Trac, I ask, "What about my BMW?"

"Brit will handle it. After he beats the fuck out of crazy Izzy, and basically totals his Escalade, Brit will find his way back here and take care of your car. He'll take it to a garage and get it repaired, then he'll delivery it to the beach house."

"You two are good to have around. Thanks for saving my ass back there."

"Rocco's father pays us a lot of money to protect you. If I didn't return you alive to your boyfriend, there would be hell to pay."

"I imagine so. You don't fuck with the Malonni's, do you?"

"Absolutely not."

# # # # #

Two hours later, I'm dropped off at the beach house. Dragon stays seated in his Sport Trac. Since he knows I'm safe at Rocco's side again, he zooms away to some Mafia-related event that needs his prompt attention.

Rocco welcomes me into his sturdy arms once I'm back at the beach house. We stand together in the drive, next to the garage. His hulking limbs press around my body with comfort, and his lips meet my lips with heartfelt concern.

Following an endearing kiss and hug, he pulls away from me and asks, "What the hell happened to you today?"

I come clean, confessing everything.

He walks me into the beach house, not at all surprised by the details of my adventure with Izzy Ramon. The guy knows about enemies and everything nasty since he's in the mob. Once inside, as he makes me a strong drink, which consists of blue gin over crushed ice, he admits, "I did have a soft spot in my heart for the man at one time."

"Obviously you were delusional then. I'm sure we all go through stages in our lives like that."

He sort of chuckles, passing me the chilled drink. In doing so, he shares, "Izzy was always bipolar, and he had a pretty bad temper on him. You must have really pissed him off."

"He's psychotic. I'm talking two or three or four different personalities in that body."

My lover shakes his head, sitting across from me at our two-person table in the kitchen. "He's harmless. Izzy purposely makes people believe that he's insane."

"He almost murdered me today. I told you he shot at me."

Rocco defends his ex and rattles off, "I'm sure he was only playing with you. Obviously he didn't hit you."

Whatever. If Rocco wants to believe this, let him. I personally know Izzy Ramon is a basket case; nothing will change my mind.

Instead of explaining this to my boyfriend, I ask, "Do you really think Izzy has anything to do with the murders?"

The handsome and alluring man across from me shakes his head. "I really don't." He reaches for my drink, takes a hearty sip, cringes because he's not a big fan of gin, and passes the tumbler back to me.

"Why do you think this?"

"Izzy is into prostitution and drugs. He's not into diamonds and murdering people. His business is separate from what's currently going on in our lives."

Curiosity nags at me, eating me from the inside out, and I inquire, "What kind of prostitution does he do?"

"A string of boys work for the man. He feeds them drugs and has all the sex he wants. He was even doing that gig when we were dating."

"Sounds like the fine life of a crazy mobster."

Rocco rolls his eyes. "I honestly don't know what I was thinking by almost marrying him."

"Surely, you were thinking with your cock."

He dabs a fingertip against my nose in a cute manner and shares, "Maybe I was."

"I mean … Izzy did have a nice cock after all. The thing is about as wide as fuck."

He balls up his right fist and slowly glides it into my right cheek in a playful manner and greedily smiles. "Shame on you for admiring another man's cock."

"Trust me, his cock will never be as nice as yours."

"Good answer, Derek."

"I'm so bad," I reply, finish off my drink, stand up, move around the two-person table, and drop to my knees in front of him.

The goon turns in his seat and faces me. Mischievously, he asks, "What are you doing down there, babe?"

I look up into his almost-purple eyes and rattle off, "I'm a little hungry. What do you have to feed me, Mr. Italian?"

"What kind of food are you in search of?"

"Well, I'm definitely a carnivore. Meat is my thing." I reach between his legs with one hand and cup his goods with a straying palm, which provides his tools with a temple-numbing and dick-hardening squeeze.

"Looks like you found what you're looking for."

I lean forward and brush my lips over his swelling knob. My mouth meets his denim in such a naughty manner. Kisses are provided, a dry suck, and now I pull off and away from his goods. I reach for his buckle and zipper, willed to take care of his sexual needs, and share, "I intend on riding your cock in a matter of minutes."

"You're a tease. You wouldn't dare. What kind of man are you?"

"My ass is begging for your dick," I add, slipping one of my hands inside his jeans, where I find exactly what I'm looking for: eight hard inches of guy-tube, which is ready to be licked, sucked, and driven into my firm bottom.

Coyly, Rocco says, "The park is open. You get a free pass for an-all-day ride."

I wrap a palm around his stick and pull it out for a hearty suck. Before my lips fall over his stiff pole, I cordially say, "Promise to hurt me."

"Hell yeah," he seductively whispers, into our flesh-gig.

CHAPTER SIXTEEN – PIN HIM DOWN

Twenty minutes later Rocco has my stomach pinned to our bed with my legs open and his eight inches of firm stick inside my tight opening. While riding my puckering hole in and out with his massive club, he whispers, "Take it like a man, Derek."

I take everything he has to offer: his light spanking; bites to my shoulders as he presses his torso's weight against my back; his heated and damp breath as it massages my earlobes; his emphatic name calling that causes bubbles of pre-sap to leak out of my hose, onto the bed's sheets. I allow him to ride me in rushed motion without protection. Lube seals our bodies together as we glide against each other in prosaic bliss.

"Ramming you," he chants. Again, he spanks my bottom and causes me to jump under his weight. One thrifty spanking after the next ensues, which turns my bottom a stinging-red that mixes with a lustrous pink hue.

I mumble with satisfaction beneath him, cling my fists to the sheets, and perspire on the Egyptian fabric. With just the slightest movement of my ass, I thrust upward, become a power bottom for the goon, and send us both into a state of satisfaction.

"I want you to carry my load inside you," he chants, creating our destinies.

Granted, it's not the sexiest thing to hear while bottoming, but it will suffice; Rocco will surely have to improve his bedtime talk in the near future, though, with or without my assistance. Not that I'm complaining about our romance on the tangled sheets, of course. Thrust after cumbersome and painful thrust occurs to my rump. The mobster rides me with chaotic lust, bangs my bottom with all of his might, and pushes me against the bed with his forceful weight. "Fucking you," escapes his mouth as his pole meets my center again and again. He huffs, "I love you, Derek," and pumps all of his mass inside me, pulls off and away, and pumps me again.

Repeatedly, I do semi-push ups on the bed, grind his cock with my rear, press my weight against his, build an extraordinary moment of bliss between naked men as we combine together, fall apart, and combine again.

"Banging you," he chants, drives his pole inside my tight end, extracts himself, and continues this action for what feels like hours.

"Harder," I instruct in a waning moan, wanting nothing more than the guy to bash my rump with his stick, breaking me into man-pieces of succulent pleasure on the bed.

The guy of my dreams is not at all new to trespassing inside my man-hole. Seventeen minutes of his pump-ride turn into twenty-some minutes. Heavy sweat and heat is found between us and glazes our bodies together.

"You're hot like this," he prattles, and almost finds his state of bliss, preparing to blow his gooey freight into my middle.

"Ram my hole," I utter, changing into a naughty boy, and rather liking my notorious behavior.

Unfortunately, he cannot contain his load any longer. Huffing and puffing for breath, he chants, "I'm going to shoot."

"Do it. Spray it inside me," I coach, ready to consume his load into my ass-canal, wanting his sticky swimmers inside me.

One final jolt occurs to my bottom: roughly, blasting my core, and nonstop. He lets out a monstrous grunt, fires his spray in my middle, fills me with his cream, and decorates my hub with his wet and gooey Mafia-ooze. He pants as he blows, and eventually grows limp over my body.

In a matter of seconds, my own euphoria is found. An explosion of cum occurs between my legs and squirts against the sheets and my firm belly. I let out a moan of satisfaction as every drop of sap finds its way out of my system. Just for fun, I thrust my shaft between the two surfaces and feel the last of my creamy shipment flush out of my throbbing cock.

Spent now, limp on the sheets, ready for a post-sex nap consisting of an hour or more, he knows I've come. The man rises from my back and pulls his sticky shaft out of my core. Forcefully he flips me over and mouths, "Hungry." Now, he immediately dives over my ripped stomach with an extended tongue and begins to lap up the leftovers of my load, moaning with pleasure.

Enjoying his company, thrilled to be his Mafia-accepting lover, I open my legs for him to become more comfortable and feel his slippery tongue lick up every drop, creamy line, and smear of man-juice from my flesh. Helplessly, I reach down to his skull with my right hand and run my fingers through his onyx-black hair, obey his thirst for my skin and the meal I freely offer him.

"So good," he murmurs, devouring my chest.

"Just the way you like it," I reply.

"Bittersweet love."

"Exactly."

# # # # #

"We work until we find Croon," Rocco says the next morning while overlooking and consuming the beautiful Gulf with its blue-green waves, balmy sunshine, and gliding seagulls. Both of us are naked and lounge in the sun, enjoying the early morning rays with warm croissants and freshly pressed Nicaraguan coffee. He turns to me and admits, "If Izzy says Croon is behind the murders and the missing diamonds, then it's true."

Again, I check out the Italian's hard body, relish the glistening fuzz on his bare chest, his pert nipples, and the limp cock against his torso. Attempting to limit my sexual action with him, building up spurt in my balls, I allow my future husband to crave me to his fullest. Instead of teasing him, I draw my attention away from the stud and ask, "Do you trust him because he's your ex-boyfriend?"

"Absolutely not. I trust him because he has nothing to lose in telling us the truth."

"A most interesting comment, Rocco."

"Hey, I wasn't born pretty."

I share some light laughter with him and eventually ask, "Where do we find Croon?"

"He's hard to find and hides well. Blending is his nature. I imagine he's burrowed in The Reach. Where else could he be?"

"Good question."

"I know. That's why I asked it." He finds my chin with his palm and gently rubs its curved flesh in an affectionate manner with the two fingers. "You bring out the smartass in me."

I ignore him and say, "We leave in an hour for The Reach. What do you say?"

"You took the thought right out of my mind."

"At least I'm good for something, right?"

# # # # #

Our hunt for Croon takes us to The Reach during the middle of the day, which glistens with a winter's blue sky that seems gentle with a light chill in the air. My sexy sidekick's good mood enables us to share a second round of heated and quick male-inside-male action before this adventure. The sex between us is fun, sticky, and porn-perfect. Neither of us complain about it, of course. Now, we have work to accomplish before such adult guy-play transpires again.

The Reach is dead during this hour of the day, completely uninhabited. The drug dealers and many hustlers are safe in their dirty crack houses and rat-infested one-room apartments. Snipers are hidden away like vampires until dusk. Meth users are semi-dead in shadowy corners.

Rocco and I sit in a cherry red Chrysler 300 with armored doors and tinted windows; another vehicle from his prized fleet. Together we study a calm, cool, and collected Sier Street. Jonesing for some conversation, I ask, "What's the plan?"

My lover turns into a smartass and rattles off, "I'm going to call Croon at his posh palace and invite us in for some English tea and sugary crumpets. I'm sure Elton John will be joining us."

"Don't be a dick with me."

"I like being a dick … because then I know you'll suck me."

I playfully punch him in his right shoulder. "I can beat you off, too."

He takes my hit like a man and chuckles. "Right now you're hitting my shoulder. Maybe later you can hit my ass with your crank. What do you think?"

I sock another punch into his muscled shoulder and prattle, "Fuck you, Rocco Malonni. I'm not going to marry you now if you ever ask me to. You're going to be a single man forever. Good luck in finding someone better than me."

"I love threats. They make me hard. Spew is already bubbling out of my dick because of what you said." He's just about to lean into me for a world-spinning kiss when a bullet shatters the Chrysler 300's windshield, whizzes between our seated bodies, and exits through the tinted, rear window.

Crystals of windshield shatter and fall to our feet and laps as if it rains glass. The sound is ear-popping, like it's the end of the world. He and I both slump down in our seats, wide-eyed and terrified. Afterward, he asks, "What the fuck was that about?" and more bullets garnish the vehicle's grill and hood, spraying everywhere.

Prepared to drop a load in my Diesel jeans, I hide behind the dashboard in a ball. My eyes are now completely closed and my heart rocks within my chest. Someone who hates us is obviously on a mission to kill Rocco and me. God knows we have enough enemies to create our own army of angry men. Terrified, I ask him, "What's the plan now, smartass?"

"Glove compartment … open it."

I open the glove compartment as more bullets decorate the 300. The tiny area is filled with a TomTom, Kindle, unused condoms, a traveling tube of lube, a handy Colt .45, a pack of chewing gum, an unused cell phone, and two round objects that look like hand grenades.

"The two flashbombs ... Pass them here, please."

He never fails in saving our succulent asses, does he? Once a hero, always a hero, I guess. Forever he will be my protector, whisking me out of trouble among the city's dangerous mobsters, drug dealers, killers, and whatnots.

I remove the grenade-like objects from the glove compartment, hand one over to him, now the second one, and ask, "Should I follow your lead?"

"Exactly," he shares, winks at me, and glows with a masculine ear to ear smile that is unquestionably charged with testosterone.

I watch him pull a lever on the palm-size flashbombs and gently toss both onto the hood of the 300. Thick, black and gray smoke surrounds us, shadowing our whereabouts. The flashbombs make exploding sounds like World War III has just started. A ball of fire lights up the day like Hiroshima. Quickly, I find the Colt .45 in the glove compartment and snatch it up. In doing so, he grasps my left hand within his right one, and says, "Let's get the fuck out of here before we get killed."

Hastily, we exit the 300, which is possibly totaled because of its abundant bullet holes, busted windows, and smoke infestation.

Sier Street is mostly an all-residential area of run-down houses, one Section 8 apartment building with six floors, and a porn shop. Rocco and I head through the dense smoke, cross the street in heavy folds of black atmosphere, and escape into the porn shop called Hump and Bump's.

I'm out of breath while entering the adult store. Rocco is at my side, assisting me. He looks from his left to right and takes our surroundings in. Neither of us has ever been in Hump and Bump's before, particularly since it's located in The Reach. To the left are rental DVDs of naked, big-breasted women. The back wall holds racks of dirty magazines, both gay and straight, a variety of dildos, and other toys. To the right is the kingdom of homosexuality. Posters of naked porn stars hang on the walls: Dean Flynn, Bo Knight, Adam Wolfe, and

Cole Ryan. Queer DVDs feature beefy jocks, military men, twinks, sexy office workers, greasy mechanics, lumberjacks, and hairy daddies. A shelf houses the latest fiction by STARbooks Press, Alyson, and Cleis. Near the front of the store is the register area and waist-high counter to ring up sales. Behind the counter is a pimpled-face young man with blue hair, pierced nostrils, stitched lips, and nails driven into his temples.

Rocco asks the blue-haired kid, "You have a back way out?"

The kid is high on something, stolid and numb, and stands behind his register area with a dazed and confused look on his face. Obviously he's on the latest street pill and is mentally sabotaged.

My sidekick isn't fucking around and ignores Blue Hair. Between the fetish DVDs and display of ten-inch dildos is a door that says KEEP OUT. Nothing prevents my boyfriend from keeping out of anything, though. Quickly, he pushes the door open, pulls me through, and we stand in an alley filled with rusted Dumpsters, mounds of smelly garbage, vehicle-size rats, and ... surprisingly, Buli Croon.

# # # # #

Croon is dressed for the weather, sporting a leather ankle-length jacket and matching hat, gloves, and Ray-Ban sunglasses. A pair of dazzling D&G calf-high boots cover his feet. In his right hand is a cellular phone. His left hand holds a Remington automatic rifle.

Rocco faces Croon and makes eye contact with the nasty goon. The two men stand only about four feet apart; either can make the first hit.

Croon never expects to see or run into us in the alley. In fact, the look on his face is of sheer surprise, completely caught off guard.

With one fell swoop, my heated, Italian lover bolts forward, flies through the air like a crazed gymnast, and lands on the goon, knocking the rifle and cell phone out of his hands. Both are sent clattering to the red-bricked alley and out of reach. As Rocco pounds his right fist into the goon's face, flipping his hat and sunglasses off, I find the rifle from the alley, retrieve it, and aim it at Croon's bloody face.

Rocco, to my relief, has Croon pinned to the alley's bricks. He practically sits on the guy, bashes the bitch's face in with a right fist, and pins him down by the shoulder with his left, free grip.

The goon is a bloody mess. One tooth flies out of his mouth and an eye immediately turns red, which begins to bruise. Croon lets out an obnoxious growl of pain and chokes on his own blood. Slashes of oozy blood splatter against his cheeks, forehead, and neck, which prove that he becomes helpless in the alley, under Rocco's superiority.

My future husband holds his fist up in front of Croon's face and inquires, "Do you want to be murdered today?"

Croon delicately shakes his bloody head.

"You want to live, is this right?"

The bad boy nods his head in fear.

"Because I can have you killed right here and now. No more Croon. No more life. What do you think, motherfucker?"

I'm bone-hard between my legs, loving Rocco in his macho mode. Man-sap leaks out of my joint and decorates my Aussiebums; this is how excited and horny I am at the moment.

My rough boyfriend peers up at me and winks. He asks, "You'll fucking shoot him, won't you?"

"Hell yeah," I whisper, ready to pull my zipper down, find my hard shaft inside, whip the muscle out, and poke my lover's face with it until I blow a sticky load inside his mouth and throat, lathering his core.

"I told you he would fucking kill you if you don't cooperate." Rocco now holds both of Croon's shoulders, digging into his leather jacket. With a quick pull, he lifts the goon's upper portion of his body off the brick and smashes it back down with much force.

The rear of Croon's head snaps off the hard surface and he possibly suffers from an instant concussion. A gurgling sound escapes his mouth and a fresh string of blood exits from his lips. Croon blinks a number of times and mutters, "I'll help you."

"Answer a few questions, dickhead," Rocco blurts.

"Yes."

I stand above the two enemies, aim the rifle at Croon's head, and still sport a solid boner between my legs. God only knows why I find Rocco the sexiest when he fucks somebody up with his fists or handy inanimate objects. Frankly, I feel some leakage happen in my underwear as goo drips out of my flag and decorates the cotton. Helplessly, I sigh, overjoyed with the moment, intoxicated by his abusive manhandling and Croon's apparent fear. Here, I fall in love because of the alley confrontation, acting like I'm a professional mobster.

"Did you murder Tang Meadow, his assistant, and my houseboy, Mantabaun?

Croon looks like a frightened puppy with his pallid face and half-open mouth. Saliva collects on his bottom lip like a kid with Down's syndrome. He mutters, "It wasn't me."

"Who was it?" Rocco continues to shake Croon, pounds his head off the ground, and bloodies the rear of his skull.

"Zulan," Croon barely gets out of his mouth.

Rocco literally gasps and whispers, "Zulan Cane … from Spingbok, South Africa?"

"Yes. He has your diamonds. And he murdered those three people."

"Did he also blow up Rocco's Hummer?" I cut in, asking in a demanding tone.

"No. That was my work."

"Did you torch The Skin Artist?"

"Yeah," he responds; a man of few words. "I like to set things on fire."

"How do we know you're telling the truth?" Rocco brutally asks, knowing he isn't in any danger while I hold the rifle against Croon's head.

"I'm in no position to lie. You were determined to catch me."

169

"Where are the diamonds?" I ask, sounding gruff and to the point.

"I don't know."

"Zulan has them, though, right?"

"He does."

"Why did he kill Tang and the other two men?" Rocco asks.

"It's all about the diamonds," Croon says with terror in his voice.

"What else do you know?" Rocco questions, shaking the bad guy again, and smacking his head off the alley's bricks one more time.

"Nothing. You got everything from me," Croon pleads.

Rocco asks for the gun from me, which I hand over. In one fell swoop, he bashes the rifle's butt against the side of Croon's head, knocking him out cold. My boyfriend stands, brushes himself off, returns the weapon to me, and says, "We have a lot of work to do, Derek. Let's get out of here and get started."

Ready to spew a load of goo inside my pants, totally hot for the Mafia man, I follow him down the alley and head for the Swiss-cheesed Chrysler.

Rocco looks over his right shoulder and winks at me.

"I'm right here," I rattle off.

"Glad you're behind me. I like you there."

I smile, glow inside for some odd reason, and think, God only knows what we're going to get ourselves into next.

CHAPTER SEVENTEEN – QUEENVILLE

Walter Landing decides to throw a congratulatory book party for himself regarding his success in sales with *Bottom Tales*. The gathering is at The Romeo, a fabulous high-end hall with marble pillars and alabaster floors inside, a Sistine Chapel ceiling, sweeping stairwells to a second floor balcony, and crystal chandeliers the size of Bentleys.

The event is a black-tie affair with just a hint of arrogance. Rocco cannot make it to the party, having business to attend in Jacksonville, so I end up going alone. I dress in a Velentino tuxedo with leather patent G&B heels. My coif is perfect and I smell like a robust palm with a dab of masculine niceness.

While carrying a flute of golden champagne around, mingling with the all-male guests (city lawyers, private college professors, porn stars from Gladiator Media Limited, models, editors, a priest, a librarian, two police officers, and booksellers), I'm discovered by Fisk, Walter's sexy and alluring boyfriend. The man is all smiles, beaming with a testosterone-boosted prettiness that you only see in fashion magazines. The handsome Italian with his well-built bod embraces me and provides my torso with a little hug that I find quite remarkable. He whispers delicately into my right ear, "I've missed you, Derek. Peru was lonely without you."

I note that his tongue dabs one of my earlobes in a sexual manner, which causes me to immediately back off and away from him. "Now, now, Fisk. Behave yourself. We don't want to start any sexual trouble between us."

He accepts my wisdom and snatches up his own flute of champagne from atop a silver-plated tray that whisks by in a waiter's grip. He downs the golden liquid in one swallow, licks his pretty boy reddish lips, and says, "I truly did miss you. We are best friends, are we not?"

I nod my head, realizing I was being a little too judgmental regarding his tongue meeting my earlobe. "We are. I've also missed you. We have a lot of catching up to accomplish now that you're back from Peru."

"That we do," he admits, and can't keep his glowing stare off my tuxedo-covered body.

For the next hour I stand with Fisk and we discuss his tales of Lima, Peru. I determine clearly that he did not have an affair on Walter while traveling alone and afar. In truth, I'm his best girlfriend and he'll dump on me all the cock-stirring details if such an event or sexual escapade did occur in South America. Such a topic doesn't unfold, though. Instead, our shared discussion entails: food, guinea pigs, Andean music, a beverage called Pisco, potatoes, hand-woven tapestries, and Lake Titicaca. Fisk is a vat of information, explains to me that he has had the time of his life in Peru, and will return to the country sooner than later, hopefully with Walter at his side because he dearly misses the man.

We determine that Walter's *Bottom Tales* event turns into Queenville, which is inhabited by mostly queers of power, wealth, and prestige. Of course, donations are collected from the guests, and fed to the local GLBT center. A new foundation in Flamingo Cove is called Homes, which offers help to homeless gay boys and girls; the non-profit organization will also be given a healthy check after this evening's uppity event. Honestly, the party is a smash with loads of money, Walter's signed books, men in handsome tuxedos, and a promising mission. Everyone drinks and eats and mingles happily.

Fisk is drawn away by the Gaitlin brothers, two gorgeous gay blonds who own Gaitlin Hardware in Turtle Bay, a smallish suburb of Flamingo Cove. Greg and Gary pull my pal into a circle of athletes to discuss the upcoming March Madness festivities in the gay community, which some of the local sports nuts will be gambling on.

I am not alone for a single second when Walter zooms up to my side, places a comforting kiss on my right cheek, and informs, "You look delicious this evening, my love. I want to rip your clothes off and fuck you."

I laugh at his tease and add, "All the pretty boys tell me this."

"You're such a whore, Derek, which I love about you." He faces me, enjoys my chiseled looks opposed to those among us, and adds, "I'd like to make a toast to the success of this evening."

I raise my flute of yummy champagne and we clink our crystal together. I add, "Also to friendship."

"Most certainly," he says, which is followed by a wholesome sip. Now, pulling the flute away from his lips, he asks, "Where, pray tell, is your better half this evening?"

"Jacksonville on business with a sweet looking coworker by the name of Nivo, whom I hope and pray he is not currently fucking behind my back."

"Did daddy Boss send him there?"

I nod my head and reply, "The Mafia godfather did. I'm not really sure why, though."

"Such an interesting life the Malonnis' entertain. I do enjoy them, if the truth be known. They always give me ideas to write about."

"I adore them myself. Particularly the youngest mobster's son," I admit. "It's never a dull moment being Rocco's boyfriend or in the company of his tough family."

"When will this boyfriend of yours turn into a husband, if I may be so bold to ask, my love?"

I shrug a shoulder. "I'm not really sure. Perhaps sooner than later. Every princess awaits for her prince to ask."

"I simply can't wait for another wedding in our gay community. I love weddings, darling. I'm sure yours will be absolutely fabulous and something to remember."

"Time will tell, I assume." I sound rather perturbed, but really, I'm not. Mother Barbara always tells me that I was born with an exceeding level of patience, which I apply now. Frankly, there's no reason to be up in arms about Rocco's marriage proposal, whenever he decides to carry it out. I'm not going anywhere, of course. And nor do I think he's going anywhere, even if he's working with a delicious looking sidekick named Nivo.

173

Our conversation continues for the next fifteen minutes. Topics include the newest mystery he labors over, his delightful and new houseboy named Jade, and Fisk's endearing love for the older man. Eventually, the author exits my side because he has guests to attend. Before scuttling away, he politely embraces me in a firm hug, brushes our chests together, and whispers in my left ear, "As always, Derek Reed, I adore you. Thank you for coming tonight. You are very supportive of my life, writing, and whatnots. Thank you so much, darling love. What kind of man would I be without you?"

Quickly, I respond, "Walter, you're the queen and royalty of Queenville, and one of my dearest friends. I wouldn't have dreamed of not coming."

His smile melts me as he waves good-bye and floats into the crowd like an Empire butterfly.

# # # # #

Of course, I have way too much to drink at the mystery writer's book event. Flute after flute of golden champagne knocks me in the ass and slaps me across my face. Dizziness is found and oxygen is lost the following morning. I coddle a nightmarish hangover that consists of head-splitting pain and a heavy stomachache. Here, in my shared bedroom with Rocco, I lie awake in a miserable state, unable to move a single muscle, and possibly suffer from dehydration.

Approximately at ten-thirty in the morning, my boyfriend returns from his trip to Jacksonville and finds me half-dead in the beach house. Immediately, he rushes to my side, sits down on the bed near my left hip, brushes a hand against my right cheek, and inquires in a calming voice, "What happened to you, Derek?"

I groggily respond with: "Walter's book event and fund-raiser was last night and I had way too much to drink."

He chuckles at me.

"It's not funny. I think I'm half dead."

He places a kiss to my dry forehead, smiles down at me, and whispers in his soothing voice, "It's hysterical. Shame on you for drinking too much. You should have known better."

I grumble something unintelligible and feel like vomiting. Quickly, I push him away, run for the bathroom, and ...

The porcelain god of alcoholic beverages welcomes me inside its shaming shrine. Here, I am embraced by its chest-vibrating tremors. Helplessly, I vomit once, twice, three times, and promise never to drink again. And here, I kneel over the white bowel with my head almost tucked inside its convex structure, continuing to puke.

My boyfriend finds me, kneels at my side, and decides to rescue me. He wipes my face off with a wet towel, carries me back to bed, and promises to look after me for the next few hours, willing me back to good health.

# # # # #

Barbara demands our attention this evening; Mother has a leak under her kitchen sink. Instead of calling a plumber, she decides to call me. Why she does this is quite baffling. Never have I worked with tools well. In fact, I can't tell the difference between a pair of needle-nosed pliers and a chalk string.

My mother is so high maintenance and problematic most of the time. The older she gets the worse she becomes. When she yells, I have to jump. Sometimes I wish I had a sibling to fill in for me when she helplessly careens into one of her futile and needy rampages. Other times, I feel like finding her an assistant on Craigslist, someone who looks and sounds like me, paying his salary for the year, just to keep my mother managed and out of my hair.

Rocco and I drive over to her house at 2069 Peninsula Way. I sort of bitch the entire way, sounding pissed. I ask him why he answered my cell phone and took my mother's call while I was milking my hangover under the comforter and among many pillows in our shared bedroom.

He looks across the seat of his Lexus LX, since his Chrysler 300 is in Vinnie's Auto Body being repaired of its bullet holes and shattered windows, and says in a rather snippy manner, "Barbara is not the villain you make her out to be."

"Oh, but she is. If you only knew how she tortured me as a young boy."

"She's your mother. Respect her."

He and I have always had a difference of opinions regarding Barbara. He defends her on a regular basis, and I just want her to sometimes go away and live in Peru or Ecuador. "Respect is earned. It's not given away like penny candy."

The conversation ends with this last comment. He really doesn't want to start an argument with me that I just might win. Being quiet is his subtle way of telling me I win the verbal entanglement, which I'm perfectly fine with.

# # # # #

Ten minutes later, my mobster man is under Mother's kitchen sink. I admit, the Mafia warlord is terribly hot on his back as his shirt rises and he shows off his hairy belly button. I literally have to look away or I will sport a boner while standing next to my mother, above him.

The kitchen is minute in size with a dish washer, electric range, and massive refrigerator. Rocco clanks tools together under the sink, attempting to determine exactly what's wrong with Barbara's pipes.

Standing over his legs, Mother gently grasps my right elbow and chants, "Rumor has it that the two of you beat up Buli Croon. Is this true?"

"Who told you that?" I inquire, surprised that she knows about our gig with Croon in The Reach.

"Dane Duncock. He stopped by here to visit me. He was looking for the both of you. He just so happened to mention your little episode with Croon."

"How do you know Dane, Mother?"

"Why wouldn't I know Dane, darling? I know all your friends. You do realize I keep track of your social calendar, right?"

I'm quick to say, "Dane is not my friend. He's a very dangerous man that I highly suggest you stay away from."

Rocco clinks and clanks pipes together with tools. He calls out of his plumbing tomb, "I think I found the problem."

"What is it, darling?" Mother bends over, facing his crotch, and asks.

"A crack in one of your pipes. You're definitely going to need a plumber. I suggest Enzo Batterman. He can help you."

"I adore Enzo," Barbara says. "He's one of the most beautiful men on the planet. All those muscles and his handsome face. The man causes me to melt."

I roll my eyes and hiss, "Mother, stop it. I'm getting sick. The man is my age."

She waves a hand at me and rudely says, "Get over it, child. A woman doesn't have to be dead when she's living her sixties. Her biscuit doesn't dry up and fall off, mind you."

Thank Jesus in heaven that Rocco climbs out from under the sink so I don't have to listen to another one of my mother's snippets that pertains to her sex life. He stands and pulls his shirt down, covers his adorable navel, and wipes his hands with a supplied rag that Mother passes to him. In doing so, he asks Barbara, "Why would Dane Duncock stop by to visit you?"

"He told me he went to your beach house, but you weren't there. So he decided to pay me a little visit, which I was delighted with. We had some tea and lunch and … that man is amazingly handsome. If he weren't gay, Derek, I'd have to rethink my girlfreindhood with Melvin."

"That is too much information, Mother," I say, guffawing. Sometimes she crosses a line and has to be put back in her place. I'm the person to do this, of course, having no qualms about it.

She turns her attention directly to my handsome plumber and says, "Dane has information for you regarding the murders. I asked him what his information was, but he chose not share those pertinent details with me."

"I'm not surprised," I provide.

She immediately spins around and faces me. Demon eyes (slanted and on fire) peer at me, and she spits, "What do you mean by that?

Occasionally I have to watch what I say in front of her, or to her face, forced to back down. This is what happens now. She is in no mood to have her buttons pressed and shows her fangs and claws, ready for a battle. To deter such a moment from occurring with her, I retreat from my attack, and cordially say, "Nothing, Mother. Tell us more about Dane Duncock."

"There's nothing more to tell. He simply stayed an hour, found my tea and lunch delicious, as was expected, and off he went on his merry way."

Rocco finds some paper and a pen in the kitchen. He jots down his recommended plumber's number and says, "Don't forget to call Enzo Batterman about the sink."

"Of course not, Rocco. Thank you for helping me out. You're always so kind."

I become a little disgusted when the two hug and kiss. An eerie vibration skirts up and through my spine. Willies find my stomach and dryness forms at the back of my throat. Their kiss is short and sweet, but still unfathomable to digest. Thank God it ends quickly, or I'd have to commit suicide or risk murdering them both.

# # # # #

We leave Mother's in a matter of minutes. In doing so, driving back to the beach house, Rocco says, "We need to review things."

"It never hurts to do that."

"Let's start at the beginning. What do you think?"

"Julie Andrews says it's a very good place to start," I reply, quoting a line from the song "Do-Re-Mi" in *The Sound of Music*.

Rocco laughs at me, keeping his eyes on the road. "One, Tang Meadow's body is found on the beach."

"Stabbed to death," I add, getting my two cents worth in.

"Then his assistant is murdered."

"I liked Nate. He was a nice guy."

"Then Mantabaun was murdered."

"We still have to figure out why, and if he was involved with Dane, Izzy, Croon, or Zulan."

"The Hummer exploded," I add. "Don't forget that."

"Croon likes to set things on fire. He's responsible for the Hummer."

"Once an arsonist, always an arsonist," I proclaim.

Rocco chuckles because of my comment and says, "The hidden storage room in The Reach must also be important."

"Yes, exactly. I almost forgot that."

"And The Skin Artist was burned to the ground."

"Which Croon confessed to. Do you believe him?"

Rocco scratches the side of his head while driving, and admits, "I do. Something tells me he wasn't lying to us."

"I concur. What about the e-mail sent from Tang?"

"I imagine it was a warning of sorts. A calling out that something horrible was about to happen. Something he knew about but couldn't tell you face-to-face because maybe he was being watched. The guy purposely wanted to be anonymous."

"His e-mail included clues to the first murder, right?"

"I'm leaning toward yes on this. It makes sense."

"What about the diamonds? You retrieve them from Springbok, South Africa and they end up stolen from the beach house."

"You're very good at this, Derek. What a great memory you have. I think Zulan took them himself. Nine chances out of ten, he hid them somewhere. I'm quite sure he managed to get Croon and Izzy to do the dirty work for him and ..."

"Izzy and Croon knew what was going on?"

Rocco nods his head. "I think that, but can't prove it as of yet. Zulan probably hired both of them to work for him. He has the power to accomplish something like that."

"They were paid to murder three men?"

"Exactly."

"Because Mantabaun, Tang, and Nate knew about the diamonds?"

"Yes. This is what I believe."

I sigh heavily, thrilled with my knowledge and comments. "And now Dane is back in the picture, wanting to share valuable information with us. Do you think it's a setup?"

"I don't," Rocco seriously utters. "Dane isn't the antagonist we've made him out to be. I'm sure he does have some crucial details about the murders for us that he wants us to hear, but he's not a killer."

"Do you also think he has information about the missing diamonds?"

"Perhaps. I'm not sure. But these are really great questions you're asking."

"He knows about Zulan's role in his murdering gig, doesn't he?"

"Absolutely."

"So where do we go from here?" I inquire, drawn into our conversation, unwilling to take my eyes and ears off Rocco.

"We find Zulan and take him down."

"You mean kill him?" I question, already scared shitless with his plan, knowing I'm not the killing type. I can handle some violence at a moderate level, but not the stuff the mob gets involved with. There'll be no butchering horses on my hands.

He shakes his head. "That's too violent. One, we find out where the diamonds are. Two, we take the diamonds back. Three, we let

Zulan know that we know he's behind the murders. Four, we beat the fuck out of him, but not kill him. Busting his nuts will feel plenty good after everything we've been through in the past few weeks."

"It sounds brutal," I say.

"Life is brutal. Nothing is pretty if you think about it. Everything has a rawness about it that makes it bloody."

"You're hot when you're brutal, Rocco."

He laughs behind the steering wheel. "I knew I could still turn you on, pal. What do you say we go home so I can use some of this hotness on you?"

"I'm game," I reply, ready for a bed-romp with him, or an over-the-sofa-romp, whatever he has in store for my skin.

"And I'm gay," he says with laughter.

"That too. Better to eat you up whole, if you know what I mean."

"Keep talking," he says. "I've got a boner the size of the Gulf between my legs and I don't want to lose it."

"I'll do my best," I respond, and reach over between his muscled thighs, find exactly what I'm looking for: his mound of hard erection, which is just waiting to be kissed, licked, and dramatically sucked because of my produced appetite for his skin.

CHAPTER EIGHTEEN – FLESH GIG

Our hunger for each other is limitless. Clothes are ripped off once we're inside the beach house. We kiss passionately with entangled tongues and huff for breath. Hands move up and down over solid chests and private parts swell with a life of their own. Rocco and I stand next to the sofa in the living room, naked and panting. When he pulls away from me, he whispers, "I've been dreaming all day of my body colliding with your body."

"Ready or not, make me come, man."

He laughs, thrilled with the idea.

My fingers find his left nipple and gently provide it with a squeeze. My lips connect to his corded neck and supply it with a crazed lick. A palm races down and over his hairy chest, drawing fingertips against his rippled abs and puckered navel. Curiously, they find the man-scaped patch of tangled hair between his rigid legs, and travel southward bound in search of his upright tool. A fingertip happens to discover the apex of his cock and shares a pleasurable squeeze with it. Ooze leaks out, proving that he's excited with the notion of our combined fun, and I remove it. Now, I draw the dribble to my lips for an evening snack of bittersweet lust between colliding men in love.

"You're hungry for me, aren't you?" he asks with his hands planted on my naked hips and a steady fire of bliss-filled lust caught in his magnetic eyes.

"I love you," I whisper, overjoyed with our connection, knowing we are about to have heated sex again, here and now in the living room, exactly like untamed animals.

"And I love you," he provides, falls to his knees, licks my limber body, and obeys his thirst for my salty skin. Lips connect with both nipples, my solid abs, creased and muscular navel, and fall heavenly to the area of desire between my pumped legs. Predictably, he laps at my tool's head, and seems to be enjoying himself, moaning. One lick occurs. Two licks. Three licks. And now he pleasantly presses the tip of my shaft into his mouth, releasing it just as quickly.

I murmur idiotically above him while hanging onto his bare shoulders, attempting to balance myself. A forward hip motion takes place, but I pull away immediately, waiting to plow his face with my throbbing pole. Perspiration builds on my rippled torso, sweat-dotted shoulders, and wrinkleless forehead. The warm sweat drips off my flesh and falls on my companion's head and shoulders, possibly stinging his flesh. A moan escapes. Two moans. Three moans. And now I become feeble above him, wavering to and fro, dizzy by the mobster's unending lick-fest.

His fingers find the smooth ball sack between my legs and begin to gently stroke its flesh-covered orbs. His other hand is placed firmly on my left hip, assisting his balance while on his knees. Steadily he continues to lick my shaft in a north and south direction, pausing a few times to gently slip my cock's head between his semi-parted lips and carefully sucks on the piece of timber, which purposely sends me into a bout of everlasting joy. Strings of saliva connect his mouth to my stick. A satisfied moan escapes his face as he ends his licking spell and decides to orally satisfy my manly needs by placing his lips over my rod. I slide the beef deep into his mouth and down the passageway of his throat.

Thrusting occurs; I cannot help myself otherwise. Speedily I bolt my hips forward, jam my extension inside his system, quickly pull the bitch out, and jam it inside his core again.

Beneath me, the mobster gags on my size. More strings of saliva drip out of the corners of his mouth. He attempts to hold his head still while I bash my tool inside him, fucking his throat. More graphic sounds of pain mixed with elation surface from his mouth and rise into my ears.

The feeling of my engorged cock inside the narrow pathway of his throat is mind-numbing. Euphoria is discovered, which causes me to become semi-unconscious above him, reaching into a state of pure satisfaction and relentless wooziness.

His firm grip on my left hip loosens and my boyfriend's fingers find their way up to my left nipple, providing it with a tender twist of delight. The fingers soon pull away from the nipple and dance down and over my rolled abs, eventually decide to toy with my navel, and brush against its flawless skin.

Weakly, I continue to buck my hips against his face. Each and every time I bolt forward, my triangle of V-hair brushes against his upper lip and conceals the guy's nose. Again and again I pound my weight with his face. Enjoying the moment between us, I huff and puff, perhaps ready to burst a load in a matter of seconds. Of course I want to coat his throat with my sticky explosion, drowning him with my explosive seed. Why not, since he is my lover and future husband?

Rocco knows I'm about to blow my sap inside his mouth and backs off and away from my tool. In doing so, he wipes his right hand across his face and inquires, "What do you say you sit on my face so I can eat out of your ass?"

Truth is there isn't anything better than the man's Italian tongue entering my bottom. Perhaps this act is one of my favorite things we share, obliging to his craving almost every time he asks. In response, I say, "Make it last … I'm not ready to shoot yet."

He lies down on the Oriental rug behind the sofa, winks up at me, and informs, "I'm ready anytime you are, pal. Let's get that ass licked."

# # # # #

Inch by inch I lower myself onto his face, happily in an S-position with my legs open and my glory hole available for his pleasure. I face his feet and slowly fall against his extension of tongue while holding the erected beef between my legs in my right hand. "Lick me," exits my mouth and I close my eyes, ready for our man-with-man connection again.

He balances my ass with his palms, securing my weight over his mouth. My balls touch his chin first and graze his five-o'clock shadow. A light moan escapes the man as he finds a simple and short episode of bliss. Beneath me, he whispers, "Almost there."

When the tip of his tongue rubs my core, a single sigh of contentment is released from the narrow passageway between my lips.

The thin cords that line my neck tighten and my shaft bounces within my palm, ready to be manipulated.

"Lower," he murmurs beneath me, directs me to seal my bottom with his mouth, and combine our queer worlds together as one.

I listen, always taking his needs into consideration, so very much willed to supply his desires with exactly what he demands. Slowly, I lower myself onto his mouth and feel his slippery tongue enter my firm rump. An intoxicating murmur escapes me as a jolt of lively bliss drives throughout my middle. I gently throw my head back in deep satisfaction, feel his tongue slip inside my body, roll around, pull out, and slip inside again. My world spins above him: chaotically, blindly, and lively. I rise and fall on his tongue-work, immerse myself in his passion, and feel as if I will topple forward where I will inevitably collapse on his body in pure man-elation.

Rocco decides to lightly spank me once ... twice ... three times as his slippery motion progresses. He groans with deep satisfaction beneath me, into our flesh-gig. His untouched staff lies perfectly straight against his torso, leaks pre-bubbles of ooze into his pitted navel, and fills the attractive divot with white goo. Another spanking is felt on my bottom, a swirl of his tongue on my rear, and a hearty grunt is heard that exemplifies pure ecstasy beneath me. The mobster is relentless under my rump's subtle spell, fueled by our connected passion.

Fruitfully, I begin to stroke myself off as I continue to ride his mouthy tool. Here, I rise and fall on his outstretched tongue as I jack off. The strokes are smooth and swift, hurling me into a state of no return. Twelve working strokes turn into three dozen. Challenged by the moment, I fill the living room with my verbal passion, whimpering, "Rocco, eat my ass."

His spanking seizes for a few seconds. My lover pulls my end apart and presses his entire face into my outlet. The tip of his nose, reddish and warm lips, and part of his scruffy chin enter my core. The man is extremely sloppy at work, but very satisfying at the same time. He adds saliva to my bottom, releases the juice from his mouth, and lubes my hole for a future ass-connection with his inflated cock. Murmuring sounds escape his face as I continue to ride its model-like handsomeness. The sounds are erotically cleansing and passionately rewarding; exactly what I want to hear while applying my bottom to his handsome features.

More stroking ensues on my part. My right hand bolts up and down on my shaft, and wills its excess skin to glide over the muscle and sensitive nerves underneath. I buck a drop of cream out of my shaft with utmost pleasure and watch it fall onto the sexy goon's hairy chest, approximately an inch away from his solid, left nipple. Two more drops slide out of my cock's rounded head and drip on the Italian's ripped chest.

Hunger finds me; shame on me. I gently lean forward, feel my leg muscles tighten, and extend my left hand to his cream-filled navel. Here and now, I collect his pre-load with two outstretched fingertips and draw them to my lips. A second later, I open my mouth and slip the fingertips inside. Immediately, I consume Rocco's hearty spent: a mixture of sweetness and bitterness. "More," escapes my throat and lips as I discover unlimited pleasure between us and consume every drop of my boyfriend's ooze down the back of my narrow throat.

He greedily finds my sack of blond balls between my legs and provides it with some fond palm-massaging. He rolls fingertips around their drooping niceness and tenderly shares a squeeze and pull, which causes two more bubbles of preliminary sap to trickle out of my flesh-covered hose.

I gasp above him with complete satisfaction. Behind my lids, my eyes roll chaotically into the back of my skull. Quickly, I pull my hand away from the erect stem between my legs, and admit to my sex-buddy, "You'll have to stop or I'm going to shoot."

His tongue is released from my tight hub and his comforting grip frees my balls. No longer does he spank me, ending this moment of man-bliss between us, but only temporarily. Beneath me, he heavily breathes, attempts to gain oxygen again, heaves for air, and groans, "Take a ride on my stick. I want to cream your insides."

Using some of my own ejaculated man-sap that decorates his chest, and a little of his own sticky cream from his navel-filled pool, I grasp the swollen crank between his legs and begin to lube it up.

A guttural whine of sheer glee escapes him. Beneath me, he coaxes, "Jump on it. I want to fuck you this way."

I admit, I feel a little greedy to have his shaft inside my center, which is hungry for his length and girth. Facing him now, standing overtop his still body, bareback and unsafe, I lower myself onto his condomless-pumped rod, and direct the ooze-covered tubular slab inside my ass, inch by inch. Tears ebb at the corners of my eyes and breath is lost. I pant from our naked connection, slowly and deliberately steer his stem into my middle. Eventually our bodies seal together by cock and hub – exactly how we want to be coupled.

He coaches, "Ride it, man. Make me shoot."

"Fuck me!" escapes my mouth with surprise. "Fuck me hard, Rocco!"

As he bucks upward, I plunge downward. Our motion is hurried and carried out with synchronized enjoyment. Together we work in north and south movement that only offers the both of us a sense of euphoria, building our climaxes. The man clings to my hips and bolts his dick into my crack. I aptly apply gentle twists to his rigid nipples. Thick perspiration is like a sealant between our bodies, molding us together in bliss. Fire is discovered as he humps my interior and I vivaciously ride his joint. Together we find a fused rhythm of rising and falling action against each other's body. Up and down we shift, pant, sweat, moan, and huff.

"I have to spray," he eventually announces, pink-faced and perspiration-covered. "My cock is going to fire off inside you."

"Do it," I proclaim, ready for his load, willed to be dangerous with his monogamous body and shooting spray.

With his teeth clenched and his forehead covered in tiny wrinkles, he announces, "I'm bursting, Derek."

"Bring it," I whimper, continue my ride, and assist him with his combustible load due to our friction.

We shoot together, heave for air, and become doused with sweat because of our frenzied motion. Rocco bolts his firm rod into my center one final time, ejaculates his load inside my hub, and floods my intestines and other masculine organs with his sticky and swimming gunk. A moan of bliss takes over his vocal cords and releases into the room; it sounds eerie and demonic but quite gratifying for the man at the same time. Sweat clings to his forehead, shoulders, and chest, which proves that he is obviously putting all of his sexual effort into our embrace.

His firm grip on my tool jacks me off with exuberant skill. No longer can I tamp my load, feeling it rush through my plump and veined erection. "Blowing," exits my mouth and white juice splatters against his hairy chest, rounded chin, succulent lips, and rosy-red cheeks. The stuff clings to his flesh, decorates his handsome face and upper torso, and seals our bodies together as lovers.

Spent now, the urge to satisfy my naughty lover becomes overwhelming. I find globs of white goo on his chest and gather the thick spurt with my left fingers. One by one, I slip the fingers into his mouth and smear his face with my seed. Sneering down at him, I chant, "Eat it all up, guy. You know you want to."

Indeed he does. The goon opens his mouth and allows my fingers easy access to his tongue, which is lathered with the creamy spent. One finger after the next is gently rubbed against his slippery tongue. We mix bodies together like this and prove our unstoppable ardor for each other.

Following our messy episode of man-sex, I lean over his bulky torso. The man's cock is still in my ass as we breathe wildly together. Quite roughly we connect chests and I dab my lips to his lips.

He wraps his arms around my back and keeps me as a parallel prisoner against his sticky chest. Following our kiss, his model-handsome face lights up with a brilliant smile, and he asks, "Do you have any idea how much I love you?"

"I don't. Tell me."

"Of course you do."

"Maybe I do. Tell me again."

"I love you more than my family … and my own life."

"You don't," I reply, perhaps blown away by his confession.

He dots a warm kiss to the tip of my nose, boyishly giggles, and replies, "Shhhh … I do. Just don't tell anyone."

"It will be our little secret."

CHAPTER NINETEEN – GARRETT, UNDRESSED

Between scheduled houseboy interviews, I decide to catch some sun on the beach, since the day is bustling with rays of blistering light and offers ninety-plus degrees. I lounge in a Rio Blue beach chair and a pair of Rocco's Rufskin trunks, which are a little snug against my middle and showcase my manly goods with eye-zeal. Diesel shades cover my eyes. Here, I think of the past interviewees for the new houseboy position since Mantabaun passed:

Rodriguez Padilla was twenty-years-old, dark-skinned with aqua-colored eyes, had a five-ten frame, thin as a rail, and enjoyed pot, which I smelled all over him. As my questioning proceeded I learned that the young man had already had a job. His employment was part-time hustling on Mandarin Street in Flamingo Cove. In short, after learning these details, I politely asked Mr. Padilla to leave and thanked him for his time.

Can Con was gorgeous, a nineteen-year-old jock taking business courses at the local community college. He arrived ten minutes late for his interview, but I really didn't care. The guy was wearing a pair of Nike shorts, running shoes, and nothing more. His body was nothing short of an Olympian's. And his smile was to die for; one of those million dollar grins that cause me to grow hard, instantly. I thought of hiring him on the spot, but the guy's cell phone kept ringing during the interview, and I realized that he was a queer social bug and was obviously going to be more involved with his friends opposed to my residence, which inevitably caused me to ask him to leave and not hire him.

Joseph "Joey" Iron was adorable; a man in a boy's body. He stood a little under five-foot, and sported freckles over the bridge of his nose and on his cheeks. Joey had beautiful amber-colored eyes and thin blond hair. His voice was soft and tender, presumably harmless. I learned the boy/man was not as innocent as he acted or sounded. Joey liked to steal things after breaking and entering into a number of

Florida homes. Once that was accomplished, he sold the stolen goods on the black market. Of course, his interview ended thereafter and I kindly asked him to leave.

Ricardo Sabado lived in Tarpon Bay, approximately ten miles away. He looked like a Peruvian god: six-two frame, 200 pounds, amethyst-colored eyes, muscles out the wazoo, only twenty-one-years-old, and ... was an illegal alien. Rocco and I could not harbor a person with such a status, although Ricardo would have worked out just fine as a new houseboy because of his good looks and apt abilities.

Enough. I needed a break and decided to find the sun. Here, I sit, absorb the rays, await my afternoon interviewees, and enjoy a screwdriver. I take a sip, swallow it down, take a second sip, and ...

"Mr. Reed, I knew you couldn't hide from me."

I look up from the sandy beach and white waves. Garrett Haute stands over me in his navy blue police officer's uniform, shimmering shield, Kenneth Cole sunglasses, and pistol connected to his right hip. I eye my high school jack-friend from head to toe, absorb his onyx-black hair and eyes, and respond, "You only found me because you missed me."

He unbuttons his shirt and exposes his bronze chest, which is delicious looking. The polyester-cotton blend blows in the wind away from his lean body like a model for an expensive and masculine cologne. I study his nipples and determine the pair quite firm. My eyes take in his golden brown abs that design his striking tummy and look absolutely edible.

"You're always joking with me, aren't you?" he inquires, moistens two fingertips with saliva, and rolls the tips over his right nipple, turning himself on ... and me.

Under the uniform and between his legs, I witness his solid tube of nine uncut inches. As usual, he has decided not to wear underwear, sports a commando look this afternoon, and is ultra-sexy (and easy) among the other officers of the law on his force.

"Stop being sexy with me. You know I'm with Rocco Malonni."

"How is your criminal of the year, anyway?"

I take offence to his question and snap, "Rocco is not a criminal. Can you nail him for anything?"

"I'd like to nail your ass and his ass at the same time, if the truth be told. Unfortunately, mobsters, their hot boyfriends, and city cops like me usually don't fuck around with each other. How upsetting."

"You're toying with me now, aren't you?"

His palm rolls down and over the splay of his solid and chiseled chest. Fingertips play with his adorable navel and eventually fall to his zipper. In doing so, the cop asks, "We have some unfinished business, don't we?"

"Melvin's tickets need to be taken care of," I respond, comprehending his visit in full now.

"And my cock needs sucked by your mouth," he rattles off, pulls out his nine inches of uncut hose, and jacks it off two times with his right palm.

I shake my head. "Just take care of the tickets, guy. You know my mother loves and cares about you. She honestly doesn't ask many favors. Do her this little thing and help her boyfriend out."

"Only if you shove my long cock down your hungry throat," he suggests again, continues to stroke his tool, and bobs his right fist up and down in a speedy manner.

Ooze drips out of his hose and falls to the sand. I admit it's a hot scene to watch him in action as he cranks his meat a few times on my private beach. Reality kicks in for me, though, and I know his true purpose this afternoon: he wants to blackmail me to carry out a sexual favor with his rock-solid tool to cover up a few lousy parking tickets. Helplessly, I lick my bottom lip and suggest, "Put your dick away, Garrett Haute. This is not going to happen between us. I'm almost a married man."

"I won't hide the tickets then."

"Fuck you," I challenge, ready for a fight.

"Of course you want me to fuck you," he chortles, still playing with me.

I pause for a second or two and think about my options. The cop is married to Whitney Hockingstock-Haute, and has three young daughters. Unfortunately, Whitney has yet to learn that she sleeps with a queen every night, who she sometimes fucks. The naughty side of me can easily blackmail Garrett like he currently attempts to blackmail me. I can easily tell his wife about his queer antics. How simply this act can be executed by snapping a pic of us in a heated embrace: a brief kiss on the beach; me falling on my knees with his hard shaft brushing against my open mouth. How unflattering this event will be when I send the picture to Whitney's cell phone and out him to the mother of his three daughters. Or, I can play Mr. Nice and ignore his ridiculous game, go on with my life the way I normally do, and just let my mother's boyfriend be a man and deal with his fucking parking tickets on his driving record like other citizens of Flamingo Cove. I ponder the consequences of each option, and eventually say, "I have something to admit to you, Garrett."

He continues to rock his joint up and down, which looks better than a stripper in motion. White cream leaks out of the beam's head and drips into the sand between his legs. Amid jerks, he asks, "What are you talking about?"

"Your wife ... Whitney."

"What about her?"

"Blackmail of course. I'm not beneath it. Rocco has taught me how to carry it out with very much skill during our time together. His details to process such an act are limitless. I guess this is something that comes with the territory when you decide to marry into the mob."

"What kind of blackmail?" he inquires, putting his jerk-off session on pause for the next minute or two. Instead, he stands motionless with his pole in his right hand, and keeps his concentration locked on my sunglasses, bare shoulders, striking torso – somewhere.

"I have pictures of you with a few men that I can easily send to her." It's a great lie on my part. Why not? What the fuck do I have to lose?

"What kind of pictures?" His interest peaks and the expression he shares with me doesn't really agree with him. He loses some color in his already tanned face, perceptibly feeling cautious by my comment.

"Can you seriously ask that? I mean, come on, Garrett. I know what you do with men in Palisades Park, among other places in the city. You're a whore with the fags. You'll fuck any guy in this town, and you're not very careful about it, from what I understand. You and I both know it. And other men know it also." Again, I layer my bogus facts, build a fine case against him, and purposely sway his decision to erase Melvin's parking tickets from the carpet seller's file.

"You have pictures?" It sounds like a whine that escapes his mouth, which is almost boy-like.

"I do. About fifteen in all. Black and whites. Your face is quite clear in all of them, among other body parts, of course. I believe you're with a few young men in naughty positions. Sometimes even with two jocks at the same time. You photograph very well, if I must admit. A triple-X star all the way, if I've ever seen one."

"And you intend on showing Whitney these pictures?"

"I imagine so, but only if you don't handle Melvin's tickets. You understand me now, right?"

"I don't want to come out to her as of yet. I'm not ready for that," he admits. His voice wavers and his face locks with fear. In truth, I see that his cock is actually shrinking in his right hand, deflating right before my eyes because of my disturbing deal with him.

"I never intended to hurt you, just so you know. As the old cliché goes: a man has to do what a man has to do to get what he wants."

"I was your jack-buddy in high school, Derek. Why do you want to hurt me now?"

"I don't want to hurt you. It is what it is, though. That might make me sound like a douche bag, but whatever. You find a way of making the tickets vanish from Melvin's record and … I'll give you the pics and proofs of your sexual liaisons with your younger men. What do you say?" I know I have him exactly where I want him – by his balls and in a state of terror, which allows me to be his puppet master.

"I'll do it," he says without even thinking about it. "I'll handle the tickets, and you stop by the police station and drop off the photos and prints." Motionless, he stands in the sand half-naked and shows off his alluring torso and cock.

"Deal," I say, although I will never carry out such an act since the devised pics are bogus.

"Deal," he agrees.

# # # # #

Behind me, I hear Rocco's voice say in an aggressive manner, "What the fuck is going on out here?"

Shit! Clearly he sees the semi-naked cop next to me on the beach, holding his wanker in his right hand. Rocco knows it's Garrett Haute, whom he despises to the fullest. I have no doubt he witnesses me ogling the police officer like a tasty slab of meat, and sees that my mouth is semi-open, obviously aroused by my ex-fuck buddy.

Truth: Rocco knows about my high school days with Officer Garrett Haute. Recently, I have sat him down with a bottle of red wine in front of an open fire and shared the steamy details with him regarding my naughty days with a younger Haute.

Fib: Rocco only thinks that Garrett and I blew each other off. Honestly, we did more. The guy used to bang me into the next day, causing my ass to sting for a week or more.

Truth: I never fell in love with Garrett. Lust drew me to his skin and nothing more when I was a young boy. Not once did I ever lose sleep over him. Never did I have strong emotions for the man. Together we only shared a naked connection mixed with intimate lust, but nothing more. I wanted his nine inches of steeping cock in my ass or mouth, and always passed on the opportunity to have his heart.

Fib: Rocco believes I had safe sex with Garrett at all times, when in fact the two of us enjoyed barebacking to its ultimate limit as young men. Condoms were expensive in our day, since we never seemed to have any money, and the plastic dick covers were very awkward to purchase at the local drug store for fear of being labeled sexually busy by its employees. Any young man who did purchase condoms was in fear of having rumors wildly spread about our small community regarding sexual activity among heathen teenagers.

Truth: A string of homemade movies of Garrett and I are out in the world of our most intimate moments together. Boys having sex in bedrooms, at a local park, in his swimming pool, in the front seat of his Honda Civic, and elsewhere. Each profiles unsafe and dirty sex between boys under the age of eighteen. Youthful lust of sixteen- and seventeen-year-old guys who were interested in nothing more than getting off, shooting their loads, and becoming spent together. The movies all define underage sex with virgin skin, high libidos, and quick explosions.

Fib: Rocco thinks these movies were destroyed, deleted from Garrett's digital camera and never uploaded onto some XXX gay site for over-sexed perverts to enjoy on the Internet. Perhaps someday he will accidentally run across one or two of our vintage flesh-work and learn of my feisty and erotic boy days with Garrett in front of the camera.

Now, Rocco rushes down through the sand and meets Garrett face to face. Without notice, he pulls his right arm back and quickly rushes it forward with a balled fist. My lover nails a surprised Garrett in his right jaw, forcing the man to fall backward.

The cop lets out an animal-like grunt as his head flies to the left. His right hand releases itself from the limp cock between his legs and flies upward. When Garrett hits the beach his navy blue shirt opens around his torso like wings and his dick flops around between his nicely sculpted thighs.

My Mafia guy screams down at the man, "What the fuck are you doing with my boyfriend? And why is your cock out?"

This is nice to see. I like it when a man defends me, even if I'm in the wrong. Talk about chivalrous. This act can cause an immediate boner to form between my legs. I'm not in the wrong regarding the cop's unexpected visit. And nor do I sport an erection. Instead, I merely watch the angry scene between the two young men unfold, craving popcorn, a box of Goobers, and 3-D glasses.

"We were talking," the cop stupidly supplies, rubbing his jaw where Rocco nailed him.

"With your cock out?" my boyfriend inquires, rage in his almost-purple eyes. He stands approximately fourteen inches away from the interloper. His feet are slightly spread and his palms are on his hips, unmoving and clamped against his jeans and leather belt, which are signs that declare that he's ready for a heated battle like a Spartan.

"We were cutting a deal together," Garrett explains, sitting up on the sand; his limp rod hangs between his legs with the tip of it touching the sand. In truth, he can easily find his Sig Sauer P226 at his right hip and blow a hole in Rocco's head, stomach, shoulder ... somewhere. Garrett realizes he is not in danger, though, and stands, climbs off the sand, and seems ready to talk this absurd moment out with Rocco like two adult men.

Rocco turns his view to me in my beach chair and asks, "What kind of deal?"

I look over at Garrett, who just happens to be zipping up his goods, hiding his nine-inch beast away for the moment, and say, "You tell him what you wanted me to do, Garrett. Be a man and fess up."

"Tell me," Rocco turns his attention back to the cop and demands with fury in his eyes.

"Melvin Caspi has some outstanding parking tickets. I told Derek I would find a way of removing them from our system if he blew me." Garrett starts to button his uniform's shirt. His eyes meet my eyes, but they don't seem to share any apology whatsoever.

"Is this true?" Rocco asks me.

A light wind blows against my body, winter still present. The sun is warm, like a thin blanket of sorts that keeps me cozy. "It's true," I reply. "I wasn't going to give him a blowjob. I told him numerous times to put his dick away."

My boyfriend's brow becomes furrowed and he asks Garrett, "Why didn't you put your cock away when he asked you?"

Garrett has two buttons on his uniform's shirt buttoned. He raises one hand and admits, "I need to get back to the station."

When the officer of the law starts to walk back up to the beach house, Rocco stomps through the sand after him. My boyfriend is in a state of irreversible rage, possibly ready to accomplish something foolish with the cop's handsome body. Beating his face in with fists is not beneath my lover, I know. Nor is breaking one of the man's arms or legs. Hell, Rocco is part of the mob and can easily plug a bullet in the pig's skull if he wants to, and Dragon or Brit can do something with the cop's cruiser and easily hide his body. Murder is not removed from the equation regarding the Mafia, of course.

I scream, "Rocco, be careful! Don't do anything stupid!" The tiny hairs rise on the back of my neck and my mouth goes instantly dry.

My boyfriend ignores me. He follows Garrett up the beach and yells at his back, "Stay away from my man! Do us all a favor and find your own boyfriend! Don't make me come after you! God knows I will. And when I fucking catch you, you'll wish I didn't."

Garrett stops in the sand, spins around, plants his right palm over the loaded Sig at his hip, and attempts to clarify, "Are you threatening me?"

"Only if you let your cock out to play with my boyfriend, then it's a threat."

"I can arrest you right now if I wanted to. You do know that, right?" Garrett has a serious look on his face that means business: stern eyes, pursed lips, crumpled eyebrows, and a tight jaw. His right palm is steady on the Sig at his hip.

"It's a draw and you know it," Rocco shares. "I can have you removed from the Flamingo Cove force by the end of this evening. What will all of your straight buddies on the force think when they learn you're fucking little boys? And what will Whitney think?"

"I'm not fucking little boys," Garrett hisses, outraged and on fire, but careful not to use his Sig.

"I can have a rumor spread around this city in a matter of seconds that you do. You'll be put on paid leave, severely investigated, and God only knows what other kind of shit. You know I can accomplish this." Rocco means business, playing one of his Mafia cards to the best of his abilities.

"You wouldn't?" Garrett asks, bites his bottom lip, and finally removes his right palm from the Sig.

"Try me, Garrett. Most men don't, but maybe you're not like most men."

The Flamingo Cove officer puts his arms up and shows off his smooth palms, surrendering. Realizing his loss today at Rocco's dual, his voice is filled with caution and unsteady nervousness, "I'll stay away. You won't see me around."

"And the parking tickets in Melvin's file, get rid of them," my husband-to-be aggressively adds. "Melvin's a nice guy. He's one of my personal friends. See that he has a clean record."

Garrett puts his arms and palms down at his sides again and nods his head, agreeing to Rocco's requests. He spins in the sand and begins his exit around the beach house to his cruiser. Over his right shoulder, he calls out, "I'll walk myself out. No need for your escort."

# # # # #

Rocco sees the helpless look on my face that says: I really don't know what the hell was going down with Garrett. Like the defending gentleman that he is, the Mafia man comes to my beach chair, bends over, wraps a gentle palm around the back of my head, kisses me on my nose and lips, and says, "I never did like that guy."

"Me neither."

"Any luck with your interviews for a new houseboy?"

"None. It's been a bust."

"Someone will come along. No need to worry." He pauses, scans my torso, middle, legs, and asks, "Are you wearing my trunks?"

"Guilty," I reply.

He smiles. "They look good on you."

"You look pretty damn good on me, Rocco."

He seems to ignore my comment and now asks, "You hungry for some lunch?"

"I am. What are you in the mood for?"

200

He slides one of his palms down and over my torso, against the trunk I took from his dresser, and cups the goods between my legs. "Meat. I'm really hungry for some meat, man."

I want to ask him if seeing Garrett's naked cock turned him on; this would be inappropriate, though. Instead, I reply, "It's an all you can eat lunch buffet special out here on the beach. I hear the meat is grade-A stuff."

In response to my comment, the gangster falls to his knees in the sand, nuzzles his face to my middle, and bites the nylon fabric which covers my growing tool.

CHAPTER TWENTY – WHERE IN THE WORLD IS ROCCO MALONNI?

This night, I have the most amazing dream while curled against Rocco's naked body:

Garrett and I are in a log cabin somewhere in upstate New York. Snow reaches above the three windows, evidently proving we are snowbound and alone, just the two of us.

The cop serves us cups of hot cocoa with marshmallows. He is dressed in his uniform, badge and all, and cuddles up next to me by the sparking fire.

"Happy Anniversary," I whisper to him, pecking his cheek with a light kiss.

He places his lips against my neck and chants, "It's been three years now, hasn't it?"

The room is wall-to-wall polar bear fur. I take a sip of my hot chocolate and nod my head. The warm brew goes down smooth, even if the log cabin's single room is filled with a troublesome chill, I warm up a touch. Following my kiss, I ask, "Are you going to seduce me?"

"How did you know?"

"I just did. I don't plan on being gentle with you," he admits.

"I was hoping you would say that."

Approximately five minutes later we're naked in front of the crackling fire. Garrett looks unbelievably sexy with his extension of nine inches between his legs and the nicely groomed treasure trail of onyx-black hair beneath his comma-shaped navel. A recent trip to Cancun has suntanned his body from head to toe, making him delicious looking. The cop winks at me in a playful and boyish manner with his shadowy eyes. A smile surfaces on his face and he says, "You ready for my mouth against your rump, pal?"

I shake my head and reply, "Better yet, why don't I use my mouth on your rump?"

"I like that idea," he admits, rolls onto his belly, and positions himself on his knees and palms. Over his right shoulder, he demands, "Suck my ass, Derek. This is no time to be shy. Be a man and get the job done."

To my surprise, the pig has a bit of curly hair that lines his puckering ass. I dig through it with my tongue, find it desirable, and take a lap at his inflexible hole.

He lets out a whimper of delight in front of me, cocks his head back like a wolf, and begins to growl. I notice that his fingers dig into the faux polar bear rug, and claw in pain and joy at the piece of fabric.

Attempting to please him, I decide to use my own fingertips on his bottom and gently pull his ass-slit apart. My extension of slippery tongue discovers his center with such ease, driving him mad in front of me. I lap and lick at the circumference of his hole and dip my tongue inside. For ten minutes or more this action continues. In doing so, I moan behind him with much hunger and sexual energy, satisfied with my work, needy for his opening, and unwilling to stop.

To my surprise, the city police officer backs into my face and calls over his right shoulder in a pleading manner, "Fuck my ass with that tongue. Do it, Derek. Don't let me down."

I'm charged with sexual fire and decide not to let the good man down. Behind him, I nuzzle my face into his cop-core. Saliva leaks out of my mouth and swabs his opening. The tip of my elongated tongue dances inside his middle, pulls out to allow me to breathe, and enters his behind again.

"I'm shooting," he groans, possibly humping the bear skin rug with his extension of inflated cock. Gasps exit his mouth and fill the log cabin, which seem louder than the howling wind outside. His murmuring becomes deep and obnoxious as he empties his load. The dream-sex is quick with the cop and he falls away from me after he blows his cargo. The guy slips off my face and rolls onto his back.

Glue-like semen sticks to the end of his knob and sculpted stomach. While kneeling over him, I lap every drop off his perfect skin. Now, I find the still-hard shaft between his legs and consume the released ooze with bliss, craving its bittersweet flavor on my tongue.

"Your mouth made me blow," he huffs and puffs for air on the bear rug. "I never had a man eat my ass out like that before."

"I'm glad you liked it," I reply, unwilling to finish my meal so soon. My right palm finds his firm pole and wraps around its base. I jerk its extra skin upward and push two more bubbles of ooze out of his spike for the taking. Ravenous for the sticky sap, I lean over his skin again, extend my tongue to the tip of his meat, and extract the excess spew into my system, spirited by its sugary and astringent taste.

Under my touch, spell, care, the cop goes numb. His eyes roll into the back of his skull and his head gently turns to the right. The officer of the law finds enough strength to murmur, "It's been a long time since you've done this, Derek."

"It's only a dream. Frankly, I'm hoping you come again when I decide to fuck your ass."

He laughs at my comment, and suggests, "Bring it on." Following this statement, he lifts his legs, bends the pair at their knees, which allows access for my timber to enter.

# # # # #

"It's bareback or nothing," I say down to the police officer. "You know the rules, man. Don't fuck this up for the both of us."

"No plastic is the way to go. It feels better without it."

"If I had a gun, I'd fuck you with it."

"Dirty sex ... I love it, Derek."

I hold the bottom of his feet and allow the tip of my flag to brush against his ball sack. As light moans escape his mouth, I release his right foot and drag my cock against his closed and tight man-opening.

Beneath me, staring up at my chiseled core, he whimpers, "That was hot, dude ... Do it more."

"You're a whore," I chant down to him, grinning from ear to ear. Now, I push the tip of my unprotected stick into his crease, watch him grind his teeth together with utter pleasure, and observe his fists as they grasp the polar bear rug.

"Fuck me," he steadily breathes, caught in his selfish act of bliss, and wants nothing less than all of my beef pressed into his tight center.

Two more inches enter his middle ... four inches ... all of the inches slide inside his body and cause his eyes to squint and his teeth to grind. Juxtaposed huffs escape the man's mouth. His chest rises and falls by my thrifty work, and he begins to sweat profusely. Garrett's head twists from left to right in fascination because of my heedless labor.

As expected, I heave in and out of him, and obey my hunger to burst my man-freight. My balls slap against his bottom as I rock to and fro above the pig. Minute after minute compiles as I plug his rear with the throbbing meat between my legs. Steady and pulsating movement is delivered to his rump, combining my skin with his.

"Fuck me," he whines with delight, a smile spread across his delicious looking face. "Don't stop. Fuck me hard."

I heed his advice, sway forward and backward, and cling my hands to his feet while blasting his hub, reluctant to be vigilant, speedy, and rather rough at work. Bang after consistent bang occurs to his core. Thrifty motion ensues for the next seven ... eleven ... sixteen minutes as I plow his behind, working all I have into him, performing like a triple-X star who works for Colt or Hot House or Falcon.

"So good," he murmurs beneath me. "Don't stop. Tell me you're just getting started."

"You're tight ... just the way I like my ass."

"Thank you for my ass-pounding, Mr. Reed. Thank you very much." He looks dazed and confused as he murmurs this beneath me.

"My pleasure," I chant down to him, sort of chuckle to myself, and know that this dialogue between us would never happen in real life.

Again, I bolt into him, pull out, push my rod into his hole, bang him hard and fast and long and ...

Like any mortal man, though, I am clearly unable to hold my load in forever. Incapable to stand the ripples of ecstasy that course through my shaft, I pull my dick out of his hub and demand from him, "Finish me off. You know how to do it."

Accepting his duty, the pig lowers his legs but still keeps them bent. He reaches down and over his perspiration-covered torso and finds my dog with both hands. The po-po whispers, "I'm going to two-palm you."

My response is rather brutish and uncivilized, "I don't care what the fuck you do to me as long as I shoot my load."

He becomes submissive in the folds of my pornographic dream. His palms thrush up and down on my spike, eager to please me. Fingertips roll against veined meat as balls thwap chaotically against my muscular thighs.

Because I find a sense of elation, I moan and gasp with pleasure. A surreal feeling of lust sweeps throughout my core and I almost lose my balance. I hold steady on my knees above the cop, unwilling to break away from our shared good time.

"Pumping it," he chants up to me and jostles my beef. "I want you to shoot it all over my chest, Derek. Don't hold back."

"Shut the fuck up!" exits my mouth, totally out of my character in real life. I think about backhanding the fucker across the face to keep him quiet, but I have better things on my mind: my rod is almost ready to burst its steamy load, emptying its creamy junk on the blue's skin.

"Blow, guy. Don't hold it in," he coaches, into our gig on the polar bear rug.

Three … four … five thrusts occur as I pound his fists. An arc of pleasant turbulence skis throughout my body, announcing my orgasm. My hips jolt one last time as I grit my teeth and growl like a rabid animal. Rushed heat zooms from one end of my torso to the other and …

"Shoot it," he coaches with a wide grin of full contentment.

A final ripple of euphoria cascades through my core and white spirals of man-gunk sprays out of my pick. The thick and creamy goo slaps against Garrett's chest, decorates his nipples, mouth, one eye, and the man's nicely sculpted shoulders. More jiz twists out of my crank and flies into his beautifully coifed hair and hangs from one earlobe, bathing him down like a circus animal.

More gasps and moans escape my mouth as I shoot the last droplets of my sticky load against his perpendicular-positioned body. And following my explosion, I kneel over his nicely built frame with his sweaty muscles and beautiful skin, and scoop up my seed with four fingers, delivering my goods to his mouth for a guy-treat that I'm quite sure he's in the mood for.

Although I half believe he's going to fight me on eating my spew, the cop doesn't. In fact, he does the complete opposite: the little whore opens his mouth and practically demands the gooey junk from me, ready to swallow my boys down, and relishes the warm spunk like candy. In a matter of seconds he consumes all of glue-like cargo, chowing it all down with ease, obviously having a hearty appetite for the sap.

Our connection ends as quickly as it begins. I finish using Garrett's skin for my personal needs and demand, "Get out. Don't even get dressed. Just leave. I don't want to see your fucking face anymore."

A helpless look crosses over the man's handsome features and he asks, "What are you talking about?"

I raise a fist, ready to pound him in the jaw, and explain, "Get the fuck out of my cabin. Rocco will find us. The man will kill you. I don't want you here."

As a blizzard's wind rips against the windows and spirals in anger outside, Garrett unhappily rises from the faux polar bear rug and escapes my side. Seconds later, he opens the cabin's door, allows a swirl of turbulent snow and wind to enter, and exits into the storm without saying a single word, simply vanishing into the winter's reckless fury, naked from head to toe.

# # # # #

I wake up this morning with a solid rod between my legs and pre-ooze that leaks out of its mushroom-shaped cap. One quick piss will take care of such morning madness, deflating the shaft. I roll over on my right side to kiss and hug Rocco, offering my company and love for another morning and day. To my surprise, Rocco isn't anywhere to be found on the bed. The spot next to me is empty of his sleeping body.

I imagine my boyfriend is in the kitchen, preparing strawberry cream cheese-filled pancakes, link sausages, freshly squeezed orange juice, and maybe a slice of toast for each of us. Or, he is in the shower, cleaning his body of night's sweat, becoming fresh for the day, willed to smell absolutely perfect for me. The kitchen is empty, though, as well as the bathroom. I check the rear patio to see if my man is sunbathing or drinking a Bloody Mary for breakfast. The cobblestone patio is empty except for a fiddler crab that finds its way up through the sand from the Gulf. Here, I wonder if Rocco has decided to take a morning run or stepped out of the house to fetch provisions from the local grocery store since we no longer have a hired boy to assist with such chores.

Rocco's cell phone sits on the kitchen table, which I find and wonder why he hasn't taken it with him, wherever in the world he is. Maybe the cell's battery is dead and this is why he's decided to leave it behind. I flip the device open, watch its screen light up with an arrangement of hues, and determine the battery is fine.

Panic starts to settle within my system. Honestly, where can Rocco be? Why hasn't he jotted a note down and left it for me to find in the beach house, regarding his whereabouts? This behavior is not like him. He is far too responsible to behave in such a manner, which is why I question his location and begin to worry.

I call Mother, just to see if she has demanded Rocco's attention without me knowing, seeking out plumbing assistance again from him. Barbara answers her cell phone after the third ring and asks, "What?" in a rather moderately rude tone; no surprise here.

"Mother, have you seen Rocco?"

"I haven't. Why, darling, is he missing?"

"I don't know yet. He's nowhere to be found, though."

"Have you tried Brit or Dragon? The pair might know of his whereabouts," she says, understanding that the two hired men tend to know where Rocco and I are at all the time, since they are our bodyguards.

"I haven't, but will."

"There's your answer."

She hangs up on me, ending our call without telling me goodbye. This is a familiar act in our lives, I realize. Barbara has always hated wasting time. Perhaps I'm just like the woman: impatient, bitchy, and unaccustomed to things not going my own way.

I heed her advice and call Dragon, who is with Brit. "Where are you two?"

"Out front smoking, Mr. Reed."

"Are you with Rocco?"

"I'm afraid not. He went for a run earlier. An hour later I saw him in the drive."

"He wasn't in bed with me when I woke up," I reply in a scathing tone, become overtly pissed off, and accidentally take it out on the man. "I suggest you two find him. It's what my father pays you to do." Truth is I don't like to speak to Brit or Dragon in this undignified manner, but sometimes I have to. Rocco needs to be found, and these men are experienced to carry out such a task. And if they don't, both know there will be hell to pay.

"Yes, Mr. Reed," Dragon responds, ending our call.

I phone all of Rocco's brothers and their wives. None are aware of his whereabouts and haven't seen or heard from him in the last twenty-four hours.

I call Rocco's father, hating to bother him, since he runs the mob in Miami. Unfortunately, Boss Malonni doesn't know where his son is. Nor has heard from Rocco in almost forty-eight hours. I promise to let him know if I find Rocco, which he is grateful for, calls me a good son, and tells me that he loves me.

Now I call Fisk on his cell phone, but he doesn't pick up. Instead, his voicemail clicks on and I leave the message: Have you seen Rocco? If so, call me back. I don't know where he is. Please, help me.

Yes, I sound desperate and a bit pleading, but whatever. Rocco needs to be found and I will go to many lengths to accomplish such a feat.

Next, I call Walter, relieved that he's home in Coconut Key, writing. Although the man is busy, he is glad to take my call. My older friend immediately hears the concern in my voice and asks, "What can I help you with, cupcake?"

"Rocco is missing. And I'm almost ready to have a fatal breakdown. He woke up early, went for a run, and was seen an hour later in the drive. Now he's nowhere to be found."

"Did he go to the store?"

"No."

"Where is his cell phone?"

"He left it on the kitchen table. Exactly where I found it."

"That's strange. I've never known him to be without his cell phone."

"Exactly," I reply.

Walter clears his throat by coughing into his fist. "Sweetie, I don't want you to panic. I'm sure there's a reasonable explanation regarding his whereabouts. The last thing you need to do is have a breakdown. Please try and hold yourself together. I can help you with this."

"I'm starting to wonder if he's alright. Rocco and I were trying to figure out the three murders and we just discovered that Zulan Cane is a mastermind behind the killings."

"Who is Zulan Cane?"

"It's a long story about diamonds and South Africa."

"This sounds very serious, Derek. I'll tell you what. Keep close to your cell phone and try not to be terrorized by this. I'm sure Rocco is perfectly unharmed and fine."

"How do you know that?" I ask, already terrorized.

"I don't. That's why I'll be there in two hours. I'm getting in my Mercedes right now. Stay at the beach house and wait for me. I shan't be long."

"I will," I reply, fold my cell phone, snug it up against the base of my chin, continue to panic, and painfully wonder where the hell my future husband vanished to.

CHAPTER TWENTY-ONE – SEXY BITCH

Who better to call than Garrett Haute when someone of importance is missing in my life, right? Following my conversation with Walter, I dial Garrett's cell number and wait for him to take my call. He does after the third ring.

When he answers, he immediately rattles off, "Derek, I knew you would come around. I'm glad you called me, especially when I was just thinking about you."

"This isn't about you," I shoot at him. "Rocco is missing and I need your help to find him."

Silence ensues. The man on the other end is probably in heavy thought regarding my situation, which I respect.

"Are you there?" I eventually inquire and wonder if he disconnected our call.

"I'm here. In fact, I'm right around the corner from you. What do you say I drop by and we can discuss your matter in person?"

I give him permission, even if he's slightly dangerous to be around, since he has always had a raging boner for me.

"See you in two, Garrett. And just so you know, I'm perfectly fine with you not wearing anything. To be honest, that would be the highlight of my day."

Before he arrives, I decide to throw on some more clothes: jeans, a vest over my T-shirt, socks and shoes. I use the attire as a shield or protection against his sexy behavior, since he's always into my skin and ready to seduce me. It's better to be safe than sorry, I presume, especially if I want to keep Rocco as a boyfriend.

The Flamingo Cove police officer arrives approximately five minutes later. He carries a paper bag in his right hand from Sparky's Doughnuts and a cardboard carrying tray with two coffees in his left hand. Upon his entrance into the beach house, the guy wears a smile from ear to ear, eyes me up and down, and shares, "You're wearing way too many clothes."

"My boyfriend would approve," I challenge and help myself to his bag of sweets and a coffee.

He ignores me and points to the bag from Sparky's and says, "I got you your favorite. Apricot turnovers."

"You're an angel." I place my coffee on the end table to the right of the sofa and open the bag. Immediately, I smell sugar, flour, and my favorite fruit. Now, I pull out one of the turnovers, take a bite, moan with delight, sit back in the sofa, and find a sliver of heaven.

Garrett discovers a seat across from me in one of Rocco's favorite reading chairs. He crosses his legs, sips his coffee, and says, "Tell me about Rocco missing."

I tell the cop as much as I can remember: Rocco finds me on the beach; we share some rough sex together in the sand; I have dinner with the gangster and eventually head to bed where I snuggle in his arms. "When I woke up this morning, he was gone. I called his brothers and their wives. They haven't seen or heard from him. I called his father. He told me he hasn't talked to Rocco in forty-eight hours."

Again, Garrett takes a sip of his hot coffee, drawing the waxed paper cup up to his beautiful lips. Following this act, he inquires, "What about Dragon and Brit?"

I shake my head. "Neither has seen him, but both are on a promising search to find him."

"Anything ordinary happen in the last few days?"

I give him a look of confusion: raised eyebrows, sunken eyes, and a slightly open mouth. "Are you serious? My whole life has been a whirlwind since Tang's body showed up on the beach behind my house. And I certainly don't need your antics right now."

"I mean in the past few hours," he clarifies, takes yet another sip of his tepid coffee, and swallows it down. "You need to take a breath and calm down. We'll find Rocco."

"I can only hope. You need to know about something odd that has occurred."

It's now his turn to raise an eyebrow at me, which he does. "Such as?"

I tell him about my drive to Watergulf and the event with Izzy Ramon, leaving no detail spared.

After listening to my story, he shakes his head in the most adorable manner and shares, "Don't make me take your apricot turnovers away from you."

"Why?" I hiss, clamping the paper bag close to my chest.

"You know perfectly well why. Izzy is trouble. I'm sure he was the one who kidnapped Rocco this morning and ..."

I abruptly shake my head and interrupt him with: "It's not Izzy. There's no way. He's crazy, but not that crazy."

"Who do you think we should be worried about then?"

"Zulan Cane."

"Who the fuck is Zulan Cane?"

I contemplate my current situation and want to tell Garrett about Rocco and his smuggling adventure with the four million dollars' worth of diamonds, which are now illegally inside the country. I also want to share with him that the diamonds are now missing. I know my lover's actions were illegal, which I've agreed to and accepted, since I knew he was doing the job. My question is simple for Garrett Haute: Will he let this itty bitty smear of law-breaking slide or not? This is the risk I have to take when spilling my guts to him. Can I trust Garrett Haute to help me or hinder me?

"Tell me," the guy demands, seeing right through my secrets. "I know who Rocco is and what kind of family he comes from. The Mafia's dealings are not as secret as you think they are. You're not going to share anything shocking with me. What's going on? Something is, and you're the guy who is going to tell me about it."

I take a large bite of the turnover, wash it down with a slug of coffee, and think, What the hell? I can throw the dice and see what happens. If I don't trust Garrett now, I never will. But I do trust him, since high school. He's a good guy who just happens to be a little sexually confused for the last dozen or more years. So I pour my guts out to him and say, "Zulan is trouble with a capital T. Rocco made a trip to Springbok, South Africa to take back four million dollars' worth of diamonds that Zulan thieved from Rocco's father at the end of October. Rocco returned to the States with the diamonds at the end of January. The diamonds end up missing from our beach house. Three bodies end up dead. The Skin Tour is purposely torched. And a list of bad guys aren't telling me the truth behind the murders or the missing gems."

"Who is on the list of bad guys?"

The names come to me like porn stars, which I rattle off, one by one: "Dane Duncock. Buli Croon. Balls Banco. Izzy Ramon. And Zulan Cane."

"That's a nice line up."

"They're all liars and thieves and henchmen."

"Those are some pretty strong labels," he says, sipping his coffee.

"Zulan is behind them all. The guy is a fucking mastermind and the devil's advocate. They are all just puppets to him and nothing more."

"Who says?"

"Izzy Ramon," I confidently clarify.

Garrett supplies me with a quizzical look and asks, "Do you believe him?"

I nod my head and reply, "I do. It's the only thing I believe, since Rocco retrieved the diamonds from Springbok."

The cop stands up and moves over to the sofa. He plops down beside me, practically rubs the tip of his nose to my nose, and asks, "Why should I help you when I know you won't suck my cock?"

"Because you're a nice guy. Plus, you have Whitney to suck your cock."

"How do you know I'm a nice guy?"

"I just do."

"And sucking my cock is out of the question, right?"

"I'm afraid so. I love Rocco, and that's who I like being naked with. His cock is the only cock I suck these days. I'm sorry to disappoint you. It is what it is, though." It's a douchebag thing to say, but whatever. He'll just have to get over it.

"Such a pity," he says in a downer mood and shifts his head away from mine.

Silence and stillness occurs. Eventually I take another bite of my apricot turnover and wash it down with a swig of hot coffee. Afterward, I inquire, "Are you going to help me find Rocco or not, Garrett?"

He spins his attention back to me and provides a lively smile. What spills out of his mouth is rather nice to hear, almost comforting: "I'm only going to help you because you make my cock hard. It feels rather great to grow a boner in your presence. I even spew a little in my boxer-briefs – if I'm wearing them – when I'm around you."

"This is good to know," I reply. What am I really supposed to say regarding the officer's shocking admission? I know he likes me, but do I really make his dick solid? I guess so, but I'm certainly not going to find out, since I plan to marry the godfather's son at some point in my future.

"I think we should start at The Reach and look for this Zulan guy and that room you were knocked out cold in."

"Sounds like a plan," I concur, rise from the sofa with my coffee and turnover, and begin our gig together.

# # # # #

Garrett and I make our way to The Reach to find Zulan. Of course, the hot cop tries to hit on me numerous times on the drive there, but I attempt to deter his actions with the best of my abilities.

Okay, I admit, the arm of the law is a sexy bitch from head to toe, an ultimate hottie and sweet to look at. Trust me, if Rocco weren't in the "big picture" of my life, Garrett would be my number one boyfriend. The cabin dream of him last night obviously confirms my likeness for him. And because of this connection I have with the adorable pig, I most surely stay on my best behavior in his presence, for fear that Rocco might acknowledge a certain weakness I have for the Flamingo Cove police officer. Yes, it's best to play nice and keep clean in the officer's presence. The last thing I need is the mob to hunt me down and plug me with a number of Colt slugs because of unfaithfulness.

To break my sexual tension, I decide to pick a monotonous fight with the man, bickering. I tell him, "You're going the wrong way. We should be turning right on Iguana Way and a left on Bay Drive."

Truth is there are many ways to get to The Reach, and Garrett is very much aware of this fact. He snaps at me, "I've got it handled, pal. You sit back and just enjoy the ride. Take a nap or something. Ogle my crotch if you want. Hell, you can even play with it, I won't mind."

I watch him steer his black Corolla around Market Center on the outskirts of The Reach. Eventually he makes a left on Bay Drive, exactly where we need to be.

Since Garrett is off duty he sports snug street clothes against his frame, which consist of Diesel jeans and a canary yellow tee that clings to every toned ab that indiscreetly line his well-built stomach. Half of me wants to be a naughty boyfriend behind Rocco's back and reach across the seat and graze a palm over the cop's rippled torso. At this precise moment, I can gently caress his abs one by one with stray fingers and enjoy the hell out of myself. I'm a faithful man and decide to keep my hands to myself, since I will surely be marrying into the Malonni family in the near future, and soon become a son-in-law to one of the most powerful mobsters in the United States.

Garrett senses my attraction to him, and my withdrawal. A boyish and mischievous laugh escapes his beautiful mouth and he asks, "You don't play around, do you?"

"I never do. It causes too much hardship and trouble in a serious relationship."

"Because I'm willing to play. You know that, right?"

"I do. But frankly, I have to pass. Rocco or his father would murder me."

"I commend you for your faithfulness. A lot of guys would be fucking me right here and now if I gave them the opportunity. I know it sounds arrogant, but it's true. You stand alone, which is noble, and a position I respect. I definitely need to find a man like you, Derek."

When he makes a right on Gulf Square Road, heading for the rundown apartment building where I followed Croon inside and was knocked out cold in that mysterious junk-filled room, I reply to him with: "You have a smoking body and a great personality. You're a nice guy most of the time, Garrett. And to tell you the truth, I'm sure a man is going to come around sometime soon and rock your queer world and heart."

He parks his Corolla, we jump out, and now we head across the street to the dilapidated apartment building. In the process, he says, "You're just being nice to me to get to my cock."

I laugh at this, enjoying his sense of humor.

"I'm glad you think my sex life is so funny."

"That's not why I'm laughing and you know it."

He changes the topic and asks, "You packing?"

I pat my right hip and say, "I won't leave home without a gun anymore."

"Thatta' boy. Rocco is training you to be a good mobster."

He leads me inside the apartment building and we climb the stairs to the right. Again, I meet an empty and dark hallway as before, except this time it's with a city cop. Garrett sees the three apartment doors to the left, and the four to the right. Surprisingly, the entire building is quiet: no screaming babies, no yelling gang members, and no gun fire or rap blaring. I lead my hot companion to the right, down the length of the hallway, and end our travels at the familiar metal door.

He tries the door. This time it just happens to be unlocked. He opens the door and we walk into another hallway that leads to the thirty steps and secret room on the fifth floor. I point to the stairwell and instruct him to proceed; Garrett listens.

Together, we walk up the thirty steps and find another steel door, which is also open. My sidekick pulls the door open and ...

The room is completely empty. Nothing is inside. No boxes, vintage furniture, or other miscellaneous items. White walls welcome us. Two windows allow sunshine to bleed into the room. Specs of dust float and spiral among the golden-white light.

Garrett turns to me and says, "It's empty."

"It wasn't before."

"But it is now."

"Look, I'm not lying. You have to believe me. This room was chalk full when I was attacked."

"I do," he replies and nods his head. "I'm sure Croon and Zulan were hiding things in here that were illegal or stolen."

"Like diamonds."

"Now, you're catching on," he responds, smirking.

# # # # #

We decide to leave the empty room, exit the apartment building, and spend the next half hour driving around The Reach for anything conspicuous that might lead us to Zulan. To no avail, we come up empty-handed, which is really no surprise.

"This is a waste," I say to him. "We're getting nowhere by doing this."

"Do you have a better idea?"

"I do."

"Such as, Mr. Smarty Pants?"

"Croon ... We need to find him. He can lead us to Zulan. Once we find Zulan, we can learn where Rocco is, and the missing diamonds. What do you think?"

He's just about to answer me when my cell phone rings. I produce an upright index finger in front of his mouth to signal him to keep quiet for a second, take the call, and learn that it's Walter Landing.

The mystery writer chants in the phone, "I'm at my Flamingo Cove place. Come and visit me. And hurry. I have some very important information for you."

"You left the beach house?"

"I did. I couldn't stand being there alone because it was far too frightening. The place is haunted now that the two murders have happened on the beach. Besides, I always feel much safer at home." He sounds out of breath, bemused, and half himself.

"What kind of information do you have for me?"

"I can't tell you that until you arrive, darling."

"I'm on my way," I reply, ending my call with him. Now, my attention is drawn to Garrett again, and I instruct, "Turn around. We need Palisades Street."

"Why Palisades?" he questions.

"Walter Landing has some things to tell me … us."

"He can't do it over the phone?"

"I'm afraid not."

"That man is such a drama queen," the cop bitches, rolls his eyes, and grows perturbed. "I swear … He's this city's biggest pain in the ass."

"Be nice. He's very intuitive and can help us find out where Rocco is. The man is a genius when it comes to solving mysteries."

"It doesn't mean I have to like him."

"You're very right. It doesn't," I respond, shaking my head, "even if he's brilliant and charming and … Just get to Palisades."

"You're a little feisty, Derek. Maybe you should calm down."

"I will when we find Rocco."

"Love forever," he sighs with a lift in his voice, attempting to take my edge off.

"You're just jealous," I counteract and attempt to relax in my seat. Honestly, though, I'm far too excited to see Walter because I want to learn a few facts regarding my boyfriend's whereabouts.

Garrett chortles, "Yes … I am jealous. Someone has to be when it comes to your sexy queer ass, my friend."

CHAPTER TWENTY-TWO – MEN AT PLAY

40568 Palisades Street is Walter's abode in Flamingo Cove, which is much smaller than his estate in Coconut Key, a very wealthy area located two hours north. The small bungalow seems appropriate for a mystery writer. The two-story coastal home has three bedrooms, two and half baths, a classic argot Florida architecture, stone base columns on the front and back, wood ceiling beams, a coffee porch, and a working fireplace. The cost of this twenty-year-old Cove home is close to a million dollars, which is nothing considering Walter's hefty bank account.

Garrett parks his Corolla in the U-shaped drive next to a cluster of palms and says, "This place isn't so shabby."

"You should see his estate in Coconut Key. It's unbelievably huge and dick-hardening. It's been in *Architectural Digest* numerous times."

We exit the vehicle and find ourselves at the front of the bungalow. I knock three times and the bamboo door is opened by two men, both of which have the bodies of models. One is completely bald with nipples the size of dinner plates, piercing green eyes, and jockish legs. The second naked man looks like Seann William Scott, decorated with a muscle-plated chest and a robust smile. The two strangers lean into each other, are all eyes, and study my sidekick and me from head to toe. Seann just happens to lick his lips, finding the cop delectable.

Nervously, I clear my throat and say, "I'm here to see Walter."

Garrett jabs me in my side and rattles off, "Fuck a visit with Walter. I'd rather play with these two studs."

Nipples and Seann share a laugh. Both step aside and let us in. In a rather brash and sexy tone, Nipples says, "Walter is writing. I'm sure we can fetch him for you from the study."

"I'd like you two to fetch my cock, if you don't mind," Garrett chides while cupping the goods at his center.

I pop an elbow into his gut since he stands somewhat behind me, and say over my right shoulder, "Can you control your cock for at least a half hour?"

He is not at all pleased with my comment. "What can I say? My dick is always hungry for guys. Besides, if you're not going to fuck me … maybe these two will."

I roll my eyes, walk through the earthy-colored foyer and into the writer's gathering room, where I find a seat and relax. For the next two minutes I take in the room: abundant with glass windows; slate flooring; many ferns and a miniature potted palm tree; recliner with brightly colored pillows; a tiny bar area to the far right; sliding glass doors to the left lead to a private patio outside. The room is fabulous; something one would surely see in *House Beautiful* or *Elle Décor*.

A gay magazine called *Men at Play* sits on a table next to a moderately uncomfortable reading chair. Before picking up the glossy-paged periodical, I watch my cohort disappear down the hallway with the two men; the three are obviously on a search for Walter.

My attention is drawn to the magazine, which sports Brad Star, Chris Ward, and Dylan Roberts in their glorious nakedness. Each are adorable and delectable with their beautiful smiles and porn star bodies. Once I push a concocted boner away, I flip to the interview between one of the magazine's writers (Clint Shellings) and Brent Corrigan, a cutie boy toy. I read half of the article and proclaim it a little dull. Next, I flip to the Dr. Hung article where he answers queer sex questions by valued readers.

One question asks Mr. Hung if eating shit is healthy. Mr. Hung dogmatically disagrees. A second question asks the doctor if it's possible to take on three cocks in one's ass, all at the same time. Dr. Hung replies, "I don't know how this is physically possible, but I'm sure you can try. Just be careful. And send a video of the festivities to me." A final question regards strong urges to sleep with a priest. The doctor professes the importance of choice, leaving the reader on his own.

A few minutes later Walter finally enters the room in a silk blue robe from Nagasaki, Japan. He holds a gin and tonic in his right hand, sits across from me, and says, "Did you happen to see my new toys?"

"Nipples and Seann William Scott?" I politely reply, raising an eyebrow. Now, I fold the magazine closed and place it back where I discovered it on the table that separates the writer from me.

"Aren't they amazing looking men?"

"Positively stunning. But does Fisk know you're playing with them?" I really want to know, particularly since I am under the impression that the two men are monogamous with each other and never become frisky outside their relationship.

The mystery writer nods his head, glows with a boyish smile, and replies, "They were a little gift from Fisk to me. I can use them up for three days. They perform for me. Both are superb at jack-scenes, suck each other off, and fuck like porn stars together. I never touch them, if you want to know. Instead, I'm the open-mouthed voyeur."

"Did you bring your sex entourage up from Coconut Key?"

He tilts his beverage up to his lips, consumes the three fingers of alcohol and tonic, licks his lips, and answers, "Of course I did. I still have forty-eight hours with the sexy dudes."

"Which means we'll make this visit short, I presume."

"A very good assumption, darling. Frankly, the young men need all the attention they can get from me, of course. Fisk is paying them quite the sum of money for their live XXX shows."

Truth is Walter looks extremely happy; I've never seen him so solid before, even with Fisk. But, who wouldn't be exhilarated while being a voyeur regarding his hired helps' carved torsos and lengthy wankers?

Enough. I'm here for more important matters. Not to digest his latest two-man fling and watch-fest. Finally, I cut to the chase and ask, "What information do you have for me?"

"Lots. You'll cream yourself after you hear what I have to tell you."

Before informing Walter to begin, I look to my right to see if Garrett is in the hallway which leads to the rest of the bungalow; the horny man is nowhere to be seen. Honestly, I believe he's playing with the two naked men, filling his time during my meeting with the writer.

Maybe he's off somewhere in the bungalow receiving and giving a blowjob at the same exact time, or surrendering his body to the duo for other intimate acts among men at play.

Whatever. I have more important issues at hand. One, I need to find Rocco. Two, I need to find the diamonds. Three, who killed Tang Meadow, his assistant Nolan Cutler, and my houseboy Mantabaun?

He clears his throat, places his empty tumbler down on the table between us, and says, "Your houseboy was not your friend. The man just happened to be your enemy."

I confess without shock, "I sensed that all along. We had a few incidents with the young man that concerned me. Stealing things, lying, and such. Rocco was the one who wanted to keep him on our staff and protected him."

"I discovered through a network of my friends – all very good sources, if I may say so – that Mantabaun worked for Bali Croon."

"I assumed as much." A sigh escapes me; one filled with embarrassment, failure, and shame, all at the same time.

"And Croon works for Zulan Cane."

"Who took the diamonds from the beach house, correct?"

"Wrong!" Walter fires at me, possibly a little blitzed by his gin and tonic. "Mantabaun took the diamonds and gave them to Croon. Zulan's number one man is Croon, who in turn, passed them onto his mobster boss. Zulan, I believe, has the diamonds and Rocco is in his custody as we speak."

"Why was Tang and his assistant murdered?" I look at Walter's gin and tonic and believe that he needs a refill to continue wetting his whistle.

"Zulan had Croon kill Tang and his assistant because they discovered that Zulan was going to steal the diamonds back from Rocco and you. It just so happened that Mantabaun was sleeping with Tang. They were boyfriends. And Tang was fucking his assistant, Nolan Cutler, on the side."

"So, Zulan had all three of them murdered for fear that his plan to steal the diamonds back would leak?"

226

"Exactly," Walter replies.

"Was the e-mail from Tang a warning of sorts for me?"

"I believe so. He was asking for help and possibly knew Zulan was going to have him knocked off."

"He and Mantabaun were in too deep," I reply. "They should have known not to mess with Zulan."

He licks his lips, desiring another gin and tonic. He passes on retrieving the beverage though, and continues, "As for your Hummer ... Croon set it on fire. The man is an arsonist by nature."

"And The Skin Artist? Did he set it ablaze, too?"

My mystery writing friend nods his head. "Of course he did."

"Where does Izzy Ramon fit into this?"

He shakes his head. "He doesn't. Izzy has no connections to the murders. Perhaps he wants to keep his badass persona afloat, but whatever. I believe the guy is more interested in drug smuggling opposed to diamonds. Izzy is innocent regarding all three murders, even if he is a little crazy."

"Who ransacked our beach house?"

"Balls Banco. He found out about Zulan's mission and decided to steal the diamonds himself."

"But it was too late. Mantabaun had already opened the safe beneath the floor and took the goods, right?"

"You're catching on, Derek. I'm very proud of you. Maybe someday you too can write a mystery of your own."

"Did Banco get a little greedy and try to accomplish a fast one over Zulan?"

He nods his head.

"What about Dane Duncock? He works for Croon. Did he have anything to do with the murders?"

"He didn't. Croon had him doing other work. He's an innocent party when it comes to the three killings."

"What happened to my boyfriend? Where is he?" I sound desperate, somewhat pleading.

Walter rubs his chin like Sherlock Holmes and carries out a constant stare at me. He whispers, "I do believe he was abducted after his run, right out of the shell driveway at the beach house."

"Who do you think did that?" I inquire.

"Zulan Cane, of course."

"How do I find Zulan and Rocco?"

"I suggest you get Dragon and Brit on Croon's tail while you find your boyfriend."

I nod my head, agreeing. "I can do that."

"It's the smart thing to do. If you find Croon, you'll find Zulan and Rocco."

"So, where is Rocco?"

"Underneath The Nest."

"In The Reach?"

"Yes."

"Who told you this, Walter? How did you learn this?"

My friend shakes his head and whispers, "I can't expose my source. Let's just say he is trustworthy and valuable; a true friend of mine."

The Nest is the worst bar in The Reach. It's filled with drug dealers, murderers, male hustlers, pedophiles, rapists, thieves, terrorists, and other horrible villains in the world. It's the last place I want to visit. But, I have to save Rocco, accomplishing everything in my power to process such a feat.

He continues, "Zulan has a private office underneath The Nest. A stairwell at the back of the seedy bar leads into the ground. I believe it's three stories down."

"Is Rocco there?"

"Yes ... With the diamonds."

228

"Is this information you're sharing with me accurate?"

"To the best of my knowledge. Again, my sources are impeccable masters at their games. Don't question them."

"You have more than one?"

He winks at me and responds, "Every writer does, darling."

"What is my fee?" I inquire, believing it is going to be steep for the writer's helpful assistance.

He shakes his head and retorts, "Don't insult me. I adore you and Rocco. I would never charge you a fee to save his life."

"When I find him, if I do, what am I going to walk in on?"

"I'm sorry. I can't answer that. I don't have those details."

"Will you join me?" I plead with the mystery writer, hoping he does in fact travel to The Reach with me, and then into The Nest below.

"I'm afraid you're going to have to do this on your own, Derek. I would rather not get involved. My aged body says to sit this one out, if you don't mind."

"I don't, Walter. I would hate to place you in a dangerous position. Our friendship is far too valuable for that."

"Thank you. I appreciate the love."

"We all do. It's why I have to find Rocco."

# # # # #

When my conversation with the mystery writer ends, Garrett enters the gathering room with his pants unbuttoned, a missing shirt, and a perspiration-covered chest. I give him a once-over and see that his hair is mussed, a semi-boner rests between his legs, and he has cum on the right side of his face. Upon his entrance, I ask, "What have you been up to?"

A smile of elation is wide on his face and he snickers, "Those men were very bad with me. Neither could keep their hands off me."

Walter does not look amused. He shares a cringing gaze with my cohort and questions, "You fucked around with my toys, didn't you?"

"They begged to eat my cock. I couldn't tell them no. And in return, I decided to eat their cocks."

"You have dick-juice on your cheek," Walter shares. "You should give it back to one of them."

I laugh under my breath, enjoying the writer's sarcasm and hostility.

The gay police officer moves a fingertip up to his right cheek and wipes the drop of ooze away. He now slips the fingertip into his mouth, between his reddish lips, and sucks on the appendage, cleaning it off.

"You're a slut," Walter fires off, purposely being unkind, rather upset that Garrett has taken advantage of Nipples and Seann.

I know it's time to leave and quickly ask the cop, "Where is your shirt?"

"One of the men wanted to keep it as a souvenir of our shared quickie."

"Fuck!" Walter hisses, rolling his eyes with an uncontrolled sigh.

I stand up and begin my exit. My attention temporarily digests Walter and I say, "Thanks for all your help. You mean the world to me, friend."

"Of course. It was my pleasure."

"And thanks for letting me fuck around with your hired help," my sidekick chuckles with an ear to ear grin.

Before Walter can utter something unpleasant and quite rude, ready to cause an argument, I buzz by the cop and leash my right hand on his left forearm. Hurriedly, I drag him out of the bungalow. In doing so, I holler at the writer, "We'll talk soon!"

"I hope without your little man-whore!" Walter yells back, meaning every word of his brutal comment.

I ignore the novelist and whisk Garrett away to The Reach, seeking out safety, Zulan, Rocco, and the missing diamonds.

CHAPTER TWENTY-THREE – STUDLY AGRESSION

Garrett and I walk into The Nest with no intentions of sharing a drink or finding men to fuck around with. Instead, we enter the sleazy bar ready to carry out business, which consists of finding Zulan, Rocco, and the four million dollars' worth of diamonds.

The Nest rocks with some classic CCR. Meth-using boys line a sticky wall, waiting for sex and cash. Some give blowjobs to middle-aged bald men with big bellies for their next meth fixes. Others sway on the red-illuminated dance floor by themselves, obviously high.

The smell of pot lingers about the bar, heavy with semen, sweat, and alcohol. A few leather daddies sit at the bar, smoke and drink, and observe the high boys on the dance floor. Two just happen to be locked together by tongues and hands, enjoying each other's company. To the far right is the U-shaped bar. A bartender who looks like Garth Brooks makes chemical eye contact with me, wanting in my jeans. The guy winks at me once and attempts to draw me towards him. When I don't pull my stare away from him he smiles at me, into my pretty boy looks, and possibly becomes hard as a rock in his clean Wranglers.

Side by side, Garrett and I make our way through the druggies, dealers, hustlers, and whatnots. A restroom sits in the rear of the bar. A shirtless bear with a Harley Davidson bandana around his head exits the bathroom. To the right of the bathroom is a door marked PRIVATE, which my sidekick and I decide to enter since it's not locked.

Once through the door, positioned on our right side, is a naked ginger-haired boy pressed against the black wall. A leather-clad daddy bangs his cock into the boy, holds his bait by the hips, and wildly rocks in a to and fro motion. A dim light hangs above the pair from the ten-foot ceiling, shadowing the couple at their flesh-work. Daddy shows us a face of perspiration with an intoxicated grin. I assume he's a guard of sorts at the door, but is far too busy fucking his toy to stop our obtrusive entrance.

As the boy's chest beats against the black wall, Garrett and I pass without a confrontation. Quickly, we make our way down the narrow hallway, enter a second door, and find ourselves at the top of an iron staircase with a flashing red EXIT sign, which hangs on the wall.

I turn to Garrett, who happens to be a reddish-black shadow behind me, and say, "This is it. Three floors down."

"And a shitload of trouble."

"I'm ready for it, are you?"

"Fuck yeah, man. Bring it."

"Bring it," I smile and step forward.

# # # # #

Our decline begins, one step at a time, careful with our footsteps, endangering our own lives as we attempt to find Zulan, Rocco, and the stolen diamonds.

At the bottom of the first flight of iron steps, a yellow-white light hangs from the ceiling, illuminating a locked cage which hangs on the wall. The cage is the size of a gym locker. A fluorescent orange sign hangs on the cage that reads DANGER – HIGH VOLTAGE.

Garrett looks over my right shoulder, studies the cage, and confirms, "It's the electric box to the building."

"I guess they have to put it somewhere."

To the right of the cage is a steel door. A red and white sticker is pressed against the center of the door, which reads PERSONNEL ONLY – DO NOT ENTER.

The cop says, "Let's keep walking, my friend. We have two more flights to go."

I heed his instruction, pass the steel door, and proceed with my decline, being cautious.

Where could a terrorist perform a better ambush, of course? Zulan's mysterious underground realm is dark and creepy, resembling a mausoleum or catacomb. To no avail, I move downward with the cop on my sexy tail. We cover twenty or more iron steps in the process, careful of what lies below.

The aroma here is biting: a mix of sewage and mold. The scent is heavy in my nose and mouth, greatly irritating. I try to hold my breath for as long as possible, but fail miserably, taunted by the stink.

Behind me, my cohort asks, "What the fuck is that smell?'

"I'd guess sewage."

"I think I'm going to vomit."

"Hold it in, buddy. We have one more floor to go."

Walking down a dozen or more steps, I see where the smell originates from. An iron pipe runs horizontally over our heads as we pass under it to the third sublevel. Shadowy green gunk drips from a seven-inch crack along the pipe. Shit falls from the second floor to the third floor, possibly forming puddles on a level below.

Ignoring the smell to the best of our abilities, covering our mouths and noses, we continue to head deeper into the earth. When we finally end our escapade at sublevel three, another steel door welcomes us. This particular door has a red System Sensor strobe above it, which is the size of a dinner plate. I observe no handle or window decorating the door. The flat surface in front of me is nothing more than a sheet of thick steel, which I'm unable to open or close.

Garrett says, "I feel like I'm in a video game."

I nod my head and chant, "I feel the same way." After my comment, the red strobe above the steel door begins to flash and quickly turns to green. The door now slides open to the right, slipping into the wall.

# # # # #

Zulan Cane stands at the open door, grinning from ear to ear. He is fully erect at six-three, weighs no more than 180 pounds, has a thick jaw, commercial white teeth, wide brown lips, aloof onyx-colored eyes, and licorice-black skin. The diamond smuggler holds an Alexander

AWS entry rifle with a matte blue finish and a synthetic stock. It's a dandy of a gun that can blow Garrett and me away in a second.

Happy to see us, Zulan teases, "A pleasure to finally meet you, Derek Reed." He eyes up my lawful companion and adds, "Garrett Haute, I'm always delighted to see you. Both of you are fine looking young men."

I look over my right shoulder and inquire, "You know him, Garrett?"

"Not personally. He must have found out that I'm a cop."

Zulan chortles, aiming his rifle at me. Once he is finished laughing, he demands, "Your weapons, gentlemen. Put them on the floor and kick them over to me. Don't do any funny stuff, queers, or I'll blast the both of you away."

I release my loaded Beretta from the nape of my back and place it on the floor. Garrett pulls a Colt from inside his jeans and does the same thing. Both guns slide across the cement floor to our assailant, who just happens to still be grinning from ear to ear, which really starts to piss me off.

As Zulan takes our guns, slipping one against the nape of his back and the other between his flat stomach and black denim, I inquire, "Rocco ... Where is he?"

The diamond thief ignores my question and says, "You're quite the sleuth, just so you know. I recognize a good detective when I first see one and you fit the bill. It's nice to know that you've done your homework on Tang, his assistant, and Mantabaun. My question for you is simple, of course: Why didn't you ask Croon where your hustler is hidden? I'm sure he can remember. Croon is a smart cookie. He's a faithful employee of mine. One of my best little monkeys I operate with."

"Tell me where Rocco is," I demand with a crack in my voice, outraged with Zulan and his negative antics.

Zulan shares an apocalyptical laugh, tilting his head back. "You two are pathetic. I've been watching you on numerous monitors since you entered The Nest. Didn't you think I would be protected? Do you really think I allow unexpected and nameless men to show up at my doorstep without letting me know first? I mean seriously, boys, what the fuck were you thinking?" Behind Zulan is an expansive desk with a variety of laptops and three flat-screen monitors. One of the screens shows Daddy working over his boy's ass on the first floor. Another screen shows The Nest with its seedy clients. The last screen is a bird's eye view of the stairwell that Garrett and I have just walked down. To Zulan's right side is a modern white leather sofa and two matching chairs from the Salina La Portina collection, a designer in Barcelona. To Zulan's left side are two doors. One just happens to be open, exposing a sink, oval mirror, and an American Standard toilet. The second door is windowless, all steel, closed, and tightly sealed with two Yale locks.

"All I want is Rocco," I say. "You keep the diamonds and we'll call it even."

"It's honorable to know that you are buying a hustler for four million dollars."

"He's not a hustler!" I snap, shaking my head.

Zulan laughs at me, thrilled with his objective teasing. A sneer surfaces on his face that tells me he's deceitful, wicked in every way, and the devil's spawn.

"This is all over greed, isn't it? You wanted the diamonds back, and whomever got in your way, you decided to dispose of them, didn't you?"

He nods his head and shares his antagonistic grin.

"I'm also on your kill list, Zulan, aren't I? You knew I would come and find Rocco, and now you can kill me."

"You're very clever. It's a shame you and your hustler won't be alive to enjoy your smarts."

Panic settles into my system and I muster the strength to ask, "Did you kill Rocco?"

Zulan's smile is eerie, almost like a creepy jack-o-lantern's in a horror movie. He clicks his teeth together once, twice, and says, "Why would I kill Rocco alone when I can knock off the both of you faggots at the same time? I mean, two birds are better than one, right?"

Garrett lets out a short gasp behind me. I wonder if he has a Beretta hidden somewhere in his jeans, or elsewhere on his body. One quick pull of its trigger can sustain Zulan and give us access to the underground pad so we can find Rocco, and possibly the missing diamonds.

Serious now, and sharing a line for a smile, our brutish enemy says, "What kind of host am I being? The two of you should come inside." He steps to his left, backs away from the door, and permits us to enter.

I hold my ground, unwilling to move. Truth is I'm trying to formulate a quick plan of attack to catch the bad boy off guard and possibly disarm him of his weaponry, having every goal of knocking him unconscious – somehow.

"Gentleman, do come in."

I look over my right shoulder at Garrett and see that he discretely winks at me, which prompts me to share a wink in return. Sarcastically, putting on an act of sorts, I ask the cop, "You want to stick around for a visit?"

Garrett, without Zulan seeing, rubs his swollen crotch, obviously packing some heat in all his right places, and responds, "I'm always up for a goon visit."

I turn my attention back to the diamond smuggler and say, "We're in. I hope you're serving us drinks. I'd like a comforting champagne if you have one, please."

"Without poison," Garrett adds behind me.

Zulan chuckles. "You two are so fucking witty and adorable. The three of us are going to have such a fun slumber party together."

Garrett and I take a slow step forward and enter the underground apartment. Both of us are prepared to do battle with the diamond goon at whatever cost we have to sacrifice to save Rocco's life.

# # # # #

I decide to be a gentlemen and let Garrett enter the apartment first. He says, "Thanks, dude, for using me as bait."

Zulan chuckles again, finding us comical.

I ignore him and begin to walk in front of his hulking mass. In passing, I pop my left elbow up with my arm and swing my fist into his face. Knuckles lock with the man's mouth, knocking one of his front teeth out. Blood gushes out of his orifice and rolls down and over his chin.

Honestly, it's an all-out war between Zulan and me in just a matter of seconds. Once he feels my blow, he decides to retaliate, which is expected of course. He swings his right fist up and into my chin, plowing me hard. I literally jump off the cement floor by the hit's force and fall to the cement and land on my back.

Zulan is not through with me just yet and decides to kick me while I'm down, nailing one of my ribs, which fortunately doesn't crack. Blood drips out of his mouth and splatters against my tee-covered torso.

The bad boy isn't satisfied with just one kick, though, which I'm well aware of. As he attempts a second kick, I swing my right fist upward and make contact with his balls.

The diamond thief lets out an animal-like grunt, cups his sack with his right hand, and sports tears at the corners of his eyes.

I'm on my feet in a matter of seconds. In doing so, Zulan decides to use the Alexander AWS entry rifle that is strapped over his chest on my face. He utters something down to me that sounds foreign because of all the blood running out of his mouth. I'm pretty sure he wants to murder my queer ass and bury my bones in a Louisiana bayou. The bad ass motherfucker positions the rifle in front of him with his trigger finger ready to blow me away and …

Garrett saves the day. He quickly finds the Beretta in his jeans, pulls it out with speed, aims it at our enemy, and says in his bad boy cop tone, "Hey, shithead," gaining Zulan's attention.

What transpires next is nothing less than testosterone-boosted action:

Zulan fires off a single shot and it nails Garrett in his right leg.

Garrett screams at the top of his voice and pulls his Beretta's trigger twice.

One bullet nails Zulan in his throat while the other takes out his heart.

The cop accidentally drops the Beretta to the cement floor and grasps his upper thigh where Zulan's bullet is nestled inside.

Zulan falls backward, away from me, clutching at his throat with one hand and his heart with the other. Blood washes down the room, sprays out of the South African, and sprits my face.

Garrett falls to the floor and immediately snatches up his Beretta from the cement. Tears ebb at the corners of his eyes from the pain that skis like molten-hot fire through his right leg. He pops two more shots off at Zulan, but both miss the man. The bullets fly into a Steve Walker print on the opposite side of the room; the painting just happens to be one of my favorites, a piece called *Creature from the Blue Lagoon*, 2006.

I hear and watch Zulan bleed to death in front of me. The liquid pours out of gunshot wounds as if he is a human spigot. One of his unsteady palms latches on the center of his bullet-ridden throat while the other lies limp on the floor. An indecipherable growl escapes the man as his body deflates against the cement.

Garrett crawls over to me and asks, "Are you okay?"

My face is splotched with Zulan's blood and my right jaw is swollen. Other than these two issues, I'm unharmed, perfectly fine. I turn my attention to his damaged thigh and say, "You're bleeding and you're hurt."

He mans it up and replies, "Trust me, I've been through worse. Sometimes a man likes to feel pain."

I want to laugh at his comment, but decide not to, knowing the cop is just acting tough to get through the sufferable moment. Instead, I watch him pull out a credit card-size phone from inside his jeans. The unit is black with silver etching. He slides it open and says, "I'm calling for help."

Attempting to lighten the mood, I ask, "What else do you have hidden in your jeans, sexy man?"

He plays with me and responds with a semi-smile and light tone, "Wouldn't you like to know, happy boy?" He dials a number into the sliver of cell phone, mentions his name, a set of numbers, and adds, "Under The Nest. Three floors down and ..."

I decide to find the key on Zulan for the two Yale locks on the steel door to my left. Maybe Rocco is still alive, hidden in the connecting room. Then again, maybe not, and I will unfortunately discover his corpse as sawed-off pieces; the most horrifying sight I will ever witness in my life.

The Yale key is in Zulan's front pocket of his denim. I kneel next to his bleeding body, slip my hand into one of his pockets, and discover the key with my fingertips. I pull the key out with two fingers, feel blood on the digits, and almost puke. In a matter of seconds I stand at the steel door next to the bathroom area and begin to unlock the Yale locks.

Behind me, Garrett slides the slim cell phone away from his adorable face and calls out, "Be careful, Derek! You don't know what's in there!"

I say over my left shoulder with curtness, "My boyfriend is in here and I need to find him." Quickly, I finish unlocking the two locks on the door and drop them to the cement floor where they clatter. Feeling my chest heave for breath, and anxiety take over my system, I pull the door open and ...

CHAPTER TWENTY-FOUR – RIMMING ROCCO

Rocco sits in a steel chair in what looks like a jail cell with wall to wall cement. A single sixty watt bulb hangs overhead, embodying him in its spotlight. The chair is welded to the floor, immovable and unbreakable. He has duct tape pushed across his mouth and cheeks. His wrists are bond behind him and more duct tape is securely wrapped around his ankles, connecting them together. The man wears nothing more than a pair of blue and white Aussiebum briefs, which showcase his ripped abs, hairy torso, and bare legs as steamy and sexy hot.

I rush to his side and brush a hand through his black hair, feel sweat and grime, but I really don't care since he's alive. Tears ebb at the corners of my eyes and a sniffle exits my nose from the excitement of finding and rescuing him. Standing in front of the mobster, I warn, "It's going to sting when I take the tape off your mouth. Handle it like a man."

He nods his head, understanding my comment. Rocco lets out a manageable grunt which I translate as just do it.

"I'll count down from three." Again, he nods his head, granting me permission. "Three ... two ... one." I quickly rip off the eight-inch piece of duct tape that covers his mouth and cheeks. A sneer of discomfort falls over my face, knowing he's in a considerable amount of pain because he loses some of his skin and whiskers above his upper lip.

My lover lets out an intimidating scream that fills the cement room, which echoes dramatically off the walls, roof, and floor. Now, tears sweep into his reflective eyes, which become as wide as garbage can lids. When his mouth is finally uncovered, free of the tape, I notice his pale cheeks and bloodless lips. He provides a roar and grunt like an animal, and rattles off, "That hurt like a motherfucker."

"I honestly didn't mean for it to sting." Hurriedly, I supply his mouth with a kiss and roll fingertips against the curve of his chin. I say,

"You cannot believe how worried I was about you. Rocco, in all honesty, I thought you were murdered. I believed I was going to find your body parts around The Reach."

The guy grumpily fires off, "I need to get out of here."

"Are you hurt?" I inquire, moving around his seated position. I spend the next minute removing the duct tape from his wrists, making a pile of it beneath the metal chair.

Once his arms are free, he rubs his left wrist first and now his right wrist. "I'm glad to see you, Derek. Frankly, I thought I was a cooked goose." Finally, he sounds rational and himself again.

As I unbind his ankles, freeing them from the duct tape, I tell him about Walter's knowledge regarding his whereabouts. "The man truly is a mystery solver. Had I not visited him you'd still be tied up, or even murdered."

"You know about Zulan then?"

"I do. Garrett took care of him. Two bullets were used. One went straight into his throat and the other one nailed his heart, which finally took him out. Zulan is probably at the gates of hell right now, begging to be let out."

"Garrett's here with you?" Rocco sounds pissed off, jealous, something. His tone becomes deep, poses judgment, and is filled with poison.

"He is. He's in the front room getting us help. The cop was very much involved in saving you. I didn't know who else could possibly help me after your morning run. You'd still be tied up in here if it weren't for him. I really think you should make pretty with the man now, and thank him for his help in saving your life."

"At least he's good for something. I'll consider it my tax money at hard work."

It's a reply I really don't want to hear and find grating. He can be so rude at times, particularly if he's under pressure and without food or water for two days. Truth is I ignore his obnoxious comment while helping him up from the steel chair. The Mafia man falls to the left a little, loses his balance, but I catch him before he tumbles to the cement floor. After cradling him in my arms, and connect his chest to my chest, I say, "By the way, you look like shit."

"Thanks for noticing. I knew you loved me for a reason. It's not like I was abducted and kept in the dark for the last forty-eight hours."

"You're pretty rank, too." I close my mouth and nostrils from his sour smell, knowing he needs a shower.

"I thought you loved the scent of strong man-sweat?"

"Not that much," I honestly declare. "A little is a turn-on for me. What you have going on is indescribable."

He licks the side of my neck in an endearing manner, shares a soft sounding growl, seems happy to see me, pulls away from me, and says, "You're making me hard."

"You're always horny."

"Only for you, babe," he says, and caresses my left cheek with a dirty palm.

As Garrett, three other Flamingo Cove police officers, and EMS arrive in the underground room, I ask Rocco, "Did Zulan beat you up?"

"Following my run, he placed a gun at the back of my head in the drive. A rag was placed over my mouth, I passed out, and woke up in here. He didn't beat the shit out of me, but I did think he was going to kill me, but he didn't."

"That's a blessing. I refuse to have a boyfriend who's missing half his face. I really thought he was going to kill you."

"Not a chance," Rocco says in a confident manner, still rubbing one wrist after the next, obviously enjoying his freedom.

"Where are the diamonds?" I lean into him and ask in a discreet tone, making sure those around me can't hear.

He presses his lips up to my right ear, points over his left shoulder, and chants, "You can find them in the room behind us. I saw Zulan carry them in there. "

243

"How do we retrieve them?" I ask, watching all of the cops and EMS aimlessly walk around the room, absorb the situation, and allow our moment together.

"I'll deal with the pigs and you fetch the diamonds. I'll meet you back at the beach house in a few hours. I'm sure I have to go through some questioning, heavy protocol shit, and be checked over by the EMS."

"Sounds like a plan. You'll be in good hands. The police won't hurt you. I know Garrett will take care of you."

He rolls his eyes, snuffs with distaste, and admits, "Trust me, he's the last man that I want to take care of me."

In a matter of seconds he begins to be questioned by the local authorities about his doings with Zulan Cane. It gives me enough time to sneak into the connecting room without being seen. Here, I stand among purple-dim lighting, a cement floor, an artillery of guns that decorate the walls, and various steel tables that are covered in everything from small purse-size handguns, grenades, tazers, pipe bombs, and automatic Uzis.

I look around the room and see the diamonds in a navy blue canvas bag the size of two fists. The satin bag sits on one of the steel tables. Just to make sure they're inside, I open the tied fabric, stare into its confines, grow eager with a smile, and chant, "Bingo."

Now, I discreetly carry the diamonds out of the purple-dim room, find my way through the group of working men, and begin my travels to the beach house without being stopped, questioned, or hassled by any of the lawmen. In doing so, my Mafia lover makes eye contact with me as a medic takes his blood pressure. He winks. I wink back. All is good for now between us, another mission accomplished.

Frankly, it's the easiest escape I have ever carried out while in the company of Rocco Malonni. Before I know it, I surface from the underground rooms, exit The Nest, walk to the edge of The Reach, and hail a cab back to the beach house without any questionable nuisances.

# # # # #

Once at the beach house, locked behind its doors and windows, I take a deep breath for a few reasons: one, Rocco is safe and practically unharmed; two, the diamonds have been rescued and will soon be returned to Boss Malonni, Rocco's father; three, Zulan Cane has been taken care of, washed out of society's goodness; four, I can easily rest now with Rocco at my side, awaiting our next adventure together.

# # # # #

Freshly showered and wearing nothing more than a tight pair of yellow and blue Rufskin briefs, I open a bottle of white wine, drizzle a few strawberries with some semi-sweet chocolate, change the sheets on the California-size king bed, find myself on the bed, and wait patiently for my better half to return for an evening of male-with-male seduction.

The chocolate-drizzled strawberries sit on a silver tray to the right of the bed. Next to the fruit is the iced bottle of white wine and two crystal glasses. A storm begins outside and wind whips against the side of the beach house, which presents a soothing sound that I find rather comforting and harmless.

Unfortunately and unexpectedly, I become tired and doze off. My sleep is dreamless and consists of nothing more than a dark room with a few sprinkles of diamond chips. How long am I asleep for? An hour? Two hours? Almost three hours? I'll never really know.

At some point I groggily wake up to Rocco's beautiful face as he sits on the side of the bed and sports nothing more than a white towel around his middle, and droplets of shower water on his rigid shoulders and pecs. His right hand is flat against my hip and he gently glides it against my body's frame. My boyfriend smells of ash-scented soap with just a hint of honeydew. His hair is damp from a few minutes in the shower, washing the past two days' worth of grime from his ultra-cut body.

"Hey, sleepyhead."

"Hey." I rub a fist in my right eye, removing sleepies. "When did you get home?"

"A few hours ago."

"You should have nudged me awake."

"You needed your sleep. I'm sure you were just as stressed as I was in the last few days."

I smile, enjoy his palm on my hip, and his presence within the room. "Did you eat?"

"Everything I could find."

"Did you drink some water?"

"Loads of it. I was very close to being dehydrated."

"And you showered, of course, since you're still wet."

He stands up, drops the cotton towel from his chiseled middle, presents a semi-boner in the dim golden light offered by the room, and confesses, "There's something else you forgot."

I shake my head and tease, "I'm sure I remembered everything."

"Everything?"

"Yeah," I reply, nod my head with a shitty grin spread over my face, and visually consume his chiseled looks. "Everything."

"I'm sure you forgot something," he chants as he kneels on the bed's mattress with one knee and positions the tip of his cock at my mouth.

Without caution, I lean forward and lick the tip of his swollen prick. My tongue travels around its smooth cap in a speedy manner. Saliva drips to the freshly changed cotton sheet, spotting the fabric.

He tries to steer his veined tool between my working lips, wanting to receive a cordial blowjob from me, but I'm not ready to put out just yet. A masterful grunt escapes his face, a slap to my right cheek from his dick ensues, and he demands rather brutishly, "Suck it, boyfriend!"

Fingertips discover his balls and begin to play with their hairy orbs. In doing so, I still lather the tip of his shaft with my tongue, drive him mad above me, and send my lover into a robust tizzy of excitement.

The mobster presses his right hand against the back of my head and demands again, "Suck it, Derek! Eat my cock!"

Because I starve for his meat-tube to reach into the back of my throat, and because I desire him as much as he desires me, if not more, I gently open my mouth and allow his stem to slide inside and begin to gag me.

"Yes," he expels overtop me. "This is what I want."

Without a timely warning, he bolts his hips toward my face and nails his beef into my narrow hole. All eight inches of his rock easily slide down the back of my breathing passageway and begin to gag me. Of course, I take it like a man, wanting him to fuck my mouth. Here and now, I apply a plethora of friction to the excess skin that covers his working pick.

"Jesus, Derek," he bellows, caught up in our act of combined naughtiness. His bolts continue to work my throat, one after the next, steadily and without a sense of gentleness. He murmurs odd sounds above me as I toy with his ball sack, massage it in my right palm, and turn him on like no other time before.

My own erection pops out of the yellow and blue Rufskin at my center. Sap clings to my rod's head, wanting to be licked away by my partner's roving mouth and tongue. To no avail, though, this moment is about him. I'm willed to do nothing less than to please him and allow the back of my mouth to become his hole to fuck, knowing that he's going to blow at any given second.

More salvia drips to the bed. And even more ooze leaks out of the throbbing shaft between my legs. The moment between us becomes intensified with our testosterone, steers us into sexual bliss, and whatever else we can delve into together, while we enjoy each other's company.

"Can't help it ... I'm shooting," he heavily exhales.

Before I can retreat from his pumping hose, man-fluid is ejaculated from his tool and fills my insides. The creamy, thick load blasts my throat, mouth, and leaks. The bittersweet glue sticks to my teeth and tongue, satisfying my needs and hunger for his sticky seed, desiring nothing more than this moment between us – lust between men, a reunion of naked and spirited bodies in motion that helplessly discover pleasure in unison.

What transpires between my own legs is nothing out of the ordinary and over-the-top joy mixed with a little sexy. As he continues to beat the inside of my mouth with his joint, my own untouched dick releases a stream of cream against my abs. The jet is thick and pungent, sticks to my navel, the elastic rim on the Rufskin, and the triangular area between and beneath my pecs.

"Holy shit," he announces with excitement. "Your rock just burst without even being touched."

In truth, I'm far too busy gagging on his spent, attempt to swallow his liter of goo into my system, and crave every drop of the mobster's paste with porn star bliss.

"Damn, you're amazing with your mouth," he confirms. "I don't know who taught you your skills but … shit, I love them." He pulls out of my face, jacks himself off twice, and enjoys the last string of shifting elation inside his center.

I wipe my mouth with the back of my left hand and begin to sit up on the bed, but the goon pushes me back down and insists, "You're not done yet, Derek. In fact, we're just getting started."

# # # # #

Not even a minute later, Rocco kneels on the bed with his awesome looking rump in my face. He coaches, "Lick it. Don't be shy."

I do as I'm instructed, enjoying his command. Not once do I feel belittled or at all insignificant. I rather enjoy my sexual romp when he is in control, detailing my every move for both of our pleasures. Listening again, positioned on my knees, I peel his tight ass cheeks open with my fingers and begin to swirl my tongue around his tight orifice. One swirl turns into a dozen or more, causing the Godfather's son to whimper in front of me.

Out of my briefs, still providing an erection between my legs, even if I have already fired out a sticky load, I eventually dart the tip of my tongue into the man's bottom, pull away quickly, and please him again in the same manner.

"You'll make me shoot a second time."

Catching my breath, a few inches away from his bulbous rump and its pink-tight center, I announce, "Cream away, Rocco. I hope you do."

Again and again my mouth finds his core. Unconditionally my tongue probes his middle. I delve the slender and wet tool inside his body, pull away, and continue this act for the next eight … eleven … fourteen minutes until he begs to have it replaced with my chunk of veined cock.

I don't have to be told twice. In fact, I reposition myself behind him, steer my plastic-free wanker into his single, puckering eye, and eventually apply palms to his hips, and balance myself like a good Rocco-fucker.

What transpires next is nothing less than lust between men. I continuously swing into the mobster, release my pick from the unyielding target, and find it necessary to bang his bottom yet another time. Jolt after jolt manipulates his outlet. Inches of fleshy sword pulverize his behind, exit, and pulverize it again.

In front of me, he pleads, "Fuck it … Fuck it hard, Derek."

"I'm on it," I chant, bang him with all my weight, and endlessly hump his rump with high velocity and minimal grace. I become animal-like with my task, devouring the bad boy with a relentless libido.

As I bolt inside the goon, pull out, and buck his center again, he finds the pumped apparatus between his solid and sweaty legs and starts to jack its fleshy and plump tube. Truth is I'm so involved with my own gig, I don't know what he's doing between my legs.

Behind him, holding his firm hips with my steady palms, I drill him, "Rock into me."

"Gotcha," he murmurs, obeying my desire. Before I really know what's happening, the mobster becomes a power-bottom, and shifts his weight backward, quickly pulls away, and seems to enjoy his ride on my granite-like dong.

"Take whatever you want," I inform.

Continuously he bangs into my pole. And ferociously I bounce into his opening, digging my fingernails into his skin. Together we work with skill, share a to and fro action of delight, both caught in a combined act of man attempting to get man off, and vice versa.

We heave for air and expel violent sounds from our torsos. As a ripple of euphoria sweeps throughout my interior, I thump his ass one last time. Following this final thrust, my orgasm is reached. Liquid fires out of my hose, into his hub, and unites us together.

Out of breath with my unprotected bolt still locked inside his center, with his system flooded with my gooey churn, I question over the splay of his muscular back, "You came, didn't you?"

He crawls forward, releases my dick from his opening, and separates our bodies. After this act, now facing me, he confesses, "I couldn't help it. I jacked myself off two times and ... spray went everywhere."

Between us, splattered on the bed's sheets, are strings of his white shoot. Hieroglyphic symbols of gay lust decorate the cotton. Half of me wants to lean over and consume his spent off the fabric, but I really don't have the opportunity since he leashes a palm against the back of my skull and forces a kiss on me.

I melt against him, lost and in a world of fag-wonderment. The kiss is like a drug I have never taken before, enjoying it to the fullest. My entire body goes numb under his mouthy spell, and I immediately feel intoxicated, drunk and high on his relentless passion.

When the kiss ends, he touches the tip of his nose to my nose, and he whispers, "You want to go for round three?"

Excited, feeling my cock bounce between my legs in agreement, I reply, "Give me a half hour and I'll be ready."

"Thirty minutes it is," he confirms, shines with an exuberant smile, and kisses me yet again.

CHAPTER TWENTY-FIVE – THREE DAYS LATER

I know that Buli Croon is still MIA, and Dragon and Brit are attempting to find the man by using their best efforts. Rumor has it that Croon flew out of Miami and is making a new home in Hamburg, Germany. Honestly, I really don't believe this. My intuition tells me that he's living right here in Flamingo Cove, where he stays hidden in The Reach and keeps underground like the troll he is.

Rocco disagrees with me. He insists Croon is in Germany and explains to me that Dragon saw the bad boy take a flight to Europe.

I persist, "Rocco, I'm sticking to my guns on this. Croon is right here among us. The man wants to get revenge for our nasty take-down."

My boyfriend of almost a year opposes my opinion. He rattles off, "We agree to disagree then?"

"Absolutely."

Enough said on Croon … for now, anyways.

I ask Rocco, "Where are the diamonds?"

"In hiding."

"Who has them?"

"Who do want to have them?"

"Your father."

"That's who has them."

I'm pleased with this information, tell him such, and want to sleep.

# # # # #

Since Dragon and Brit are on Croon's tail, they are unseen to me. Sometimes I hear Rocco on his cell phone with them, grilling the pair as if they are young boys instead of grown men who always pack heat. My lover becomes agitated with the duo because they haven't discovered Croon as of yet. When he hangs up the phone with Dragon, mostly angered because of the man's failure, he tries to take it out on me. This is when I usually leave the beach house and take a walk along the Gulf, staying clear of his tyranny.

I do have both of the employees' phone numbers, but calling them for a progress report on Croon will only irritate Rocco; this is not what I want to accomplish. Instead, I mind my own business, enjoy my lover's time, body, companionship, and prepare for the next step in our lives together, whatever this may entail.

What I do learn from Rocco regarding Dragon and Brit is no surprise. The duo become a serious and sexual couple, and enjoy each other's bodies to their fullest interests. Rocco imagines wedding bells in the near future for the two, which I fully support, and believe the couple well-suited to each other.

# # # # #

Walter's newest work in progress is called *Killing Cupid*. The man writes constantly, ignoring my cell phone calls, text messages, instant messages, and e-mails. I even bug him on Facebook, but he disregards me. The mystery writer is very dedicated to his work, immersed in his bizarre characters and twisted plot; another enjoyable mystery to read by the pool or in the bathtub in the near future.

Occasionally he will phone me, but our conversations are short and sweet, always to the point. He rambles about his novel: word count, what chapter he is currently drafting, and various problematic issues/events. Characters are always discussed, as well as dialogue, rising action, and the occasional sex antics between two beefy men.

Eventually I get the opportunity to talk about my life. To no avail, the aged faggot interjects one of my tales with his own business and continues to talk about his novel.

When I tell Rocco about Walter, he instructs me to suck it up and be a man. "He's a writer. It's what he does. I'm sure he would rather spend time with his keyboard opposed to you."

"You're unruly," I tell my boyfriend over a spaghetti dinner with red wine and fresh Italian bread.

"You like unruly, don't you?"

I tell him the truth: "I do like it that you're unruly. I just don't like it that you sometimes protect Walter and not me."

Rocco rubs my chin with two fingers and frowns. Eventually he says, "I hurt the poor baby's feelings, didn't I?"

"Fuck you," unintentionally slips out of me.

It doesn't matter, though. He takes me in stride, sort of giggles, and eventually ends up providing my body with a firm hug, a few kisses, and irresistible sex.

# # # # #

Walter visits with a fruit tray and bottle of white wine. We sit out on the rear cobblestone patio that overlooks the Gulf. The day is rather warm, lively, and offers a fresh spring around the corner. Over his edible gifts, he tells me that Fisk left for Lima, Peru again. To my surprise, my writer friend doesn't seem at all hurt by this news; in fact, I think he expects Fisk to act in such a manner.

Of course, I'm a little stunned at first to hear this frustrating fact, but try not to let it appear on my face. Curiosity gets the best of me and I ask, "Is he with his Latino friend?"

"The field worker?"

"Yes, the field worker. Is he having an affair with the man?"

The writer promptly shakes his head, looks up from his sliced strawberry and replies, "He's not. Alejandro, I have learned, is a long lost relative of Fisk's. The two men are distant cousins on Fisk's mother's side."

I absorb his information and eventually respond, "The man is French, Italian, and Peruvian?"

"Fisk is a mixed breed. I shall be joining him in a few weeks in Peru. Alejandro wants to meet me. Right now I just need some time to myself to work on *Killing Cupid* and then I'm off."

"It's good to know he is faithful to you. A one man's man."

My friend grins from ear to ear. "It's why I love him. I honestly wouldn't know where my life would be without the young man. I adore him and hope we spend many years together. He is my soul mate and other half. The Yin to my Yang."

"You sound very happy, Walter."

"I am. Perhaps one day I'll create a fantabulous gay romance based on our relationship and the events in Peru."

"I will surely devour it, old friend."

"And I will continue to devour Fisk … for however long he will have me."

# # # # #

Vest secretly watches my every move. I'm quite sure Boss Malonni pays him very well to do so. Not that I mind, of course. In truth, I realize that everyone has a job to do. Vest's job just happens to be to watch over me in case I have an emergency of sorts. My Mafia position as Rocco's boyfriend can never have too much protection, right? At least Rocco doesn't think so, or his father.

# # # # #

I pop in on Barbara, Boob, and Melvin. My mother's boyfriend happens to be at his store, Carpet Ride on Tarpon Street in downtown Flamingo Cove. Barbara is in her kitchen baking a homemade triple layer chocolate cake. Flour wafts about the room and the sink is filled to the brim with dirty spatulas, pans, measuring cups, and icing-covered beaters. The room smells like eggs, milk, and chocolate.

Boob sits in front of the oven and wags his tail. His tongue sticks out the right side of his mouth and he waits for something to fall on the floor to eat. When he sees me, a growl escapes his furry face and his ears go up.

Mother scolds Boob, "Silent, darling! Be polite to your brother. Derek means no harm."

"Who is the cake for?" I inquire, looking over my mother's shoulder as she spreads a thick layer of icing over the top of the chocolate layers.

"Melvin's birthday is tomorrow."

"And what did you get him for his birthday?"

"Two tickets to Australia, which brings me to my next topic. Boob will need a sitter while Melvin and I study the Aborigines."

I think: Absolutely not! Boob hates me. He's just waiting to sink his teeth into one of my legs, arms, or my neck. I'm the furry bastard's nemesis and know it. A week with him is trouble and I won't have any parts of sitting him.

"You will help me, won't you, Derek?"

"Perhaps my company isn't best for Boob. You should let him stay with someone he enjoys. If you really want to know, I'm not on his friend list. We are hardly the pals you think we are."

She consumes my information while humming something from *The Little Mermaid*. After her noisemaking, she responds, "I'll leave him with Walter or Garrett. He will be in good hands with either man. Boob will have to decide who he likes a little better."

"A fine idea," I agree, kiss her on the side of the head in an endearing manner. "Speaking of Garrett, has he handled Melvin's parking tickets yet?"

"Yes, he has. Melvin has been set free. No longer is he a felon running amuck in Flamingo Cove. Garrett is such a nice man. I love him as if he were my own son. I'm still stunned that you're not lovers with the man, Derek. Instead, you bed Rocco Malonni, who unsettles me a bit."

I roll my eyes and back away from her. The last thing I want to do is have the Flamingo Cove copper be my lover. To keep my sanity, I abruptly force the thought out of my head. Coming too, preventing myself from vomiting, I tell her, "My heart belongs to Rocco. Love leads us all astray."

My visit lasts a little more than two hours. I help Barbara ice Melvin's cake and also help her clean up the destroyed kitchen. Following this adventure, I decide to leave, kiss her goodbye, and tell her, "I love you and will see you soon."

She clamps my cheeks with her palms, dots a kiss to my nose, and replies, "Don't be a stranger. I like having you around."

# # # # #

Following my visit with Mother, I end up at Pallyo, sit at its bar, and order a gin and tonic with a sliver of lemon and two ice cubes. The Taylor Lautner look-alike bartender waits on a few other guys around the bar, mostly middle-aged men in suits and dapper looking smiles. I pick up my gin and tonic, take a long sip, swallow the sip down, and …

"My love interest," Officer Garrett Haute says while he finds a seat next to me at the bar.

I turn my attention to the handsome man and see that he sports his sexy cop uniform, minus his gun and hat, which I presume he has left in his Corolla, having ending his shift at the downtown station. "My friend," I reply. "What brings you here?"

"Your sexy man-scent of course. I can't keep myself away from it. You drive me mad, Derek. Every day you remind me of how badly I want you. I would kill for you just so you know."

I'm on my best behavior and choose not to respond to his flattering comment. Instead, I take another sip of my drink, swallow it down, and merely consume my childhood fuck buddy's good looks.

He orders a light beer from Taylor and rattles off to me, "I'm here for one particular reason that you should know."

"Is it police business?"

"My whole life is police business, man."

"Tell me what I should know," I say, giving him the most serious look: straight brows, pursed lips, concern in my eyes.

He heavily sighs, looks down at the bar, and admits, "I realize that I can never have you as a lover."

"Because I'm Rocco's."

"Yes, I know that. I still think we should be friends, though, and I'll seek professional help regarding my feelings for you." His bottle of pale beer is served on a napkin in front of him, but he doesn't take a swig. Instead, he carries out some severe eye contact with me, nods his head, and smiles. "Do you believe me?"

"I do, Garrett. I highly recommend Dr. Trisia Blake. She's superb regarding your situation."

"She's on Crab Street, right?"

"Yes. She works with her brother Zeb."

"Zeb is hot," Garrett confesses. "I wouldn't mind if he hypnotized me and took advantage of my skin. There is something sweet about his dimples, thick black hair, and rippled Colt-chest."

I know he's joking, which prompts me to share a laugh. "I'm glad you have come to your senses. This is very big of you."

"It doesn't mean I'm going to stop flirting with you."

"I expect that."

"Because what fun will life be if I can't tease you with my good looks?"

"And vice versa," I admit.

"Yes. And vice versa."

We shake hands like straight men, enjoy our drinks, talk about how sexy-hot Zeb Blake is, and enjoy the next hour in each other's company.

I learn from Garrett that Zulan Cane's funeral service is being held tomorrow at St. Christopher's Episcopal Church on Cuba Key Road.

Neither of us will be attending. Other informative details surface during my hour with the cop: Balls Banco was arrested the night before for manslaughter in Watergulf; Izzy Ramon is being watched closely for drug smuggling; and Dane Duncock has intentions of building a new tattoo parlor where The Skin Artist once stood.

"You're a vat of knowledge," I tell the cop, finishing off my third beer.

"I'm your gossiping friend and you love it."

"Ain't nothing wrong with that, is there? Frankly, I kind of like you this way."

"We're going to get along just fine as friends," he admits.

"You took the words right out of my mouth, Garrett. I'm glad you're my friend."

"Likewise, Derek, I wouldn't have it any other way."

# # # # #

When I return to the beach house I see three young men in the living room. The trio is around twenty-years-old with bright and shiny smiles. I step into the living room and their beautiful faces light up with exuberance, filling the room with natural energy and radiant joy. Centered among them, I become curious and inquire, "And who may I ask are you three?"

"Simon," a gorgeous brown-haired beauty with tiger-yellow eyes and a bit of scruff on his chin says.

"Alvin," a ginger-haired cutie with broad shoulders, emerald green eyes, and a cleft in the middle of his chin shares.

"Theodore," the last male vixen says, beaming Caribbean-blue eyes, a Colgate smile, and L-shaped sideburns with an adorable raven-colored crew cut.

I consume their names again – Simon, Alvin, and Theodore – and shake my head. "You're shitting me, right?"

"It's just a coincidence," Simon says. "We didn't come as a set. In fact, we don't even know each other."

"I concur," Alvin adds.

Theodore simply ogles me and enjoys what he sees.

"What are you three here for?" I inquire, scan their handsomeness again, this time from left to right.

Rocco enters the room in a pair of Diesel khakis, a tight Aussiebum tee the color of the blue sky, and Spanish sandals. He hears my question and replies, "The young men are here for interviews regarding an available position as our new houseboy."

"I think we should hire all three," I quip, growing semi-hard between my legs at the foursome of men around me.

My lover excuses us from the young trio and whisks me into the dining room. Here, he holds me against his hulking chest, meets his cherry red lips with my lips, and asks, "Where have you been today, guy?"

I tell him about my afternoon of baking with Mother and my drinks at Pallyo with Garrett Haute. For the next few minutes I inform him about Dane, Banco, Zulan's funeral, and Izzy Ramon. I confess, "I'm sure Izzy is still hard for you, my love."

"I have what I want right here in my arms."

"You're just saying this because you want in my pants."

"Don't tell my little secret to our friends in there. It's just between you and me."

"Which one will you be hiring?" I inquire.

"I haven't interviewed them yet. I think we should both do it together. What do you think?"

"I'm leaning toward Simon. The man is boyishly cute."

"I like him too. We'll save his interview for last." He supplies my core with a tender hug, leans into my nose with his lips, and shares a kiss to the tip of it. When he pulls away from me, he asks, "Did I tell you how much you mean to me, Derek Reed?"

"Never. You're a very abusive man. I need therapy because of you," I kid.

He now stands approximately one foot away from me and reaches into the front, left pocket of his khaki shorts. He pulls out a navy blue velvet box the size of a Zippo lighter, falls down on one knee, and peers up at me with tears brimming at the corners of his eyes.

"Dear God, you're going to ask me to marry you, aren't you?" I'm blown away, nervous for him. What the hell is he thinking? And why hasn't he done this sooner?

He nods his head while opening the navy blue velvet box and asks, "Will you make me the happiest man in the world and spend the rest of your life with me, Derek Alexander Reed?"

My heart wavers to and fro within my chest as I study the gold band inside the velvet box: size eleven, thin with curly cues etched into its surface, nothing cheap or ghastly. My legs begin to wobble and I feel light-headed. To no avail, a smile reaches my earlobes and I reply, "I would love to marry you, Rocco Malonni."

He stands and retrieves the ring out of its velvety home. He now places it on my right hand like a gentleman. Following this action, he studies the ring and finger, and says, "Derek, I love you more than anything else in the world. You're making the smartest decision of your life. Forever you will be protected by me. Forever I will love you. I promise this with all my heart and soul"

"You really want in my pants now, don't you?" I reply, playing with him. "Marrying me means you get to fuck me anytime you want to now, and vice versa. Are you ready for that?"

"I do that already," he shares, and pats my lips with the pad of his left index finger.

"I love you, too," slides out of me with ease. "You make it simple to love you … even if you're in the mob and kill bad guys."

"I've never murdered a bad guy on purpose."

"I accidentally fell in love with one," I whisper to my future husband and stroke a hand over his head.

He shares a life-jolting kiss with me, blowing me away. One of his palms cups the goods between my legs and teases me. When he completes the kiss, he pulls off and away from me, and chants, "Why don't we get these interviews over with so I can take advantage of your skin?"

"The skin artist returns."

"Only for you, babe. I'm going to keep you now and forever."

"That's so cliché. Tell me something better."

He laughs and dots a kiss to the tip of my nose. "I'm always about clichés."

"I really like clichés, Rocco," I chant with bubbles of elation that pop throughout my system, lead him out of the dining room and into the living room, and desire nothing less than to keep him close to my heart now ... and forever.

THE AUTHOR

R. W. Clinger is the author of *The Pool Boy*, *Skin Tour*, *Soft on the Eyes*, and *Just a Boy*. His novellas include *The Drifter* and *The Weekender*. His short stories of man-on-man action have appeared in numerous STARbooks Press compilations. His hobbies include photography, football, and antiquing. R.W. Clinger is currently at work on a third Derek and Rocco *SKIN* tale called *SKIN FLICK*. He can be reached at kenitorico@verizon.net.

g any underwear. "Excuse me," I said, having a hard time looking

ed by that bulge in his crotch, "but don't I know you?" "Maybe," h

of t   bout a m

Ray   God, you

er?   in?" he as

'Lik   s stronges

ody   e on Gree

he l   I ever sa

to t   any ideas?

king   he same

coul   ery long t

rac   ne swell.

with   e in store

go c   behind sc

see t   in public

' he   vent to the

acy.   grabbed i

d. I

raci   t, so firm

t, ha

h my   bing dick

ng, I   n cock, be

sound of unzipping filled the small space. I don't know who's hand

t before I knew it, I had his rod in my hand, and mine was in his. "

do?" he asked, his tone challenging. I knew exactly, and sank to n